The Immortal Coil

J. Armand

ISBN: 0996119116, 978-0-9961191-1-5

Cover illustration by Greg Opalinski

Table of Contents

"The two most important days in your life are the day you are born and the day you find out why."

— Mark Twain

Chapter One

"Take your shirt off," were her first words as I entered the room, leaving behind any semblance of confidence I had at the threshold. There was something to be said about a woman who knew exactly what she wanted. This was already moving faster than my other encounters today and I couldn't help feeling a bit nervous. "Turn around for me." Her voice made an almost passable attempt at being sweet, but I could sense there was little to no thrill left in her from doing this anymore.

I complied and glanced around the room, trying to remove myself from the intimacy of the situation. Aside from one small window breaking up the monotony of the stark white walls, there wasn't much in the way of distraction. The purpose of the sterile decor was most likely to not take attention away from every young piece of meat that walked through her door. My only job right now was to use my bare skin against this backdrop to pique her interest, at least until she was satisfied and ready to move on.

No matter how many times I was told to, stripping down in front of a complete stranger wasn't getting any easier. I had to admit there was some excitement in the idea of grabbing someone's attention with just my body, but in practice, I felt vulnerable. There's nothing wrong with a little modesty, I guess, as long as it doesn't hold you back from collecting a paycheck.

"You're in great shape. Very cute, too. I like your look," she said, as her eyes traced up and down every inch of me with increasing enthusiasm. "I'm loving the eyes. What are they, light blue?"

I don't know how people do this for a living. I barely had my foot in the door and I was already feeling dirty. This was what I came to New York City for, though, so I had better start getting used to it.

"Oh, um, they're gray, actually." That was clearly stated in my portfolio in front of her, but it was probably part of her job to be sure I wasn't too brain-dead to take directions from a photographer.

"Five foot ten, I see. A couple inches short for the runway. That's too bad." The same harsh reality I had heard from the other two castings today, along with the observation that I badly needed a tan. Whoever said size doesn't matter was clearly over six foot. "We're doing a shoot on Saturday for our autumn line. I want to see you there. It will begin promptly at 8 AM, but make sure you arrive an hour early to get fitted. Don't show up any earlier or you'll just be in the way. Oh, and get a good night's sleep. We'll be working straight through to dinner."

On my way out of the agency, I looked at all the nervous young hopefuls still in the waiting area. Never had I seen so many beautiful people all in one place until today. It reminded me of the popular clique's table in my high school cafeteria, the table I didn't sit at. Sure, there were a few girls in my class who thought I was cute, but growing up back in Boston I always managed to fly under the social radar. I kept my grades up, I just barely held my own in gym class, and I avoided extracurricular activities and wild parties like the plague. I was more or less invisible, but not unhappy about it. Once I became a teenager I started to feel like there was something different about me from the other kids, and in high school that is the last thing you want. When I looked in the mirror I didn't like the boy staring back at me. All I saw were the lies.

Now here I am, two years and two hundred miles later, taking my shirt off for a modeling agent in the Big Apple. This wasn't me. In fact, I'm still not sure how I got talked into this.

"How'd it go?" It took me a second to pick out the voice in the crowd. One of the male models I was sitting next to while waiting to be seen waved me over. "Did you get called back?"

"Yeah. I didn't think I would, but I guess —"

"Hey, nice, so some of us were talking about going out tonight to celebrate. You should come."

"You got called back too?"

"You must be new around here. I always get the call back once they see me." He laughed and hit me on the arm. "So, you in?"

"Oh, uh, I actually have plans already. Thanks though."

"Sure you do. Whatever. It's all good."

It was dark when I got back out to the street. I had a text message and two missed calls from my mom. Now I remembered my reason for being here.

"Hi, honey!" For the typical overprotective mother, she was way too enthusiastic about her son taking a break from college to move out of state and pursue a modeling career.

"Way to pick up on the first ring, Ma." My parents were always supportive of anything I showed an interest in, as long as they double- and triple-checked that it would be safe first. It wasn't until I was older that I understood why being a parent meant so much to them.

"I can't help it. I haven't heard from you all day. How did it go? Did you find the places okay? Were you on time?" Since I got here last month, we have started a tradition of her calling me almost every day. That's not including the text messages that she learned to send just for me.

"It went fine. I have my first photo shoot this Saturday and one next Tuesday."

"I knew they'd love you!" I could hear her repeating everything to my father in the background.

I'm an only child, and adopted on top of that. My parents devoted their lives to medicine. My mom is a veterinarian and my father is an emergency room doctor. It wasn't until they were nearing forty that they realized there was more to life and wanted kids. Unfortunately, they weren't able to have any of their own.

They adopted me when I was only a few months old. I never knew who my biological parents were and never really cared. I was loved unconditionally and that's all that mattered to me. My mom stopped working until I was in high school so she could always make me breakfast and take me to school and kiss me goodbye. There wasn't one day that she didn't pick me up after school, or a holiday that the entire house wasn't festively decorated. My father never missed a chance to take off for extended family vacations or school plays and concerts — anything to find a reason to pull out his video camera. They thought the world of me, and the feeling was mutual.

They were always strict about studying to get into a good school, so I was shocked when my mom suddenly changed gears. At first, predictably enough, my father was against the whole idea of leaving college, but somehow my mom convinced him. It was even more surprising that she convinced me. I had my heart set on finishing school to become an architect and sitting in an office the rest of my life sketching blueprints or watching my creations come to life on a construction site.

"Ma, they liked a lot of people. I'm not the only one in the world to have stood in front of a camera. Who's actually going to want to look at pictures of me anyway? Let alone pay me for them?"

"Come on, Dorian, you have to be at least a little excited! Stop being so resistant to trying new things. How will you ever know who you really are if you hide yourself away?"

Excitement was the real issue here. School was my life until tenth grade, when I got a part-time job at a local gym. The money I saved up went to a car, which only helped with getting to school and work more easily. Once I became an adult, they realized I was going down the same rigid path they had. Mom didn't want me to be in my forties one day and looking back, regretting that I never took the time to enjoy myself. She was also not too subtle about wanting grandkids before she got too old to know who they were.

Working at the gym hadn't been completely by choice either. It was one of only two places that would hire you if you were under eighteen. The deli was my other option, but it seemed like half my class was already employed there. The gym job was easy enough. All I had to do was scan membership cards and wash and fold towels.

This left me with a lot of downtime that could have been spent doing homework, but then I'd have no excuse to get out of being smothered by family time after dinner. Instead, I took advantage of the machines to work out. Even after leaving my job to focus on college, I kept up exercising at the campus gym out of habit. The more stressful the courses became, the more time I spent burning off steam in the gym. Nothing helped build stress like calculus and physics. Sometimes it felt like I was making more progress lifting weights than calculating them. That was all it took for my mother to formulate this convoluted plan to start modeling.

"This wasn't exactly the first step I would have chosen to begin finding myself. I'm excited, but I'm also very tired. It's been a long day of taking my clothes off for people."

"Don't say it like that! It's only nine. You should be going out and having fun. Have you made any friends there yet?"

I could hear my father in the background protesting her idea of me partying it up. He had driven down here three times to check my apartment out and talk to the landlord before we rented it. He was openly paranoid something would happen and I would be out on the street.

"Um, yeah, I'm, uh, some of the guys I met at the open call tonight invited me out. I have to go, Ma. I'm getting on the subway now and I'll lose service."

The truth was that my plans for tonight were the same as every other night; curled up in bed studying an architecture book for my inevitable return to Boston University. I hadn't extended myself to meet anybody here. Most of my time was spent fixing up my place and checking out all the coffee shops. As crazy as it sounded, the only reason I agreed to come to New York and give modeling a shot was because I knew I could blend in. Nobody cared about who you were on the inside when taking your picture. Insecurity was ingrained in my psyche since adolescence, so it would take a lot more than a few mediocre casting calls to reprogram me.

"You're a terrible liar, Dorian. Call me tomorrow? It would be nice if you'd call me for a change. Oh, and your father and I have a surprise for you when you come back for the Fourth of July."

"I would if you gave me a chance to call first. I love you. Say goodnight to Dad for me." I had to tell myself not to feel guilty hanging up on them, but they were one step away from installing cameras in my apartment. On one hand, the freedom was a much-needed breath of fresh air. On the other hand, being so far away from home and all alone, doing something I wasn't crazy about to begin with was making me homesick.

It wasn't that I didn't want to have fun or find myself. The problem was that I didn't know how to after years of trying to keep a low profile. I was having a difficult time getting back in touch with the real me that I had buried long ago. I could tell that my parents knew something was up. I valued their support and encouragement, but the harder they pushed, the more I wanted to be left alone.

The subway ride to my apartment on the Upper East Side was turning out to be colorful, as always. My favorite part about living here was the people-watching. No matter what store, street, or subway car, there was always such a wide spectrum of different people. You never really knew what to expect from each crowd and there was always something new mixed in.

Among the tired businessmen returning home from the office, the frazzled parents shepherding their children, the hipsters, gangsters, and couples of every shape, size, and color, was a rambling homeless man. Of course, the only available seat was to my right. To look busy, I took out my phone, hoping to be left alone.

"They're after me, they're after all of us ..." There was a sudden rancid smell of body odor next to me. This was going to be a painfully long ride.

"They're going to get us. It isn't safe anywhere. They're going to get you too." I could tell the bum was speaking to me by the feeling of his hot, humid breath on the side of my face.

"You can avoid me, but you can't avoid them. Not forever, you can't! I see them, I seen them killing people off the street, in the alleys, in the park." The stench of dog food and fresh vomit on his breath continued to violate my sense of smell.

"Never a body left behind, either. Not a drop of blood or a shoe, not anything left for a big fancy funeral. The police are in on it, too. The whole government is! Why do you think we never hear about it on the news?" The smell was so bad I could taste it in my mouth now.

Against my better judgment, I looked at him. He was dirty and unkempt as expected, but the expression on his face threw me off. He didn't look nearly as deranged as he sounded. His eyes were filled with concern, not insanity.

"You wanna keep it to yourself, buddy? There are kids here," said a man standing in front of us alongside his two children.

As we made another stop, the passengers joined in shushing the homeless man, who began ranting more loudly.

"There are monsters out there on those streets. They look just like any one of you and you won't know until it's too late!" he shouted, before waddling out onto the platform.

"Don't you pay him no mind," said an older woman sitting on my other side. "There are all sorts of crazies that come out every now and again. It's gotta make you wonder what kind of plan God has cooked up for their sorry souls."

I smiled politely and kept my head down for the remainder of the trip. At least I could breathe again. As I left the train, I could see blood on the seat where the homeless man had been sitting. For a moment, I toyed with the idea that there was some truth to the man's ranting. Maybe the conspiracy theory part was farfetched, but considering how scared he looked, he could have been attacked.

The 6 train dropped me off at East 77th Street, so I still had to walk four blocks before I was home. I could hear the sound of police sirens in the distance as I made my way uptown. It wasn't uncommon to hear sirens at all hours of the night, but I had a funny feeling in my stomach as I turned the corner and saw a line of cop cars in front of my building.

An ambulance was pulling away from the scene as I joined the crowd. I could see my neighbor, Shannon, standing on the sidewalk.

"What's going on?" I asked her.

"Hey, I don't know. The police have been here since I got home an hour ago. They evacuated the building and haven't said anything since. They just finished loading a stretcher with someone on it into that ambulance that left."

She was wringing her hands nervously and didn't stop watching the scene as she talked. "Any idea who it might have been?" Not that I knew anyone else in the building besides her and the landlord, but it seemed like the appropriate thing to ask in this situation.

"I heard someone say it was Lynn on the floor below us." Shannon finally broke away from staring at the police to look at me. "She didn't show up to work for a few days and wasn't returning anyone's calls. Her family lives in Arizona, so the landlord had to let the police in."

It seemed strange that they were still keeping everyone waiting outside if they had already taken the woman to the hospital. Our landlord, Mr. Stahl, was talking to a couple of cops off to the side. I tried to avoid him as much as possible after my father repeatedly questioned his credibility when we were apartment-hunting. There were a few police chatting it up and leaning against their car looking restless.

"I'm going to see what they have to say." I excused myself from Shannon.

"Rookie, why don't you go on a food run? Looks like we're going to be here awhile," one of the officers said as I walked up. He appeared to be in his early fifties and, judging by his stomach overhang, food should have been the least of his worries. The "rookie" he was speaking to was an athletic young man with blond hair. I almost felt sorry for him having to take orders from someone who probably broke out into a sweat writing a ticket.

"Can I help you?" the third officer of the group asked. He was somewhere in the middle of the other two both in age and body type. Looking at the three of them together was like observing the sad timeline of a police officer's figure.

"Hi, I was just wondering if you know when we'll be able to go in?"

"Not anytime soon," the same officer said, and pointed behind me at the building. It was being blocked off with yellow police tape.

"What happened?"

"We can't discuss police business. Do you live here?" By his tone and body language, I could tell that my questions seemed to be bothering the older cop. They had probably been asked the same question at least ten times, so I couldn't totally blame him.

"Yes, on the fifth floor. I don't really have anywhere else to go," I said, trying to sound as polite as possible so maybe I would get more information.

"You don't have friends?" Now he was being rude. At least I didn't have to feel bad about judging him for his weight now.

"I just moved to the city a month ago." I hoped that made him feel stupid.

"And what's your name, son?"

"Dorian."

"Do you have a last name?" he said, and motioned sarcastically with his hand for me to continue.

"Benoit."

"Well, Dorian Benoit, we will try and hurry our investigation along so you won't be inconvenienced any further. In the meantime, why don't you make friends with some of your neighbors here so they'll stop asking us questions." He seemed pleased with himself for being an ass. He chuckled and looked at the other two to see if he had gotten a rise out of them.

Neither seemed too amused, which made me feel a bit better as I walked away. "There's a hotel a few blocks away on 77th Street. You can probably get reimbursed for it by the city," the rookie offered.

"Thanks," I said. "I know I can't ask what happened, but any idea when you guys will be done?"

"Check back in the morning. That's all I can tell you. We don't know much more."

Shannon was suddenly beside me with two of her girlfriends, rattling off questions to the rookie now that he was away from his colleagues. "Is it true you guys found the woman dead in her apartment?"

"I'm sorry, ma'am. We're not allowed to discuss it."

I backed out of the conversation as he patiently answered all of the same questions over again. The thought crossed my mind to call my parents, but it would only freak them out. Knowing them, they would be on the road down here before I hung up the phone. I'd just rent a room for the night and hope they didn't see the charge on my credit card before I got the chance to explain in the morning.

I stopped off to get coffee at a corner cafe before going to the hotel. I never even drank coffee before I moved here, but it seemed like everyone in Manhattan was always walking around with some form of caffeine.

It was just after 10 PM when I walked in. The cafe was completely empty except for a man behind the counter reading the newspaper. They had a bunch of flavors I had never heard of, but not my favorite caramel latte, so I had to settle for regular coffee. I continued on to find the hotel with my disappointing drink in hand.

It cost me four hundred dollars, but I was able to get one of the last available rooms. According to the concierge, there were already quite a few people from my building staying there. Shannon and her friends were walking up to the front desk as I entered the elevator.

I could hear most of their conversation while they checked in until one of the girls erupted into a coughing fit. She was so pale that the veins in her face were beginning to show. No more than fifteen minutes ago, she appeared completely healthy, but now she looked like she had been suffering from pneumonia for weeks.

The elevator doors closed and took me up to my floor. I couldn't help but feel bad for Shannon's friend and the lady I saw being taken away from my building. It was for reasons like that that I could never follow in my parents' footsteps and go for a career in medicine. Somehow they became experts at shutting out emotions when dealing with patients. I must have been in fifth grade when I asked my dad if he had ever lost a patient. He told me he had lost many, but didn't let himself think about it. If he got emotional over every loss, then he would never be able to move on and save the next person.

I got off on the sixth floor to find my landlord waiting for the elevator. His expression when he saw me said that he would have rather it had been anyone else in the world but me getting off of that elevator. He was probably dreading the pending complaints from my parents.

"Hi, Mr. Stahl." I spoke first. "Any news on what happened?"

"Lynn Sutherland, fourth floor. She moved in right after you. She didn't show up to work or return anyone's calls for a few days. Her family called the police to check on her, so I let them in."

He finished there and walked into the elevator. I put my hand out to stop the door from closing.

"Is she all right? I saw them taking her away."

"She was sick, real sick. I hear she travels a lot. She just got back from overseas somewhere. EMT says she might have picked up something."

He looked spooked.

"What do you mean *something*? The police don't evacuate a building because someone is sick." I was beginning to think it might be a good idea to call my parents after all. At least they could offer professional advice.

"No … no, I suppose they don't."

He definitely wasn't telling me everything. He kept pressing the elevator button to go down as if I wasn't even there.

"Where are you going?" I asked him.

"I've got to pick up a few things from my place there. I left so fast to get a room I forgot half my stuff."

That made me realize I had also come here with nothing.

"Do you think they'll let us back in? I want to get some of my things if we're going to be here awhile."

"No, you stay here. No sense in both of us getting in trouble in case they kick us out. Besides, I don't think your father would appreciate hearing that I let you back in before everything was checked out."

Mr. Stahl was still staring down at the elevator buttons like they were part of the conversation. I let the door go and walked to my room, seeing as this wasn't getting me anywhere.

I was pleasantly surprised when I opened my door. The room was definitely worth the money spent and almost made me regret having to go back to my cramped apartment. It was nice to stay in a room where you could actually see the floor and the bed wasn't covered with laundry in true bachelor-pad style.

My cell phone battery was dying, and without a charger or my laptop, I felt completely cut off from the outside world. I didn't have my architecture book to study from either, so all I could do to pass the time was watch TV.

I put on the evening news thinking there might be something about the police at my building, but I guess it was too boring to report compared to celebrity babies and breakups. The next best thing was spending a few bucks on a movie.

I found the old black-and-white version of Frankenstein from the 1930s, a personal favorite. I must have seen this a dozen times since first watching it in the third grade. My father told me people actually used to be scared when the film first came out. If anything, I felt bad for the monster.

An hour through the movie, the sound of a woman crying in the hall caught my attention. Hopefully, whatever was going on at the apartment was done by now. Sitting around in the hotel room was making me antsy and I wasn't going to be able to fall asleep any time soon after finishing my coffee. At least if I could get a change of clothes and my toothbrush, I'd feel more comfortable staying here overnight. I grabbed my phone, which was dead by now, and my bag, and left the room.

The crying was coming from up ahead by the elevator, but whoever it was sounded like they were calming down. Shannon walked around the corner, looking down at her phone in one hand and holding a bucket of ice in the other.

"Hey Shannon, are you all right?" She looked miserable and then I remembered her friend from the lobby.

"Oh hey Dorian, I didn't know you were here too. It's just my friend, Michelle. She was feeling really sick earlier tonight so another of our friends took her to the hospital. It had me really freaked out and then I got this call from the friend that took her. Some homeless druggie in the emergency room started attacking people, so now they aren't letting anyone in to visit. I have no idea if she's okay or not."

I'm terrible at comforting people, but I felt like I had to say something.

"I'm sure she's fine. Hospitals are set up to handle that stuff. It's pretty much the safest place you can be other than a police precinct."

"I hope so. This whole night has been a big mess. Did you hear anything about going back to our place yet?"

"No, but Mr. Stahl went about an hour ago. He said this was all because that woman was sick. Her apartment is nowhere near ours so I'm hoping they'll let me in to pick up some stuff in case we're stuck here for a while. If you need me later, I'm staying in room 602."

"Thanks," she smiled as a tiny vein under her eye grew darker. "Let me know if you find out anything."

Chapter Two

Walking through my neighborhood was a lot more peaceful without all the commotion. Nighttime was never an excuse for Manhattan to quiet down, but at least this area was far away from any tourist hotspots. The only noise on my block was the hum of air conditioners in tenants' windows. I could see my building across the street as I approached. The yellow tape had been torn down and there were lights on in some of the apartments. The police cars were gone now, replaced by a single CDC van, and the front door was left propped open. This was a good sign. If the officials had started to clear out then the building must be safe.

I poked my head in and wasn't met with any immediate resistance. There was a light coming from the landlord's place. He had the door open, and with no other way upstairs, I would have to sneak past to avoid being caught. From the stairs opposite Mr. Stahl's apartment, I could see him inside with his back turned to me. As I climbed the stairs, I heard the sound of footsteps coming from each floor.

Shannon's door was open too, but the lights weren't on. I checked inside from the hallway and saw a man in a facemask and sanitation suit with the letters CDC printed on the back. He was crouched down, working in the dark. I started getting nervous that they would actually find something hazardous, especially with my apartment being right next to hers. It must have been pretty bad if they were checking the entire building and not just the victim's floor.

The door to my place was still closed, so they must have not gotten to it yet. Before I saw the worker next door, I was thinking of staying here. Now I felt like they would need to examine my place, too. And what if they actually found something? It could be West Nile virus, or even anthrax or the bird flu. I hurried into my room and began throwing clothes in my bag, along with my toothbrush and anything else I could realistically fit.

There was a strange growling sound coming through the wall from Shannon's apartment. It could be one of those police dogs they used to sniff out trouble, but why would the CDC need that? When I listened more closely, the growl was actually more of a guttural croak. I had heard it once before at the veterinary office where my mom worked; it was the sound of a sick animal dying. A wave of sadness washed over me as I listened to the poor animal's struggle for breath grow louder. Coming here was a terrible idea after all.

Back in the hallway, I could still hear the unnerving death rattle from Shannon's place as I locked my door. I peeked in to see the CDC worker still crouched in the dark. There was no dog that I could see, but it sounded as if the noise was coming from him instead. He got up slowly. When he turned around, it hit me: the weird noise I was hearing was the respirator of his mask.

Feeling a little stupid for letting my imagination run wild like that, I quickly walked away and took out my phone. Of course, it was still dead, and in my haste, I had left the charger behind. I ran back into my place, tripping over piles of laundry and unpacked boxes as I rummaged around in the dark.

The sound of footsteps entering the apartment put a stop to my search. I had left the door open when I came in, so the CDC worker probably thought this was the next room to check. Right now I wasn't even worried about being kicked out, seeing as how I wanted to leave as soon as possible anyway. I stepped out to the living room where the worker was standing to announce myself.

"Sorry, I'll be right out. I was just picking up some stuff."

If this thing was airborne, I might have already exposed myself to whatever it was in my stupidity. Now they were probably going to need to decontaminate me. Dad would know what to do in case I did catch something, but that would mean going home.

"There you are." I spoke to the charger while reaching under the bed for it.

A gloved hand clamped down on my shoulder from behind. I jerked away, putting the charger in my bag, and got to my feet. It was the CDC worker coming to reprimand and evict me.

"Look, I'm really sorry. I just wanted to come in to get some of my stuff. I know it was stupid, but my landlord said he was coming in so I figured it would be fine ..." I didn't get to finish firing off excuses before he reached out with both hands to grab me.

I backed up into my night table, just out of his reach. He smelled awful, like he had just vomited. I recoiled from the stench, trying my best not to be rude about it. I would have expected a chemical smell from sanitizing, but the smell reminded me more of the homeless man on the subway.

"Okay, okay, I'll go with you," I said, louder this time so he could hear me over his respirator.

Headlights from a passing car illuminated the room just enough for me to get a good look at the man behind the mask.

"What the hell?" I shouted and backed up further.

His mask was cracked and large cysts covered most of his face. Immediately, I realized it wasn't the respirator on its own making that noise. The man's mouth was covered by the growths, making any attempt at breathing or talking result in an eerie death rattle that reverberated in the breathing device. Some sort of black fluid had leaked out and covered the front of his suit, causing the horrible stench.

Part of me thought this was some sort of sick dream I was having. Maybe I'd fallen asleep during the movie. I had never seen or even heard of anything like this happening to a person. I went to move past the poor guy, but he blocked my way and lunged at me.

"Stop! Get away from me," I pleaded.

He wasn't listening. He still had a surprising amount of strength left for someone in as bad of shape as he was. When he got closer, I saw that the whites of his eyes were black and the iris was grayish like a film negative. His skin was so white and flakey it was like it had been painted.

I ducked under his grasp and backed into my living room, but the man wouldn't stop coming after me. He made a mad dash through the apartment, plowing through everything in his way. I almost escaped when he grabbed my bag, pulling me back inside. This guy had completely lost his mind. I had no choice but to let my stuff go and make a run for it.

I slammed the door shut on him and called for help, hoping one of his buddies was still around. As I ran down the hall, the mutated man kept banging and clawing at the door from the other side. I was halfway down the corridor when another of the CDC workers coming up the stairs answered my screams.

"Hey, you have to help me. One of your men is in my apartment. He's hurt really badly and going crazy ..." My voice trailed off as he turned to me.

He was in even worse shape than the other guy. This one's suit was ripped down the front, exposing most of his body, which was lined with blackened veins. Bulbous tumors swelled through the cracks in his chalky skin. He was missing a glove, which showed how badly deformed his hand was. The tips of his fingers jutted out in the form of sharp claws.

This had to be a nightmare, but it seemed too real. I doubled back, looking for anywhere I could hide. The first man was still pounding on my door to get out and now the other man was right behind me. He was running alarmingly fast for someone who looked like he should be limping.

The only place easily available was Shannon's. I ducked inside with the crazed man at my heels, but something on the floor caused me to slip and fall. I didn't even want to think about what the wet, sticky substance was, nor did I have the time to check.

I was scrambling away when I felt him grab my hair and pull me back. The claws from his ungloved hand dug into my scalp as I attempted to break free. All I could do to defend myself was strike wildly behind me in an effort to break his hold. The man was hissing and snarling like an animal. I could hear his jaw chomping the air as he tried in vain to bite me through his mask.

By using all of my strength, I twisted his wrist around until I heard it snap. He didn't even flinch in pain or back off at all. His broken hand flailed lamely at the end of his arm as he continued to reach for me. I scrambled around in the dark for something I could defend myself with, but Shannon's apartment was immaculate except for the CDC's mess.

The only useful thing I found was a wood chair. I had to try and knock this guy out so I could make a run for it. I dodged to the side as he came at me and then swung with enough force to break the chair, although it didn't stun him for long. I had just enough time to slip past and get out the door. I wanted to lock him inside like I did the first man, but this one was too fast. His fingers were stuck between the door and the frame, preventing me from closing it. It was an uphill battle trying to keep the door closed with him being so much stronger than me.

I would never make it if I ran. I let go and kicked the door to knock the guy backward so I was able to close him in. The horrible sound of both mutated men and their frantic pounding on the doors filled the hallway. Out of breath, I staggered over to call the elevator with my heart pounding in my chest. I would have taken the stairs, but there were probably more of those things on every floor.

My hands and pants were smeared with blood, which must have been from my fall earlier. This wasn't anthrax or any disease I'd heard of. No wonder they were trying to quarantine this place — "trying" being the operative word. Mr. Stahl mentioned that the woman they took to the hospital had just come back from a trip abroad. If she went somewhere in the jungle, this could be a flesh-eating bacteria that caused hallucinations or schizophrenia. I'd never heard of anything turning blood black, though.

Now that I thought about it, back in the hotel lobby the veins in Shannon's sick friend's face were unnaturally dark.

The elevator was on the floor below me when I heard a thumping sound coming from down the shaft. I'd have to take my chances on the stairs, going one floor at a time. I had barely made it to the stairs when a loud crash startled me. My apartment door fell off of its hinges, releasing the maddened worker into the hall.

I raced down the stairs, praying I wouldn't draw attention to myself. The sound of a police siren out on the street was the first bit of relief I'd felt all night. I checked from the window on the stairs to see a single police cruiser parking in front of the building. The young officer who had answered my questions was getting out of the car.

I started to run downstairs to meet up with him when I heard several pairs of footsteps on the floor below. The officer was going to walk right into them if I didn't warn him in time. Hopefully, more police were going to show up, but what was he doing here on his own anyway? I crouched down on the steps waiting so I could get his attention when he came up, but more footsteps back on my floor ruined that plan. Now I was trapped between floors with nowhere else to hide.

It seemed like the cop was taking far too long to reach the stairwell. *Please tell me these things didn't already get to him.* The footsteps from the floor above were coming closer. I went down a few more steps to the next landing until I heard they were right above my head. I tried to hold my breath so as not to make any sound, but there would be no way to get the cop's attention without alerting the mutant above me too.

What's taking him so long? Don't tell me he left.

"I was beginning to think nobody was here." It was the officer. From over the railing, I spotted his blond hair two floors below. I bolted down the stairs after him, hoping I got there in time. "Where's the rest of your team?" He was walking further away, trying to make contact with one of the infected CDC workers.

"No, don't go near him!" I screamed.

The officer whirled around and put his hand on his firearm. "What are you doing in here? Civilians aren't allowed —"

"We have to get out of here! Something turned everybody here into monsters!" I pleaded, keeping my eyes on the worker down the hall.

"Have you been drinking, sir?"

"I'm not drunk. This is serious! We are in huge danger here."

Footsteps were coming down the stairs now and the man down the hall he had been trying to talk to was turning in our direction.

"Is that blood on your jeans? Show me your hands," the officer instructed, and took out his firearm.

I put my hands up, realizing just how bad this must look.

"Please, you have to believe me. I didn't do anything." Words weren't going to matter. The more I talked, the crazier I sounded, and we were about to get sandwiched by mutants.

The cop was aiming his firearm at me. My heart was racing faster than ever as I stared down the barrel of a gun. I had never been in trouble in my life and now I was in an infested apartment with a police officer pointing a gun at my head.

"Get on your knees and put your hands behind your head. No sudden moves." I hesitated, unsure which would be worse: a quick shooting death or being torn apart. "Do it!" he demanded.

I did as I was told, lacking the courage to openly defy an officer of the law while at gunpoint. He stayed out of range and had started to use the radio on his shoulder when he was interrupted by the sound of running behind him.

"Look out!" I tried to warn him, but it was too late.

The infected CDC worker tackled the officer to the floor. They wrestled on the ground while I watched, frozen for a moment. The other mutant coming downstairs spotted us and charged. I ran over to help by kicking the worker in the head so the officer could get the upper hand on the mutant and put him in handcuffs.

"There's another!" I pointed to the one from upstairs who was blocking our way out.

"Get back down and don't move, do you understand?" He sounded like he thought I still had something to do with this, but I followed orders anyway.

The handcuffed man was snarling and thrashing on the ground.

"Stop right there. I don't want to shoot you, but I will if I have to, sir." He was aiming his gun at the second mutant now.

"Look at their faces. They won't listen. They're not even people anymore," I explained. Sure enough, it dashed right at him. He took a shot and hit it in the leg at close range, but the infected man wasn't slowed down at all. The officer fired another shot at its leg, but didn't do anything to stop the mutant from advancing. There was another loud crash upstairs, followed by the sound of running, like when my door broke off its hinges.

"Get up." The officer retreated toward me. He remained focused on the man in front of us as we backed away. "I don't want to have to fire another shot, sir, but you're leaving me no choice."

After the mutant ignored his warning, the officer fired two more shots into its chest, still to no effect.

"There's no way," I heard the officer whisper to himself. He took a final shot between the mutant's eyes and laid it out right alongside the one in handcuffs. There wasn't much time to rejoice. The mutant with the broken hand was down on our floor now and coming after us just like the last.

As if things weren't bad enough, the one in handcuffs also managed to break free. "There's an open apartment behind us we can hide in," I pointed out.

The cop fired another shot at one mutant's head, but it did little more than stagger. The mutant we thought was dead was getting back up now too. "How is that even possible?" the cop exclaimed. "Get to the open apartment, but stay close."

We flew down the corridor with all three mutants in pursuit. It took both of us to push the door closed with them trying to get in. "I can't call for help," he said. "That thing broke my radio, but other officers should be here soon."

"I know it looks bad, but I swear I don't have anything to do with this," I said, pleading my innocence again.

"What are you doing here anyway?" he asked. "This building was under investigation to be quarantined."

"I live here. Well, upstairs. I came back to get my stuff after I heard my landlord was coming to do the same. I didn't think it was anything like this."

"Neither did I. I was on my way home when I heard over the radio that we lost contact with the CDC crew. They were supposed to do a sweep of the building and check in every hour unless they found something. I should have never come in without backup, but I was already in the area and it sounded more like a lazy crew than anything."

"I'm glad you came when you did. I would probably be dead by now if you hadn't, or turned into one of those things." I switched the lights on and looked around the room, hoping for a phone or something to defend ourselves with when the door inevitably got broken down. "What was the CDC expecting to find, anyway? What the hell causes that?"

"All I know is that neighbor of yours they took out of here was said to have looked suspicious. I didn't get to see her myself, but I heard it wasn't pretty." The cop joined me in scoping out the room. "No fire escape. Great. We're not even facing the street to call for help. Nobody would hear us from here."

"We should barricade the door." I let him know all about my encounter with the infected workers while we moved furniture. He was doing a decent job remaining calm during all of this.

I wasn't sure what kind of training the NYPD went through, but if he was just a rookie then we should be in good shape when the others got there.

"Hey, whoever lives here must collect swords." I pointed out two medieval swords mounted on the wall. "We can use them to protect ourselves."

"They're just decorations." He looked over from the window. "I'll check the kitchen for something better, but I'd rather we didn't get that close again to needing it."

The mutants weren't giving up their rabid assault outside. The sound of splintering wood from the doorframe of our sanctuary was almost more frightening than the unnatural howling. At this rate, we had another five minutes at most before we were overrun.

"So, by 'suspicious' do you mean terrorism?" I was beginning to think the police knew more about this from the start than they were willing to let on. "There were a lot of police for one sick woman, and the CDC was called in pretty quickly."

"I told you I don't know anything, and even if I did I couldn't discuss it. Let's just worry about staying alive for now." His words made me more curious than ever, but I ran out of time to question him. The door finally gave way, letting in the trio of mutants. "Get in the bedroom, close the door, and hide. I'm going to hold them off," the officer said, taking his gun back out.

"You're crazy! They'll kill you. You won't have enough ammo to take them all down." He couldn't have been any more than a couple of years older than me, but he was ready to face a painful death for some stranger. I wanted to believe it was an act of heroism, not insanity, but in reality, it was probably a bit of both. Heroism would sound a lot better at his eulogy, though.

Sirens blared in the distance. We just needed to survive a few more minutes until the rest of the police got here. The mutants clambered over the barricade, completely undeterred by the officer's last few bullets.

The clicking sound of the gun's empty clip made my heart sink.

He looked back at me while taking out a knife from his back pocket that he had gotten from the kitchen. I could see his resolve starting to waver. "I told you to hide!"

I didn't know what to do. All three mutant creatures were on him now. The way out was clear now, but I couldn't just leave him here to die. Two of the infected men's masks had come off during the fight. They were doing everything they could to bite the cop, but he was just barely managing to pull away in time.

Using the knife, he stabbed one of them in the side of the head. As the cop twisted the knife a few times, the worker finally collapsed lifelessly.

One of the remaining mutants almost bit into the cop's wrist, but, on impulse, I jumped in and pulled it off.

"Get out of here! Go find help, the others should be here by now," he said, looking up at me. He had killed one, but he looked like his energy was fading fast. The last two had him pinned and were doing everything they could to maim him.

I used my body weight as leverage to tear one of the infected away from the officer. A sudden sharp pain in my ankle stopped me from helping with another. I looked down in horror. The one we thought was dead gripped my leg.

"Why won't you just die?" I screamed and kicked it in the head. The creature's jaw broke, but it still kept attacking. It knocked me off balance, making me fall to the floor near the cop. This was becoming more and more hopeless by the minute.

Out of the corner of my eye, I noticed the swords up on the wall. Ornamental or not, they still looked sharp. If only I could get one of them to buy us more time. I reached out for the swords, even though they were across the room. "Please, why do you have to be so far away ... just come a little closer," I begged, imagining them flying to me in response.

The swords began to quiver in their fixture. I wasn't sure if I was being too hopeful, but I kept calling for them in my mind. The officer was still grappling on the ground with two of the infected workers. He had lost the knife during the brawl and was reduced to punching them in self-defense.

I needed both hands to keep the mutant on top of me at bay, but I also didn't want to lose sight of the swords, which were now shaking violently against the wall. The creature's face was dangerously close to my own. I could feel its chilling black and gray eyes staring down at me.

"Don't get up," I told the cop, not that he was in any position to anyway. A whistling sound cut through the air as the swords flew from the wall. One of the blades plunged deep into the torso of a mutant attacking the officer. The second sword impaled both of the ones remaining and continued out the window with their bodies. "I can't believe that worked."

"What the hell was that?" the cop said, staring at me in shock. He threw the last mutant to the floor, took the sword out of its body, and stabbed it through the forehead. Finally, the creature gave one last spasm before crumpling to the ground for good.

J. Armand

My moment of elation came to an abrupt end. The officer recovered his knife and wielded it defensively in my direction.

"What the hell are you? What did you just do?" he yelled.

I was probably more afraid of him than he was of me. I should have known something like this was going to happen, but I thought saving our lives was a good enough reason to reveal my secret. After how heroic the cop had just been I wanted to believe he'd be more open-minded, but he was acting like I was one of them.

"I, I saved us —" I stammered. "I'm a person, not like them! Please, I can explain."

He kept his eyes on me with a look of distrust, but put the knife in his back pocket. His expression hurt me more than the lingering pain in my ankle. This is exactly what I was afraid of. One day my secret was going to come out and whoever it was would disregard everything else they knew about me and only see my inner demons.

"Let's get out of here," he said right in time. The mutant skewered to the floor was beginning to come back to life.

I shut the door behind us and ran down the hall toward the sound of voices coming from downstairs. On the floor below were three police officers, who promptly raised their firearms at the sight of us.

"I'm NYPD. Officer Turner, 23rd Precinct." The cop I was with held up his badge to identify himself.

The three turned their attention to me next.

"It's fine, he's with me." I was relieved Officer Turner vouched for me after how he acted. I expected him to turn me in and treat me like I was one of those creatures.

"Sergeant O'Donnell." One of them stepped forward. "What is a civilian doing in a quarantine zone, officer? And why are both of your clothes torn and bloody?"

I let Officer Turner do the talking, since it would sound a lot better coming from him.

"He lives here, it's a long story. We have to get out of here, Sergeant. This is going to sound crazy, but something mutated whoever was working here into ... well, into monsters, sir."

The three cops looked at each other.

"Officer, we've been through every inch of the first couple of floors. The only thing suspicious here is the two of you soaked in blood and the absence of the CDC. Tell me why you didn't call for help and how that's supposed to look from my perspective."

"My radio broke while engaging them. We trapped one in an apartment upstairs," Officer Turner told the others. "I'll take you to it, but call in backup. We have no idea how many more there are."

Going back upstairs was a death sentence, even with guns, but they weren't going to listen. After everything we had gone through, I'm sure Officer Turner wasn't looking forward to going.

One of the other officers spoke up. "You trapped a CDC employee in an apartment?"

"He's more of a nightmare than an employee." I felt bad listening to him try to explain, but I didn't want to get involved any more than I already was.

"I'm going to have to ask you to hand over your gun and the knife," Sergeant O'Donnell said. Officer Turner complied without protest and allowed the sergeant to check his gun. "The clip is empty."

"Yes, sir. I had to defend myself and the unarmed civilian." Officer Turner stood his ground even though this wasn't going well at all. Part of me wished one of the mutants would come running out just to prove him right.

"Escort Officer Turner upstairs. If you find anything dead other than 'monsters,' put him under arrest. I'll be keeping his firearm for now in case it's needed for evidence," the sergeant ordered. "I'll take the civilian down to the hospital to get checked out."

"I'm fine, really. I'm staying at a hotel not far from here." The last place I wanted to be right now was a hospital.

"Son, you're lucky I'm not arresting you for trespassing and whatever else is going on here. The fact is, you are here against the law and potentially contaminated now, based on the CDC's findings. So you tell me, will you get examined voluntarily or do I have to put you under arrest?"

Actually, jail was the last place I wanted to be. I agreed to go with the sergeant and followed him out to his car. At least I was free from that nightmare, but what about the others still in there?

Chapter Three

The ride to the hospital was filled with awkward silence. I thought the sergeant might grill me on what happened at the apartment, but he didn't speak. Judging by my reflection in the backseat window, I looked as bad as I smelled. My brown hair was usually a case of chronic bed head, but now it was matted with dried blood.

It was taking a really long time to get to the hospital. I knew we had been driving for almost half an hour by the clock, but was scared to say anything. They might have a special site set up to handle this, but why would it be so far away from the apartment?

We were driving alongside the Hudson River and I could see a series of docks ahead. There were no medical buildings around here that I knew of. I finally spoke up. "I thought we were going to the hospital."

He didn't answer me. Something was very wrong. The knot in my stomach tightened as we pulled onto the docks. The area was dark except for a few scattered lights along the pier, but I spotted a group of thin men in business suits up ahead. They were standing around watching as we came to a stop in front of them.

Sergeant O'Donnell parked the car and got out, locking it behind him with me still in the backseat. The men greeted him and exchanged a few words that I wasn't able to catch. They kept looking in the car, which creeped me out.

There was a sudden gust of wind around the group, and out of nowhere another man appeared. This one had a much more muscular build than the rest of them. He was wearing only black shorts and boots that looked like they were armored or reinforced. The others looked taken aback by his sudden arrival. He showed them something that he held in his hand, which sent them into a panic.

I wasn't able to make out what the object was until some of them moved out of the way. It was a severed head belonging to one of the men in the group. Now I noticed the body it was missing from as it fell over. The shirtless man looked right at me and grinned before punting the head out into the water.

He disappeared as fast as he had arrived. There was another gust of wind and the killer materialized just like before, this time holding two short *katana* dripping with blood at his sides. Behind him, the businessmen fell to pieces in a pile on the dock.

I was a sitting duck in the police car. There was no way to unlock the doors from the back and a partition of bulletproof glasses separated me from the front. Sergeant O'Donnell was the only one left standing. He had his gun out and was taking aim at the back of the man's head.

The swordsman flipped both *katana* up in the air and sheathed them at his hips in one smooth movement. Sergeant O'Donnell opened fire, but none of the bullets hit. Somehow, the man dodged them all, barely moving a muscle or even turning around. His speed and reflexes were so phenomenal it was inhuman.

Putting his arms behind his head, he stretched dramatically like he was inviting the sergeant to try again. His incredibly toned physique could put any of the world's top fitness models to shame, let alone an amateur who had just booked his first job. In fact, this guy's body was so perfectly sculpted he looked as if he had walked right off the cover of an elite bodybuilding magazine.

Sergeant O'Donnell took another shot, but the man flicked the bullet right back at the cop's forehead, killing him instantly. The man vanished for a split second and was in front of my door before I could blink. I had thought I was home free once I escaped the mutants, but now I was going to be killed by some sword-wielding psycho.

The man ripped the car door off and threw it behind him like it was a toy. All I could do was stare in terror. Now that we were up close I could see he wasn't much older than me, maybe in his mid-twenties at most. He had dark blond hair hanging almost to his cheekbones, and matching stubble. His angular features were rugged and masculine, yet his tan complexion was as flawless as if he had been airbrushed.

He grinned and disappeared once again. I took the opportunity to flee the car. I wasn't expecting to get far, but it was better than waiting around for him to end it. For some reason I stopped to stare at where the dead bodies were. But there was nothing there except piles of dust mixed with the suits they wore.

"You're welcome," a voice called from above. I hadn't even noticed him high up on a metal storage unit. His tone was filled with arrogance, and he seemed completely unfazed by all of the carnage he had caused.

I weighed my options as I looked up at the man, who was crouching like a tiger ready to pounce. I noted several sets of tattoos on him that I hadn't paid attention to before. They were all Asian characters, like he was part of a Japanese gang or cult, except he was clearly Caucasian. He had three symbols on his left pectoral, several rows lining his right flank, and more down his right forearm. One tattoo in particular stood out: a huge claw mark along his left flank that didn't seem to fit the theme of the rest.

I snapped out of my stupor, let adrenaline take over, and turned to run. My goal now was to get back to a main street where there would be people. I was almost off of the docks when I checked over my shoulder to see if he was following, but he was nowhere in sight. There was an alley between two warehouses only a few yards away that looked like it would take me out to the street.

"What's wrong? Don't tell me you've never seen a dead body before." He appeared before me as I turned down the alley. It almost sounded like he was teasing me. I froze in place and just stared at him as he blocked my way. He crossed his arms patiently and leaned against the wall to my left. "Not the talkative type, I guess," he said, mocking me again. He began advancing toward me with a macho swagger in his walk. It reminded me of a rock star showing off to his audience. I glanced at the weapons hanging at his side and began to back away nervously while keeping my eyes upon him.

"I know what you're thinking, but I'm not going to kill you. Just make this easy on yourself and come with me." My head started swirling from the sound of his words. It felt like something was taking over my mind and making it hard to run away.

He was around six-two or three, but seemed giant by comparison when we stood toe to toe. The unnatural hypnotic feeling grew as I stood there paralyzed. I could feel him looking down at me while I did my best to avoid direct eye contact. Grabbing my face, he forced me to focus on him and flashed a devilish smirk.

His deep green eyes squinted intensely as I felt him peering into my soul. My head began to fill with an even stronger, more disarming sensation than before. The inner voice that had been screaming inside, telling me to flee, was silent now.

I was drowning in a dangerous sense of complacency as my survival instinct melted away.

The sound of a police siren blaring behind me was followed by blinding light and a familiar voice shouting. I jerked away to look over my shoulder and saw Officer Turner approaching.

I was happy he had survived, but if he wasn't already suspicious of me, he had more than enough reason to be now.

Regaining a lucid state, I turned back around, but the mysterious swordsman was gone. If not for the headlights of Officer Turner's car illuminating the dark alley, I wouldn't have noticed the cop's latest injuries. His nose was bloody and quite possibly broken.

"What happened to you?" I asked, still anxious to leave the area as soon as possible.

"Where's the officer that took you here?" he asked, successfully countering my question with a better one of his own.

"Down by the water." I pointed in the direction of the massacre.

"Is he dead?" I was a little surprised he jumped to that conclusion.

"Yes, but for the record, I didn't do it," I answered frantically. "Some guy with two swords killed a whole bunch of people, including the sergeant. We have to leave or he's going to kill us too."

Officer Turner looked completely desensitized, most likely from shock. "Take me to the sergeant."

"We're going to die! How did you know where I would be anyway?" I asked.

"Police GPS told me where the sergeant's car was parked," he explained. "I spotted you without him, so I assumed the worst."

"The worst for who, me or him?"

"There was no reason for him to be all the way down here," he continued. "If there was trouble he would have called it in to dispatch, unless he was already dead."

"Not to push my luck, but it sounds like you think I killed the sergeant and stole his car, so why aren't you arresting me?" Jail might really be the better option at this point. At least I'd be safe there.

"If there is a dead body where you're taking me, then we'll talk about arrest." I wasn't sure I followed his logic, but he definitely knew something he wasn't saying.

The police cruiser was just how I had left it, but something wasn't right. The pile of men's suits was gone, as was the officer's corpse. There wasn't any blood or signs of a struggle, not that it was much of a struggle to begin with.

I was expecting to be questioned about the disappearing evidence, but instead Officer Turner took out his flashlight and began investigating the area.

"They were right here, I don't understand." I swore to myself.

I began to search with him. Not that I wanted to find a dead body, but more to make sure I hadn't lost my sanity yet.

"Let's go," he said after finishing his search of the sergeant's car and recovering his empty gun.

"You seem like you were anticipating this." Now I was starting to become suspicious of him.

"The only thing I knew for certain was that it was going to be something weird," he answered as we made our way back to his car.

"So, you aren't going to arrest me?"

"No reason to yet. Get in and I'll explain."

We sat in silence for a minute as he drove us out to Eleventh Avenue. I looked out the passenger window at the city lights. Seeing normal people on the sidewalk helped restore my sense of safety.

Officer Turner was the first to speak. "Describe in as much detail as you can remember what happened once you left the apartment."

Recalling the whole scenario was more difficult than it should have been. Everything was so surreal. I must have been in shock myself, because I was having trouble talking about things that happened just a few minutes ago. He did a good job humoring me, though.

"No offense and not to sound ungrateful, but I'm surprised you're even listening to my side of things. I figured the only thing you would care about is what your fellow officers had to say and how bad this looks."

"You're innocent until proven guilty. It's my job not to be biased. There's always more than one side to a story and right now something else is bothering me a lot more.

"Once you left I took the officers to the room we locked the man in, but he was gone. When we ran into another one of the CDC workers, the officers didn't seem alarmed at all. Instead, they jumped me and tried feeding me to it. I managed to get away when more of the mutants ambushed us, and that's when I remembered the sergeant was with you.

"Like I said before, there was no reason for him to be down here with you and no way he dropped you at the hospital and made it to the docks that fast. Sure, you could have killed him and stolen the car, but if you were a cold-blooded killer you would have left me to die in that apartment."

He was interrupted by the dispatcher on the police radio spewing official-sounding jargon. The part that caught my attention was as clear as day, though.

"All units — we have an officer down and one wounded from gunfire at the Westfield Apartments on 81st and Lexington Ave. The perp has been identified as Officer Lyle Turner and was last seen leaving the scene in his police car. A warrant for his arrest has been issued. Subject is armed and dangerous. Proceed with extreme caution."

We both stared at the radio as the broadcast repeated several times before he switched it off.

"Is that true?" I asked, but was already pretty sure he couldn't have done something like that. He seemed like too much of a good guy.

"No, they must have radioed that in to cover themselves. If I had gone to straighten this out with my captain first, then I would never have known why you and the sergeant were down here. It just didn't sit right with me."

"Well, thanks for coming back for me and everything." He definitely deserved a medal for going above and beyond.

"You don't have to thank me, but I appreciate it. I'm beginning to get used to people treating the police like the bad guys. I joined the force to protect others and be a hero, but most people don't see us as that."

"What are you going to do now?" I asked. "Can't they use GPS to find your car?"

We pulled over and parked on a quiet residential street. I looked over at him as he rested his head on the steering wheel.

"Uh, Officer Turner?"

"Yeah, I'm fine. Just call me Lyle," he said, though his answer wasn't reassuring. "We're going on foot from here. I only took the car to get to safety as fast as possible."

Lyle got out and retrieved a backpack from the trunk. He got in the backseat, where he pulled street clothes out of his bag and changed while I checked my pockets for my phone and wallet. I noticed he had the same charger as mine plugged into the dashboard.

"You should probably go to the hospital; you might have a concussion and broken nose," I advised.

"Going to the hospital isn't the best idea. Hospitals are usually one of the first places we check when canvassing an area, especially if the suspect might have sustained injuries," he said. He climbed back into the driver's seat dressed in blue jeans, an NYPD T-shirt, and a Yankees baseball hat. "We should get you checked out. Dispatch hasn't mentioned anything about you over the radio, so there isn't a warrant out for you yet."

"I just want to go home. My dad is an emergency room doctor back in Boston. I doubt we're infected; the CDC workers turned within a couple of hours of being there and it's been longer than that for us."

We got out of the car and began walking up the block. He left his phone behind so it couldn't be traced and let me take the charger. I thought about all the people we passed and wished I were as ignorant as they were about everything going on. We stopped in a store so he could pick up a prepaid phone. He paid in cash, and we moved on.

"There's something we still need to talk about," he said.

Here it comes, I thought. I guess this couldn't be avoided any longer. The elephant in the room had finally had enough of being ignored.

"What was that thing you did with the swords in the apartment?"

"It's just something I'm able to do. I don't know how or why it works," I answered truthfully. The full extent of my power remained a mystery to me.

"That's a little more than a bar trick. I'm assuming the sergeant's missing car door was your doing?"

"No, the guy with the *katana* I told you about did that. I didn't think I'd even be able to lift something as heavy as the swords in the apartment."

"He can move stuff with his mind too?"

"No, he did it with his hands." I knew I must sound like a mental patient off of his meds. I contemplated lying about the whole thing.

"How long ago did you find out you could do this?"

"When I was fifteen." This was already the most I had ever spoken about it with anyone, but I felt he deserved some explanation after everything.

Back when my power first manifested, I'd woken up in a cold sweat from a nightmare, staring into the mirror opposite my bed. I could hear the mirror start to crack before it completely shattered on my dresser. Not sure if I was still dreaming, I went to pick up the pieces. Once my hand was just over the shards, they began to float just slightly above the dresser. I inspected them in disbelief, not knowing I was the one causing this to happen. Whenever I would motion like I was picking them up, they would rise and then fall when I would stop.

I saved some of the broken pieces in my drawer for the next morning, so I could practice again. I wore the safety goggles we used in chemistry class just in case something went wrong. It wasn't only those pieces I could move. Small objects around me would randomly start to move or float wherever I was. It took a few months, but I got better at controlling it a little at a time. The more I focused and the more clearly I could see the object, the easier it was to lift. Something across the room wasn't as easy as an object right in front of my eyes.

In less than a year, I was able to balance multiple small objects in the air as long as I could keep my eyes on them. Fine manipulation was always a problem; stuff like folding a sheet of paper always ended in my tearing or crumpling it.

"Do your parents know about this?" I could sense the curiosity growing in his voice.

"No, nobody but you knows. They worry a lot to begin with. Being doctors themselves, they would want a million tests done to see what was wrong with me.

"I was always careful about practicing when no one was home or I was sure I couldn't be seen. I didn't mess around with it much anymore once I got it under control. I used to excuse myself to use the bathroom in class all the time when I noticed papers or pens start moving, or leave the dinner table when I would have to grab the salt shaker out of the air before my parents noticed. I would never hurt anyone though. I try to stay away from people as much as possible. Back there in the apartment was the first time anything violent happened."

"Good to know. I'm trying to get a feeling for why the people at the dock would try and kidnap you and how the sergeant is involved if nobody knows what you can do," he said.

"Kidnap?" The thought hadn't crossed my mind until now, but it made sense. "The guy who killed them was acting like he did me a favor. He was trying to get me to go with him."

"I know you want to go back to Boston. Hell, if this wasn't my only home I'd want to be far away from this mess too. I don't know what's going on or how any of this can even be real."

"You're dealing with this better than I am." I shoved my hands in my pockets to stop them from trembling now that the adrenaline rush was over. "I bet you never thought you'd be involved in all of this when you became a cop. How long have you been on the force? I remember that fat cop calling you a rookie."

"Three years. Three years and I already probably put an end to my career and my freedom. My father must be rolling in his grave." I must have really struck a nerve. I was trying to cheer him up at how savvy he was for being new, but I guess as optimistic as he seemed, it was still bothering him. "I come from a family of cops, all NYPD," he continued. "That's all I wanted to be for as long as I can remember."

"Innocent until proven guilty, right?" I tried consoling him. "I'm sure we'll find something that will help."

Lyle was quiet for the rest of the way. I felt bad for bringing it up to begin with, but I didn't want to push it so I left him alone.

"If someone is after you it's not safe to travel alone," he said as we neared the hotel I was staying at. "You don't want to lead anybody back to your family, either. Get some rest. I'm going to be staying locally, so call me if anything happens. Otherwise, I'll get in touch in a few hours."

Lyle and I went our separate ways once we reached the hotel. As I trudged to my room, my head was spinning from the night's events. I had nowhere else to go if I couldn't return to Boston. The thought of never seeing my family again scared me just as much as the mutants, the NYPD, and a serial killer chasing after me.

Chapter Four

It was dusk by the time I woke up. My phone was working again, thanks to Lyle's charger, and I had several messages. Two of the messages were from my parents but surprisingly had nothing to do with the hotel charge on the credit card. The other message was from Lyle about an hour ago. I sent my parents a generic text message to keep them satisfied and then called Lyle.

"I'm at the diner across the street. I'll meet you outside," was all he said before hanging up.

Lyle was in pretty rough shape when we regrouped on the street. He had gotten some medical attention, judging by the bandages on his nose and hands.

"Did you sleep at all?" I asked after greeting him.

"No, there wasn't any time. I went to a clinic to get patched up and then picked this up for you." He took an envelope out of his pocket and handed it to me. Inside was a one-way plane ticket to Boston leaving from La Guardia airport in a couple of hours.

"I thought you said I couldn't go back. How did you get this without the police finding out?"

"Don't worry about it, I got it covered. I'll take you to the airport to make sure it's safe. I can't get on the plane while there's a warrant out for my arrest, but I'll take the train to meet you."

"You don't have to do this."

"This isn't a situation either of us can resolve by filing a report. I need to get out of the city and go off the grid anyway. I'm hoping that if I follow you it will give me some evidence to prove I'm innocent."

It was clear that Lyle's mind was already made up. There wasn't much room for me to argue. I had nothing keeping me here and was all too happy to go home. The only problem would be explaining this to my parents. I decided not to tell them the whole story until I got there. They would probably think drugs were involved when I told them everything. I considered saying they were spraying for rats or whatever they do in apartment buildings, and then just acting surprised when it eventually made the news.

We took the subway into Queens. Everyone in our car got off after a few stops except for us and another man sleeping with his head down. He reminded me of the homeless man from my ride home the night before by the way he was dressed.

"Was any of this on the news?" I asked Lyle, remembering what the man had said about government conspiracies.

"No. I'm not surprised; there's a lot that doesn't make it to the news. If something can't be explained immediately, it gets withheld so there isn't a city or country-wide panic." Lyle had his eye on the sleeping guy now too. "I'm not sure how they would break the news of a mutant outbreak. I didn't hear anything else on the police scanner, so it's most likely an isolated incident the federal government will come in to clean up."

The subway reached its next stop, letting on a pregnant woman and little girl. A few minutes later, Lyle gave me a funny look and subtly motioned to the sleeping man. I checked, but I didn't notice whatever he was trying to point out.

We had to get off at the next stop so we could transfer. I looked down at the man as we left the train and instantly saw what was wrong. Black veins were spreading along his hand at an alarming rate. The doors to the subway were just closing when we both heard the familiar death rattle. Lyle put his hand to block the door and grabbed the man, dragging him out of the subway car.

"This guy is sick, call an ambulance!" Lyle shouted to a couple of cops on the platform to get their attention before disappearing into the crowd. I stood there by myself now with the man at my feet until my phone vibrated in my pocket; it was Lyle calling. "Meet me up on the street. I couldn't let them see me."

Lyle wasn't wasting any time getting out of the area. He had already hailed a taxi when I caught up to him and was waving me over to hurry up. "This is either spreading really fast, or we're being targeted," he whispered to me after telling our driver where to go.

"You know, if you want to blend in when we get to Boston, you should trade that Yankees hat for the Red Sox. I'm just saying."

"I'd rather be thrown in jail for life," he laughed. "Are you a baseball fan?"

"In spirit, I guess. I used to go to the games all the time with my dad until recently. I follow mixed martial arts now. I tried going to a match with him, but all he kept talking about was how he couldn't understand why people would put their bodies through that pain on purpose."

"Yeah, I kind of agree with him there. I grew up the same way. My dad practically raised me at Yankee Stadium and I still go every chance I get."

There was a pause in the conversation. I wanted to ask how his father died, but wasn't sure if he would be comfortable talking about it. He did mention it on his own last night so maybe he wouldn't mind.

"You said your dad was a cop too?" I asked.

"Yup. Eighteen years on the force." There was a strong sense of pride in his voice followed by another pause. I was about to drop the subject when he continued on his own. "He died a hero. I was only eleven, but I remember it like it was yesterday."

"How did it happen?" I asked.

"Some scumbag had held up a liquor store in Hamilton Heights and was fleeing the scene in a stolen car. The officers chasing him said the guy was suspected to be high on something. He was driving against traffic to escape when my dad heard the APB over the radio.

"My dad prevented the guy from plowing through a playground full of children. He intercepted the car with his own, but was killed when the scumbag T-boned him. He gave his life to save all those kids and their families. They say he died instantly, so at least he didn't suffer. If I turn out to be even half the man he was, half the hero, I'd consider my life fulfilled."

"What happened to the other guy?"

"He got sentenced to life in prison, but walked away from the wreck with only a few broken ribs, whiplash and a concussion."

"Wow. That's not fair."

"Nah, justice was served. I know my dad is up in heaven with an unlimited supply of cold beer and free access to any game he wants to watch."

"That's a good way of putting it. I don't know, I think I'd hold more animosity if I were in your position."

"Trust me, I did for a long time, but killing a person because you're angry isn't justice. My dad always told me, 'treat others how you'd want to be treated.' That's the philosophy I still live by today. It took a lot for me to get over losing him, but I'm stronger for it and I'd like to think I make him proud."

"I bet you do. He would've been impressed seeing you in action last night."

"I didn't think of it that way," he laughed. "Just so we're clear — what happened last night was real, right? I've played the whole thing over a million times in my mind."

"I'm pretty sure it was. I wouldn't be here talking with you otherwise."

We got to the airport just in time. I didn't have any baggage to check, so we went right to the security gate with only a few minutes to spare.

"I'm going to leave you here. They won't let me through unless I have a ticket or show my badge. If you see anything, tell the flight staff immediately." His words weren't exactly encouraging but there wasn't much else we could do. "You'll be fine; the flight's only a couple of hours. I'm going to meet you there as soon as I can. Have your parents pick you up from the airport and let me know when you arrive."

The entire time I was walking to my plane, I had the feeling I was being watched. I kept looking around expecting to see someone staring at me, but I couldn't pinpoint where the feeling was coming from.

When I got to the gate, everyone was already boarding. I stood there watching the line dwindle as people pushed past me. I should have been getting on this flight, but something inside my head was pulling me away. They were announcing the last boarding call now. I started to move, but instead of going toward my terminal, I walked to the next, and then the next.

I didn't know where I was going, but I kept walking until I got to another security checkpoint. I wasn't sure if the guards would stop me, but I went through anyway. The more I wandered, the more the feeling of being watched grew, until my head started pounding. I crossed over to an empty waiting area. There was nobody at the ticket-checking booth, but the doors were open to enter the plane. My vision began to fade in and out, but I was still moving forward. I could make out the word "private" on one of the signs in the terminal.

"What am I doing? I need to go back," I said out loud.

I was halfway down the wrong boarding tunnel when my head cleared. I could see the shadow of someone behind me, but when I turned to face whoever it was, they were gone. The sound of whistling came from down the tunnel. I turned back around to see the swordsman from last night standing there with his hands on his hips.

This is it. I'm going to die.

He vanished before I could say anything. Then came a sharp pain in the back of my head and everything went black.

I regained consciousness to the sound of several voices in the distance. It took a while for my eyes to adjust to the dark room. A minimal source of light came from beyond the curtains of ceiling-high windows.

The king-sized bed under me was done up like one you would see in a museum exhibit of Old World European royalty. The fabric was intricately detailed in floral patterns that matched the many different-sized pillows on either side of me. Each pillow was adorned with gold thread and tassels, which made me think they were more for show than comfort.

There were similar ornate details in the furniture. A large mirror with a gold frame stood alongside an armoire of dark wood in the far corner of the room. Two antique-looking night tables adjacent to the bed displayed elaborate candelabras complete with fresh ivory-colored candles.

A conversation broke out on the other side of the door to my left.

"Welcome home, Noah," said a woman with a French accent. "You were gone longer than expected. I had begun to miss you. It must have been nice to be abroad again."

She seemed friendly, but something about her manner of speech was overly polite and formal.

I heard a familiar voice answer, "I was enjoying the freedom." It was the swordsman.

"Well, where is it?" the woman asked.

"I dumped him in here." There was a light tap on the door as he answered.

"*Him*? I thought it was —"

"Nope, it's a person," Noah said, with an aloof air.

Why did that woman refer to me as "it"? Just what was she expecting him to kidnap?

"And what of Monsieur Price?" she questioned further. "What did he know of this?"

"I got rid of Price and his lackeys. His job was to locate and deliver the kid." Noah's response made me even more curious. Was this Price guy one of the men he killed at the dock?

I heard the tinkling of piano keys as someone started to play.

"It's too bad he didn't work out," the woman stated. "Now we will have to replace him to keep New York in our name. Finding someone who we can trust is clearly more of a problem than we first thought. *C'est la vie*, no?"

Maybe this was some organized crime syndicate like the Mafia. It would explain the kidnapping and expensive taste in decor.

The French woman spoke again. "So, what can he do?"

"Move stuff with his mind," Noah answered in the same indifferent manner. "I haven't found out anything else yet."

My body tensed as I sat on the bed listening.

"Is that of any use?" The woman didn't seem all that impressed or even interested that someone in the room right next to her could magically move objects. Then again, the man she was speaking to could move as fast as lightning.

"It kept him alive against those creatures I told you about. I saw him impale a couple." He was there watching Lyle and me while we were being attacked and we never even noticed. Was Lyle in on this from the start? Did he bring me to the airport knowing this guy was there?

The sound of the door opening got my heart pounding again. The flick of a switch lit a chandelier overhead and two sconces above a fireplace across from me.

My kidnapper entered first with his usual swagger, followed by the most attractive woman I had ever seen. They both exuded an indescribable presence that made it difficult, if not impossible, to look away. The woman, however, was so particularly stunning I remained fixated on her beauty.

She appeared to be about Noah's age. Her skin resembled fine china, white and pure, a distinct contrast to the man's golden tan. I had always hated being so fair-skinned, but she pulled it off well. She wore barely any makeup; it didn't look like she needed any help enhancing her natural beauty. Her eyes shimmered in the light like brilliant evergreen jewels.

"Oh my, Noah, you didn't mention our guest was this cute." I could feel myself blushing at the sound of her words. The French accent made everything she said sound so much more exotic and sultry.

She was dressed in a sleek black evening gown. The diamond necklace and earrings she wore looked like they could have afforded her a private island in the Caribbean. I couldn't keep myself from staring at the thigh-high slit along the side of her dress. She had legs that went on for miles and the body of a lingerie model.

"*Bonjour!* My name is Vivian, dear. And you are?" She bent over like she was talking to a child.

Noah leaned back against the far wall with his arms crossed, just like in the alley. "He's not much of a talker."

"Don't be shy, love," she crooned. I looked up at her from my seat on the bed. Her burgundy hair was styled up, with just a single lock dangling free.

"Where am I? What are you going to do with me?" I choked out.

"Do with you? What do you mean?" Vivian seemed genuinely taken aback by my question.

"He thinks we're trying to kill him." Noah didn't seem too concerned as he began fidgeting with assorted knickknacks on the fireplace mantle.

"Why would he think that?" Vivian sounded as if she were scolding him.

"We didn't really get to spend quality time," he replied, and shrugged.

Vivian sat next to me on the bed and placed my hand in hers. "No, no, my love. You misunderstand. You are safe here. We mean you no harm."

My entire body tingled the moment we touched. I looked down at her soft petite hands on mine and smiled for a second, forgetting where I was. Her perfume was intoxicating. I could smell a very faint scent of flowers coming from her exposed neck. Feeling a bit braver, I looked her over from head to toe. Vivian was absolutely gorgeous.

She smiled at me and patted my hand. "My apologies if we frightened you, it was not our intention ..." Her voice trailed off and her gaze became vacant as she stared past me. I turned around to see what was there, but all I could see were some oil paintings of landscapes on the wall.

Vivian stood up. "She's calling me. I must go greet the other guests. Play nice." She addressed Noah while walking to the door and closing it behind her.

I watched the door listlessly, wishing for her to come back. After a few seconds my daze wore off and I remembered I was alone in the room with Noah now. He was sizing me up from across the room with a predatory glare.

I inched away from him on the bed as he sauntered toward me.

"Relax already, I'm not going to hurt you," he said, putting his hands up and taking a step back.

I remained cautious and looked at the weapons still on his hips. Noah rolled his eyes and took them in his hands. I backed up another couple of inches, almost falling off the bed. He placed the swords on the mantle, almost knocking over the expensive-looking decorations without seeming to care.

"Better?" he asked.

Noah approached again and turned his back to me. More Asian tattoos that I hadn't noticed earlier ran down his spine. He fell back on the bed and rested his arms behind his head. I jumped to my feet and traded places with him against the wall. As long as he was being civil, I had so many questions I didn't know where to start.

"Why'd you kidnap me?" I figured that was as good a place to begin as any.

"Leave if you want." He waved his hand at the door. "Those guys are just going to keep coming after you, and I won't always be there to save your ass." Noah came off as so laid-back when he wasn't murdering people, but I seriously doubted he was just going to let me walk out. "You wouldn't have liked them as much, trust me. Besides, I'm a whole lot better to look at."

I ignored his last comment. "Who are they? And who are you? Are you in the Mafia or the Yakuza or something?"

"No!" he said and burst out laughing.

I felt a bit insulted by his reaction, but it was better than him stabbing me. "Then why did you bring me here? Do my parents owe you money?"

Noah rolled his eyes again.

"It's my turn to ask something." I could hear the piano still playing somewhere in the house. The increasing din of conversation and laughter sounded like there was a party starting outside. "Can you fly?" He was squinting at me like he was serious, but his smirk threw me off.

"No." I wasn't being completely honest with him.

I had made several attempts at flying since I learned about being telekinetic, and they all ended in total failure. Lifting myself up wasn't too tough, but it was balance that gave me the most problems. After multiple near-death experiences, I gave up and put it behind me with the only thing gained being a new fear of heights.

"That sucks." Noah lay back again, obviously disappointed by my answer.

"How are you so fast?"

"It's in my blood." He was looking at his boots, which were getting the clean sheets on the bed all dirty. It made me cringe thinking how angry Vivian would be if she saw.

"That's not a real answer." I surprised myself at how brazen I was being with him.

He looked at me sideways. "Neither is you saying you can't fly."

Was he reading my mind or what?

"How long have you been following me?" I asked.

Noah sat up and moved to the edge of the bed like he was more invested in our conversation now. "Not long. I only got to New York the night before we met at the docks."

"What makes you think I can fly, then?" If he didn't know before, then I had just given it away.

"What can I say? I'm great at reading people. It's a gift." He was grinning ear to ear now. This wasn't us bonding. He was interrogating me.

"Fine, don't tell me." Maybe a less controversial topic would get me answers. "What do all of those tattoos mean?"

"I don't know. They were from a fortune cookie." He fell back onto the bed and started laughing at his own bad joke. "They look good, right?"

"I think you're full of it." Let him stab me, I was getting nowhere except learning he was a total jackass.

He was playing with the tassel on a pillow now. "If you're not gonna take this seriously then I'm not either."

"Me? I am being serious. You're the one giving me all these ridiculous answers." I regretted saying that almost immediately. He sat up again at the edge of the bed and stared at me.

"So, I'll ask you again." His eyes were piercing right into me like in the alley. "Can you fly?" he said, enunciating each word slowly.

"No! Okay, sort of..." I didn't know how to respond without sounding like a total moron. He raised an eyebrow and waited for me to get the words out.

This was so uncomfortable to have a discussion about. "I've tried, but I'm bad at it. I can go up, but that's pretty much it."

He clapped his hands in sarcasm. "There we go, finally some honesty."

"Answer my question now. Why are people trying to abduct me?" I heard the door opening behind me and hopped out of the way.

It was the lovely Vivian again. She gracefully stepped into the room and smiled warmly at me. She looked at Noah on the bed and the dirty sheets. She was visibly displeased, but didn't mention it.

"Your presence is requested in the ballroom," she told him. "Please get dressed and meet us there."

Noah let out an exaggerated sigh and leaned back, looking at her. "What's wrong with what I'm wearing?"

Vivian gently closed the door behind her. I suddenly felt like I shouldn't be a witness to whatever was about to happen. Noah just lay there grinning at her as she walked up to him and sat on the bed.

"Can you please be good tonight?" She put a finger on his chest and slowly traced it down his abs, all the while staring into his eyes. Her French accent could have melted the coldest heart. "For me."

"Why mess with perfection?" Noah gave a sly wink and pulled her on top of him.

He shifted gears and got up from the bed so suddenly that Vivian was almost knocked over. Sauntering to the door, he swung it open and paused, stretching his arms against the framework and nodding to a couple passing by who were dressed for the red carpet. He disappeared in his usual fashion, followed by Vivian.

Party guests strolled by, looking in at me. Left standing there awkwardly, I closed the door, not knowing exactly what my captors expected of me. It didn't seem like there would be much resistance if I tried to leave, but this could be a trap.

Of course my cell phone was gone, so I couldn't call for help.

I stepped out of the bedroom and into a massive corridor with wide marble floors and hand-carved ceilings. The walls were decorated with oil paintings and mirrors illuminated by candlelight on either side. Every few feet were another set of luxurious baroque furniture: loveseats and sofas, dark wood end tables and gilded display cases of expensive jewelry. If I didn't know any better, I'd think I was back in seventeenth-century France about to meet the king or something.

Walking down this hallway was like walking down a city block. I must have passed a dozen rooms before I reached a four-way intersection with two grandiose curved staircases and a tremendous gold and crystal chandelier overhead. The piano still playing somewhere in the background was now joined by a string quartet for a waltz. The more I wandered toward the music, the more I got myself lost. This must be why they were so confident I wouldn't escape.

It took me a good fifteen minutes, but I finally found where everyone was. Beyond huge double doors was a ballroom the size of a football field with yet another giant chandelier hanging overhead. I felt as if I had accidentally walked into another casting call. The room was filled with beautiful men and women of all ages. A butler and a full battalion of servants did their best not to intrude upon the many conversations of the guests they served, but even they were just as striking as the rest of the crowd. Marble columns around the room reached up to an exposed second floor, where balconies held even more party guests.

Noah was lounging up on one of the balcony railings chugging wine from a bottle. Even at rest, his intimidating presence made him stand out.

I caught a glimpse of Vivian among the party guests chatting with another young woman. The other woman's back was turned to me, but I could tell there was something special about her. She was dressed in an elegant cascading ball gown made of purple silk. Long brunette hair highlighted with lavender flowed into a theatrical spool on each side of her head, like something from a high-fashion runway show.

Vivian noticed me watching and gave a coy smile that made my whole body tingle. As if in response to her silent command, the crowd between us parted to form a path.

"Oh, Dorian!" she said, and beckoned. "I wish to present you to our hostess and master of the house."

As I walked up to Vivian, the lady in purple turned to us. After meeting Vivian, I didn't think it was possible for anyone to surpass her beauty, but this new woman was in a completely different league. My heartbeat quickened with every step closer. It was more than just her flawless physical appearance or angelic features that drew me in. The woman's mesmeric radiance was such that it created undeniable sensations of pleasure.

"Aurelia de Saint-Pierre, may I present Monsieur Dorian Benoit, our guest this evening?" I heard Vivian speaking, but I was finding it challenging to concentrate in this other woman's presence.

"How do you do?" Aurelia smiled warmly and offered her hand in greeting. "It is a pleasure to welcome you into my home."

Her accent was a blend of English, French, and possibly something else. She watched me intently with gorgeous hazel eyes. I looked down, noticing that her nails were meticulously painted to match her gown. I don't know what came over me, but I took her hand and leaned in to kiss it, almost passing out the second we made contact.

There was no way she was human. Aurelia was a mere five foot six at most. Even without her elaborate hairstyle, which must have weighed more than she, she was still shorter than I, yet her presence was so electrifying all attention was inescapably drawn to her.

"Thanks, it's nice to meet you. I have to be honest though, I'm not sure why I'm here, wherever here is," I said as politely as possible.

Vivian excused herself from the conversation with a bow and disappeared into the crowd. Nobody seemed to mind that we were standing in the middle of the dance floor. The guests continued around us, orbiting Aurelia like she was their sun.

"Why, you are in France, of course, just a short way from Paris. Your life was in great danger," Aurelia spoke with grave concern. "I sent for you to be rescued and brought to my chateau where you would be away from harm."

France? That lunatic knocked me out cold for an entire transatlantic flight?

"Rescued from whom? I thought the guy you sent was trying to kill me. He knocked me out in an airport. Not to mention murdered a whole bunch of people."

"How uncouth! I apologize for Noah's brash behavior. His social graces may be lacking, but his speed is invaluable in such situations. I assure you there is no further cause for alarm."

"Who was he sent to rescue me from?" I checked out the corner of my eye, hoping he was far enough away to not hear us talking about him.

"A former associate turned traitor by the name of Maximilian Price. He became interested in your particular abilities, but that has been resolved now."

She must be talking about my powers ...

"Yes, precisely," she said, answering my thoughts before I said anything. "You were also correct in assuming that I am no mere human, nor have I been for quite some time. There is no cause for masks here, child. This place is a sanctuary for those like you and me."

She's been reading my mind this entire time.

"Please forgive my rudeness." Aurelia seemed worried that she may have offended me. "I'm not normally so intrusive into my guests' minds. You must understand, while we may all be supernatural here, you are still different than the rest of us. I must be conscious of my people's safety at all times."

I had always felt there must be others out there like me, but I never thought I would get to meet them. Most of the time I tried forgetting about my powers since I couldn't explain them. To be honest, I guess I was scared of what I might be.

"I would never hurt anyone," was the best I could offer.

"I've heard the contrary. Noah tells me you handled yourself impressively against the attackers in your home."

I forgot I overheard him telling Vivian he witnessed that.

"Uh, I wouldn't say it was impressive, not after seeing what he can do."

"Don't be so modest, my dear! I have a keen sense for talent. It was I who turned Noah, after all."

"What do you mean, you turned him?" I would be lying to myself if I said I didn't already have a good idea what she meant, but I was hoping it was just a misunderstanding.

"We are the Archios." She smiled and extended her arms out to the crowd dramatically. "Members of our coven have had many different labels imposed upon us throughout time. Regardless, I believe you would agree that we are merely beautiful, yet tragic beings lost somewhere betwixt life and death."

All eyes in the room were on me now. Vivian was watching from across the room with a drink in her hand. Noah was still relaxing up on the balcony, looking down at us. The dancers glanced over their partners' shoulders as they passed. These were not the hideous monsters portrayed in the movies, or the ones from back in New York. Everyone here was sophisticated and gorgeous, so gorgeous it only made sense that they were supernatural. I felt the same tranquilizing sensation again as I had with Noah in the alley. This feeling coming over me must be another of their powers. But what would they want with my powers when they had their own?

"As the last remaining founder, it is my will alone that governs our many houses across the world. Aristocrats, bureaucrats, and various artisans fill our ranks, but monsters we certainly are not. However, we are but one of three covens and countless strays. Those other covens give rise to your nightmarish legends, and taint our good name."

I watched her mouth closely as she talked. Sure enough, she was still reading my mind. "The Archios do not prey on humanity for sustenance like savages. We use our allure to draw in potential donors. Those we drink from are more than willing to let us in close and to feel our lips pressed to their flesh," she said, and smiled just enough for me to see her that her top two incisors were subtly sharpened to a point. "Our fangs are diminutive and purposeful; they are all that is required to draw the blood we need."

"Aren't you killing people by taking their blood either way?"

"Absolutely not! Violence is quite unnecessary. Our donors experience unspeakable bliss, so they remain comfortable and ... *satisfied* by the encounter. Not to mention that their emotions flavor the blood we drink. The taste of their arousal is something of a delicacy that our kind savors."

She covered her smile with her hand and looked away as if taken aback by her own forwardness, but I was anxious to hear more.

"Taking very little to keep each person healthy is beneficial to both parties," she carried on. "In present times, humanity far outnumbers us and it is in their nature to fear and loathe the unknown. A revolt would be disastrous to our kind if they were to learn the truth of our existence.

"All we wish is to spend our immortality in peace. I have amassed quite a considerable amount of wealth in my time. As a connoisseur, I have often made large financial contributions to help fund the cultivation of the fine arts through the ages. Unfortunately, my appearance makes remaining unseen in public an impossibility. My undead heart breaks each night knowing I can never leave these walls to offer applause at an opera or walk the red carpet in support of an artist without persecution."

I could sense a great feeling of despair growing in her voice.

"Even those outside of this coven make some attempt at remaining hidden now, although murder is much more common for them. For centuries, the Archios have been burdened with covering up such violent indiscretions. We are forced to use our powers over the mind to influence human governments and media for the survival of us all."

"That sounds like a lot of work for something that isn't even your fault. It's not fair you have to hide from persecution when you aren't the ones hurting anyone. All that effort could be used on working together instead."

It was tragic. If even these beautiful, cultured, benevolent people couldn't exist freely because humans were too close-minded, then what hope did any other minority have?

"It pleases me to know you are sympathetic to our plight. We have even established connections with blood banks to further avoid harming our delicate flock. There was once a time when we were more openly accepted among mortals, but those days have long since passed," Aurelia said, and then stopped abruptly to watch the crowd behind me.

"There is a small problem," Vivian whispered to Aurelia as she walked over. "Intruders are in the south garden. They appear to be the same creatures that our young guest encountered in New York."

"Not again, not here too," I said in a panic.

"This is unheard of!" Aurelia exclaimed. "They must have followed you here. Now I fear we are all in danger."

The party came to a halt as everyone began squabbling among themselves. They were all speaking other languages, but it was pretty easy to understand their reactions.

"Noah." Aurelia spoke and he immediately dropped down beside her. "Please handle this troubling situation with great haste."

"Good, I was getting bored listening to a bunch of whiney socialites all night," Noah said, looking around at the crowd with disdain.

"Take Dorian with you, should you need help," Aurelia offered.

"What? Why me? I have no idea how to fight!"

"You've dealt with them before, no?" Vivian gave an encouraging smile. "You are the only one here with any experience."

"You guys are probably a lot better at this than I am, though," I tried to reason with her, "and I think Noah has way more experience with this kind of stuff; just look at him!"

"At least he has good taste," Noah nodded smugly.

"Just because we are immortal does not mean we are made for war. I am still a lady above all else. I was under the impression you understood us. Surely you do not expect to send me out to face such horrors," Aurelia said, sounding hurt and appalled.

"I didn't mean it like that ..." I was digging myself a pretty deep hole.

"Please help us," Aurelia and Vivian pleaded. I couldn't refuse them no matter how badly I wanted to. They had all gone out of their way to help me and now they were in trouble.

"Okay, no problem." The words slipped out against my will, captivated as I still was by their beauty. Just looking into their inviting eyes filled me with courage. *I can do this, I did it once before. At least this time I'll have Noah with me so I shouldn't have to actually do too much.*

"Marvelous!" Aurelia rejoiced and turned her attention to Noah. "Do watch out for one another. I wouldn't want either of you to be harmed by those vile things."

"Of course, your Highness." He bowed to her with a hint of sarcasm.

Noah grabbed the back of my shirt and the halls of the chateau flew by. We were outside surrounded by a maze of tall rosebushes faster than I could blink. The mutants' threatening growls echoed through the night ahead of us.

"Well, good luck, 'hero'," Noah chuckled as he dropped me to the ground.

"What? Where are you going?" I panicked at the thought of being left alone out here with those things.

"To the far side. We'll split up and flank the enemy. Work your way to the fountain at the center. Sun Tzu, *The Art of War*, man. Pick it up sometime; it might save your ass."

I wanted to inform him how irrelevant that advice would be in about five minutes, but he was already gone along with my tiny shred of confidence.

Chapter Five

The sickly sweet scent of roses did little to detract from the horrors in store for me ahead. Light out here was scarce. The only way I could see anything at all was from the light of the chateau and some lampposts around the garden. There was nothing in sight I could use to defend myself with either, just winding rows of ten-foot-high rosebushes.

It sounded like the monsters were scattered throughout the grounds, but I had no way of telling how many of them there were. Hopefully, Noah would just take care of them all before they found me so we could get out of here. A growl came from the other side of the hedges, and it was moving fast. Those things were cutting through the maze. With no way to tell what sort of progress Noah was making, I would have to figure out some way to help, or else they would reach the chateau. Despite impending doom, the classical music from the party was starting up again as if the dancers hadn't a care in the world.

I crept to the first intersection, trying not to get ambushed from either side. The pounding footsteps on the ground followed by unearthly growls made me wish I were back in the company of the Archios. A violent rustling from a hedge nearby made me tense up. I knew what was coming, but I was still unprepared.

A roughly human figure came bounding out toward me. It was further mutated than any of the infected people in New York. Most of the mutant's clothes were torn off, but it was nearly impossible to discern what they had looked like originally. I could make out the same black veins and creepy eyes, but it was so deformed that there were no longer any discernible facial or body features. The skin was sunken-in, like it had suffered from a sudden extreme weight loss. If these people had any shred of life left in them, they were suffering badly.

One look at the monster's claws and I wanted to run, but it wasn't about to give me the chance. A thick fog was rolling in, making visibility even more of a problem. I had no clue how effective my powers would be without a weapon to use them on. I held my breath and put out my hands in front of me as the creature charged.

I hit a home run, as I knocked the creature back through the bushes much further than I expected. The fog was blinding now, obscuring the little visibility I had to start with. However, the crash the creature made when it landed must have alerted the rest of them. Their snarls and trampling footsteps were all headed in the direction of their fallen friend. The distraction might work in my favor if I could navigate the maze swiftly to the fountain where Noah said to meet.

The maze felt like it went on for miles. Turn after turn was just getting me more lost, but I could hear running water somewhere close by, so my port in the storm shouldn't be too far off. I didn't know why I had agreed to this, or how I was expected to kill these mutants, but it wouldn't be the first time in my life I had been talked into something I didn't want to do. Another one of the creatures ran past the intersection ahead, but didn't notice me. I crouched down and snuck over to where it came from to check for the fountain.

A guttural howl from above caught my attention in time to see one of the mutants descending from over the hedges. It landed on top of me and knocked me over. I panicked and tried to push it off, but couldn't. There was barely an inch between our faces as it tried biting mine off. It was hard to concentrate on knocking the creature away during the struggle, although my life depended on it.

It was now or never. If I wasn't able to use my power, I would die. Painfully.

My head throbbed as I strained to launch the mutant into the air. It soared ten feet, then twenty feet, thirty feet, until I lost sight of it. I never thought my power would have this kind of effect. I got back up and leaped out of the way just in time for the creature to collide with the ground. It was crippled and broken, but that still didn't stop it from lurching after me.

I started running toward the sound of the fountain, but was tackled from the side as another of the mutants burst out from the bushes. I felt a stabbing pain followed by the warm sensation of blood trickling down my forearm. The creature had its teeth lodged deep into my arm and was attempting to tear the meat from the bone. I was in too much shock to yell, but I managed to pry the creature off and send him flying backward.

Black viscous drool from the mutant's mouth was mixing with the bite it had taken out of me. The way to the fountain was now blocked by all of the creatures, which had heard the fighting. The first one I had encountered was at my feet, gripping my ankle. I was trapped and frantic to find a way out. More of the mutants closed in, clawing and slashing at me from behind.

Hands grabbed at the back of my shirt, making me fall and hit my head. As I lost consciousness all of the sounds of the night swirled inside my head. I could feel the creatures closing in on me. Everything faded to red and then black until finally the pain stopped.

I woke up in another of the chateau's bedrooms with a peculiar salty-sweet taste in my mouth. I put my fingers to my lips.

It was … blood?

I felt good — lucid even, for someone who had just been through hell. The cuts and scrapes on my arm were gone and I wasn't in pain or tired anymore. I checked my other arm, hoping the bite was also mysteriously healed. There wasn't any pain or bleeding, but the deep holes made by the mutant's teeth were still wide open and the veins surrounding the wounds had turned black. Staring at the infected bite made me sick to my stomach.

This can't be happening ... I'm going to turn into one of those things.

I got up to look around the room for something to wrap my arm with. The bedroom's decor was completely different from the rest of the chateau. In place of the oil paintings, display cases, and expensive vases were weapons, and a lot of them. This had to be Noah's room. All of the weapons were different kinds of *katana*, and several scrolls hanging on the walls had writing on them similar to his tattoos.

"Don't touch my stuff." Noah's voice startled me as I was leaning in to look at one of the swords.

"It would have been great to have had one of these out there," I said turning to him. "Now I'm going to become one of those things, aren't I?"

"Yeah, about that ..." Noah hopped up onto an antique seventeenth-century dresser like it was some piece of cheaply manufactured furniture. "I fed you some of my blood to help fight the infection."

"You what?" I shouted in disgust. Without the Archios using their alluring aura to entrance me, my feelings of hopelessness and dread returned.

"What is that going to do to me? I don't want to be undead or a mutant! I just want to be normal!"

"That's not how it works. You need to have died recently for my blood to turn you. Basically, your soul can't have passed on to the afterlife yet," Noah clarified. "Our blood is good for healing; as I'm sure you noticed, your other cuts are gone. It's gonna get burned off by the infection after a while though."

"How long until that happens? And what do I do when it does?"

"Who knows? But I guess we'll find out soon enough!" he exclaimed just a little too enthusiastically. Noah's callous personality was easily equal to or even beyond his physical appearance and fighting skills. I didn't think he could keep himself from acting like a complete asshole for more than a few minutes at best. "Stop admiring me for a second. This is serious. You can't tell anyone I gave you my blood. *Anyone.* Got it?"

"I wasn't ..." I forgot he could read minds. Of course, with his ego he would interpret my thoughts as a compliment, so it was futile explaining myself. "It's not like people would believe me anyway, but what does it matter if somebody like us knows?"

"Because it's forbidden. Not only does it reveal us to humans, but then we'd have people creating armies of superhumans if everyone did it."

"You don't seem like the type that follows the rules."

"Yeah, well, I didn't, and now I don't want anyone to know about it. I'm kind of old, so my blood is more powerful than that of the other Archios. If someone is still after you and they get my blood, it can be used against me."

"Just how old are you?"

"Almost two hundred years," he boasted.

"My, that is quite the exaggeration," came Vivian's smooth voice from the doorway.

"You're just an old hag, Vivi," Noah laughed, and flashed her his signature grin. Vivian gingerly unsheathed a *katana*, checking her reflection in the blade before replacing it.

"You are very lucky that age is a symbol of status, Monsieur Burckhardt." She strolled over behind him and walked her fingertips across his shoulders.

"Now, tell me why I needed to search all over for you. You know Aurelia wishes to speak with you." Vivian spoke softly in his ear from behind him. She placed her hand over the tattoos on his chest.

"Funny, I thought this was my room," he teased and leaned back against her. "Checking here first would make sense to me."

"You are only ever here if you are hiding something," she said as she dug her nails into his pecs just enough to draw blood.

"Damn it," he said, and grabbed her by the wrist. "You know I hate having to get my ink redone."

She let go and licked her finger with a mischievous smile. The cut on his chest had already healed by the time she backed away, leaving a tiny gap in the writing.

"Your tattoo should be the least of your worries. Aurelia isn't too pleased with your performance tonight. You failed at something so simple," she scolded him.

"I don't fail," he scowled. "It isn't my fault the kid can't take care of himself."

I might as well have been mounted up on the wall with the swords. They were so absorbed in their conversation they didn't notice, or maybe they didn't care, that I was in the room.

"I'm sure that will go over famously with her. At least I will be abroad when it happens."

"You're going to America? Without me? Why?"

"New York is quickly slipping through our fingers with Price no longer in control. The same creatures have besieged at least one hospital, a hotel, and a police station in only a few hours. The remaining Archios we have there are doing their best to cover it up as wanton acts of violence, but there is only so much they can clean up without a source of leadership," she said.

"How are you planning on actually eliminating the problem?"

"I will recruit help once I'm there. We must contain this at all costs, with the humans unable to do so."

"I could clear those things out with no problem," he bragged.

"Really? Could you?" she antagonized.

"Let it go, Vivi. If I had known what I was working with out there, things would have gone differently tonight."

"I worry about you, that's all," she said, and placed her hand on the side of his face.

"There's no reason to. You did a pretty good job teaching me a thing or two." Hearing Noah speak genuinely was kind of shocking. Their interactions together were always interesting, to say the least, but it was hard to tell what the relationship between them was.

"It doesn't look as bad as I had imagined." Vivian glanced over at my arm, finally noticing me standing there. "I thought he would have turned by now. I've heard in New York it was taking only a few hours upon infection. Curious that he has no other bruises. Don't you think so, Noah?"

I didn't need to be a mind reader to tell that he was already busted.

"Isn't that something?" Noah went to stare out the window, looking for a distraction to change the subject.

"Now I see why you were hiding with him here. I hope you know what you're doing. Aurelia is busy with matters concerning her sister, so I suggest you tread lightly."

"Haven't they been feuding for years? What's up with Rozalin now?"

"There was news that she was staked and burned."

"Nice, that calls for a drink. But, I'm sure she'll be back."

"*Oui*, she is unmatched in her field of magic. When she does return, she will most certainly feel that Aurelia was involved in her death and come to make trouble, so be on guard." Vivi moved to the door. "It will be dawn soon. I've arranged for one of the drivers to take our young guest to the airport. The private jet will be waiting to return him to Boston."

"I get to go home?" I couldn't hold back my excitement. Finally some good news.

"Yes, child. It isn't safe here any longer, especially during the day, if you can't defend yourself," she said and addressed Noah before leaving. "Take care of yourself in my absence, Monsieur Burckhardt."

"I'm ready to go home," I said, hurrying to the door. I couldn't care less about my arm if I could make it back to Boston.

"Not yet, you're not. You're mine until sunrise." I didn't like the sound of this.

"You're not talking about sucking my blood, are you?"

"I'm sure you'd like that, wouldn't you? But no, I don't want to catch what you have and I'm sure it tastes terrible, too."

We were outside again in an instant thanks to his blazing speed. I could see the main chateau not far across the lawn. Noah's room was actually in a smaller chateau on the property, and we were now standing on top of it.

"Ready to fly?" he asked.

"Considering I'm dying of an infected bite, no, not really!"

"The high ground almost always has the tactical advantage and you need all the help you can get."

"I don't care about tactics," I said, peering off the edge. "Tactics aren't going to mean anything if I don't find a cure!"

"You're probably going to die a lot sooner if you hit the ground from this height. Ready?" Noah didn't allow me any more time to protest. Instead, he tossed me off of the roof to my death.

It was too dark and high up to see the ground clearly. I had to fight the urge to close my eyes, since I needed to see to use my powers. If I just tried to pull myself up by my arm or leg I'd wind up tearing them off when falling this fast.

The ground was rapidly coming into view as I hurtled downward. Only a few feet were left before I made a bloody impact, and I still couldn't figure out how to fly.

My nose was in the grass when suddenly I stopped short an inch away from smashing my face in. I dangled there a moment, realizing that Noah had caught me by my shirt.

"What is wrong with you!" I shouted.

He dumped me on the ground at his feet. "You weren't even trying."

"I never said I wanted to." I got up, hoping he was done with whatever he was trying to prove.

"You don't want to because you're scared, and that's the worst excuse for failure." He pointed to the first line of the Asian tattoo on his flank. "These proverbs are what I've learned to live by since I was turned. This one means 'Fear is failure'."

It was frustrating trying to get him to listen, but I figured he wasn't going to give up a chance to hear himself speak. As long as he could keep catching me there wasn't any real harm in trying until he got bored and left me alone.

"Fine, I'll try again," I said, already back up on the roof with him. "But what I'm more scared about, if I live through this, is my infection."

"If you really want to learn through fear, then I'll give you some real motivation." I felt him push me off of the building. In a flash, he was below me holding something in his hands. As I fell closer, I could see him standing there with his swords out and ready to strike. This guy was nuts. He was really prepared to kill me over making a point.

I kept hoping he would put his weapons away, but he stood his ground. I concentrated everything I had on envisioning lifting myself up. The wind slowed against my face as I began to glide and steady myself out. I closed my eyes as I neared the ground and put my hands out, preparing for a rough landing.

My left forearm grazed the tip of Noah's sword as I passed, making me flinch and lose control. I wiped out and tumbled across the grass, ending up facedown.

"You got my sword dirty," Noah said, rolling me onto my back with his boot.

I glared up at him as he wiped his blade on my shirt. I was hoping he was reading my mind so my opinion of him at the moment would come through loud and clear.

"What are you so upset about?" he asked. "You almost flew, didn't you?" I wouldn't have called it flying, but it was progress, I guess.

"Life is never going to go back to the way it was." Noah's words cut deep. That was exactly what I didn't want to hear. "This is who you really are. It's time you stop hiding and man up, because no matter how much you pretend you can't do something, it doesn't mean that other people out there don't know. You either learn to use your powers or you'll die, sometimes twice."

All of a sudden we were on the roof again. I was still angry and hurting as I plummeted to the earth for a third time. Noah was standing guard beneath me with his swords unsheathed and there was no doubt in my mind he was ready to use them. My first thought was to knock him over, but I could see that going horribly wrong. I balanced myself out the same as before, but this time made it over him without getting nicked. The earth shook under me as I landed forcefully on my feet behind him.

I stood up triumphantly. This was the most progress I had made trying to fly, but my joy came to a quick end. I felt a sharp pain along the back of my arm, followed by the warm sensation of my blood again.

"What the heck was wrong this time?" I turned to look at him. Noah cleaned his blade again.

"You didn't fly."

"Did you see what I just did? I landed on my feet. That's close enough." I was proud of myself and that was what mattered most. "I can move things because I can see them. I can't see myself, so I can't fly. Just let it go already."

He put both *katana* back in their sheaths. "Close your eyes."

"No way. I don't even trust you with them open." Now both of my arms were stinging in pain as blood dripped down them.

Noah crossed his arms impatiently.

"Fine." I gave in and closed them.

"Touch your nose," he ordered.

"What was the point of that?" I said, having followed his directions. This was suspiciously easy coming from him, but I shouldn't complain.

"You don't need to see your nose to touch it, so you don't need to see your whole body to lift it. You know you're there and you have the power. Now put the two together."

"How do you know it'll even work?" I asked him.

"You can't do this if you keep doubting yourself. Fear is your worst enemy, not any mutant or infection. 'A sword is useless in the hands of a coward.' " He pointed to the second line of his tattoo. "It means real strength comes from courage and faith in your abilities.

"My training gave me the discipline and confidence to conquer anything; without that, you'll never overcome weakness. You need to learn to do things like tune out distractions, hone your senses, trust your instincts, and always stay aware of your environment. The more you know, the less you'll be afraid, and then nothing can stop you."

Once Noah dropped the narcissist act, he came off as pretty wise. Maybe there was more to him than swords and swagger. Maybe.

"Don't stab me, but you don't seem too disciplined. You don't act like the other Archios. Come to think of it, I don't think I've ever seen you wear a shirt."

"I like to stay in touch with the modern world. I mean, what's the point of looking this good if you talk like Shakespeare?" Noah smirked and reclined on the grass. "I'd rather walk out into the sunlight than become one of those stuffy aristocrats."

"What about the discipline, though?"

"For over a century I trained with the best warriors in Japan until I mastered several martial arts, including different styles of *jujitsu* and *ninjutsu*. I traveled all over, challenging the most skilled warriors without using my powers. It wasn't until I was sure I was the best that I mixed in my other abilities and added parkour to create my own style.

"My kind inherit their powers from the one who turns them. They can adapt over time with practice, kinda like how living things evolve. Vivi and I both inherited Aurelia's hypnotic ability, but they like to use it a lot more than I do. My specialty is speed and stealth, since they obviously compliment my hardcore martial arts training."

"That's really cool. No offense, but when I first saw you running around half-naked with swords, I thought you were some serial killer on drugs."

"They're *wakizashi*, shorter *katana* made for indoor, close-range combat and easier concealment. There is nothing sexier than twenty inches of tempered steel, except when it's in my hands. As for the shorts and boots, they're my own modified version of *haidate* and *suneate*, armor that samurais wore. Not that I really need the armor, but it looks good."

"That explains a lot." I took a seat on the grass and began ripping the bottom of my shirt to use as a bandage for my arm. The two cuts from his sword had already healed due to Noah's blood in my system, but the bite mark was as bad as ever. "I don't think I could ever manage half of what you went through."

"Yeah, no kidding. If you had a thousand years you couldn't do it," he laughed. I realized our serious talk was over and his arrogant side was back.

"Want to know why?" he continued. "You have no passion, no motivation, and no conviction. You'd rather fall to your death hoping someone will catch you than do what you need to save yourself. Whether you want to believe it or not, you're just a coward who can't accept what you are."

His words struck a nerve. It made me think of how my mom was always going on about finding myself and my passion in life.

"Stand up and close your eyes." Noah just wouldn't give up. I was hoping he would have forgotten after getting to talk about himself. I got to my feet and closed my eyes, expecting the worst.

"Don't fall," he said. There was a moment of silence as I waited for his next direction and then I felt my legs kicked out from under me.

"What was that for?" I looked up at him while flat on my back.

He rolled his eyes with his arms crossed. "Stop complaining and get up. You proved you can at least float, so do it."

I tried again, but this time he made me wait what felt like ten minutes before he made his move. By the third and fourth time, I was flinching at every blade of grass on my leg and every breeze. I caught myself right as I fell backward the fifth time. I stayed suspended in the air parallel to the ground. It felt like I was floating in a pool. I opened my eyes and took a deep breath, looking up at the moon. The sky was so clear and it would have been a beautiful night if I wasn't getting the crap kicked out of me.

Something was wrong. Noah wasn't talking about himself, giving me cryptic lessons, or hurting me. I sat up, still floating a few inches off the ground. He was gone. I straightened myself out so I was levitating in a standing position. I felt like a toddler learning how to walk as I wobbled unsteadily in the air, balancing myself with my arms out to the side.

I didn't get long to enjoy my feeling of weightlessness. Everything became a blur as the world raced past me at Mach speed. Noah threw me over his shoulder and was running up the side of the chateau again. This time when he reached the roof he didn't stop. He took a flying leap off the side and threw me into the air as he disappeared into the darkness below.

As I fell, I realized Noah wasn't waiting under me like the other times. By now, I knew he had to be planning something even more devious. I closed my eyes and let the floating sensation take over me. I slowed my fall until I was completely stopped a foot above the ground, and then carefully righted myself.

Noah appeared in front of me, sheathing his swords. I was still finding it a little tricky to balance without concentrating. At this height I didn't have to look up to meet him eye to eye. He motioned with a finger to follow him and vanished from sight. Less than a second later, he reappeared across the lawn. I glided over the grass after him, picking up speed along the way as I gained confidence. Noah played his disappearing act several more times, making me chase him around the property. Soon I was cruising at sprinting speed.

"You can fly now," he said and stopped in front of a gatehouse where a limo waited. "Don't make this a waste of my time by getting yourself killed."

"Thanks, I appreciate it." I didn't want to add to his over-inflated ego, but I was extremely grateful for his unorthodox lessons. "But what do I do if the infection gets worse?"

"This limo will take you right to the private hangar at the airport. Oh, and here's your phone."

He tossed it into the air and disappeared without answering me. There were several messages from Lyle, who was camped out at a motel in Boston. This detour was going to take some serious explaining.

Chapter Six

I was so mentally and physically exhausted that sleeping through the flight wasn't a problem. By the time we landed at Logan International, it was night again. I felt like I hadn't seen the sun in weeks.

"Hey, thanks for coming," I greeted Lyle, who was waiting for me as soon as I got off the plane.

It was good to see someone who didn't want to kidnap or kill me. I still wasn't sure how to explain things to my parents. At least Lyle would be easier to start with, since he had witnessed some of the weirdness so far.

"Yeah, no problem. Are you okay? Your message was kind of vague."

Lyle was looking at me like I had three heads. My clothes were torn and filthy and I hadn't showered in a couple of days, so I probably smelled wonderful.

"Fine, now that I'm back. Would you believe they just let me go?"

"I would believe just about anything lately."

"Boy, am I glad you said that."

"Let's talk outside before you wander onto another plane," he joked as we exited to the main area of the airport. I was relieved to be with living people again, even if they were all staring at me for looking and smelling like a homeless person.

"Ya know, I thought you bailed on me when I didn't hear from you, but the airport told me you never even got on the plane."

"I was kidnapped," I said as we left. "You were right about the sergeant and the men at the docks, but it's over now. The sword guy I told you about, his name is Noah. He was actually sent from France to help me."

I looked around to make sure no one was listening while we stood out on the sidewalk.

"My ... uh, specialty, if you want to call it that — well, someone in New York found out about it and wanted me abducted," I explained. "Whoever it was used to be business partners with the people in France that rescued me."

"If there's one thing I learned as a cop, it's that there are always witnesses. So, the French just let you go even after knowing your secret?" Lyle asked.

"I don't know. I guess they didn't want to be responsible for keeping me around." I was scared to admit that I had become a liability now that I had been bitten. It was also a little embarrassing that even with special powers I wasn't able to take care of myself. Lyle had been understanding about everything, but I couldn't take the chance of him going into cop-mode if I told him. He might want to quarantine me, or worse, put me down to stop me from turning.

"We need to find evidence that the French knew about you being kidnapped."

"What? Why?"

"You said this guy Noah killed their former business partners on our docks. He also killed the sergeant of those dirty cops. That's not justice, it's murder. We're dealing with dangerous people and from what it sounds like, the only business they're in is crime.

"There weren't any bodies left, but I'm sure the crime scene unit found at least a fingerprint from the car door that was ripped off. Maybe even a hair or drop of blood if we're real lucky. That will help to prove others were involved so we don't sound crazy.

"Did you find out anything having to do with Noah being supernatural while you were there? Did they say anything at all when they let you go?"

"No, not really," I lied. "They were hosting some big party and didn't seem to want me around once they were satisfied their ex-partner wasn't a problem anymore. I guess they just wanted to make sure he was done drawing attention to them."

Getting into the Archios would only complicate things more. I wanted to tell him everything, but I also wanted to put this all behind me.

"Then why would they let you live if you're the last witness to all of this?"

"I, uh —"

"Are you working for them now? Is that it?"

"No!"

"Then why are you lying to me, man? I put my ass on the line for you."

"I'm not. I don't know how to explain it any better right now. All I want to do is see my parents. We can talk after. I promise I'm not going anywhere."

"Come on, I'll take you home so you can get washed up and see your family," Lyle offered.

We got into one of the cabs lined up along the curb and finally headed home. The ride was quiet until my wound started to hurt under the makeshift bandage.

"What's wrong?" he asked when he noticed me grab my arm in pain.

"Nothing. I got cut, but I'm fine. It's a long story."

We made it to my neighborhood in good time. The houses around here were all spaced far apart and secluded within the woods, with long driveways for privacy. If we actually had neighbors to speak of, my parents would be the type to worry that they might see me looking like I had gone through a war.

"You can let us off here," I instructed the driver as he pulled up to the end of the driveway. I was hoping the short walk up to my house would buy me more time to think of what I would tell my parents and get rid of the knot in my stomach.

"Wow, nice place," Lyle said as we got out. "But I don't think I could ever live somewhere so quiet. Coming to Manhattan must have been a big change for you."

"It took some getting used to, but I'm definitely homesick after the past couple of days." If he thought my place was nice, I could only imagine what he would have thought of the chateau.

"Does your family know you're coming?"

"No, I couldn't think of what to tell them, so I'm just going to wing it," I admitted.

"Do you want me to wait out here until everything's cool with them?"

This wasn't going to go well either way. Lyle might not know me well enough, but my parents could always tell when I was lying, and the truth sounded worse than any lie I could come up with.

"They're supernatural," I blurted out on my front steps. "Your parents?"

"No! I mean the people from France. There is a group of them. They call themselves the Archios and live in a huge chateau outside of Paris. The person from New York who was trying to get to me used to be one of them. I didn't want to say anything before because this just keeps getting more unbelievable."

Lyle was staring at me, stunned. "I believe you. It's a lot to take in, but I figured you couldn't be the only one. And I thought I had seen everything growing up in New York City."

"It's pretty late, so my parents are probably asleep," I said while unlocking the front door with a spare key we kept hidden. "Wait down here, I'm going to go wake them."

The comforting smell of home made me so happy to be back. I knew the house so well I could navigate it even with the lights off. I should have cleaned myself up first so I wouldn't freak out my mom and dad, but it was too late now.

"Mom, Dad, are you guys awake?" I whispered and knocked on the open bedroom door. The TV was still on and they were snoring so they must have just fallen asleep.

"Dad," I whispered louder and walked up beside the bed. "Mom!"

They were both uncovered and sprawled out on the bed in uncomfortable positions. It wasn't snoring I had heard. I could see dark veins running up my mom's arm to her face. I kept calling them more and more loudly to try and wake them. They were getting worse by the second as their skin started to whiten and flake off.

"Wake up, please!" I begged, choking back tears. "Not here, not them too!"

Lyle came running up to the doorway. "Dorian, what happened?"

"They're fine, they're just sick," I sniffled with my head down, holding my mom's hand. "They can fight it."

Lyle turned the lights on and walked inside. "Oh my god, Dorian, get away from them."

"She was trying to call me," I said, looking at my mom's cell phone on the bed. She had most of my number dialed, but never completed the call. "I could have done something ..."

"It's not your fault," Lyle said after checking for a pulse. "We need to get out of here."

"And go where? I have nowhere to run anymore, there's no point. They're all I have."

"We can go back to New York."

"Manhattan is about to be overrun by those things," I interrupted. "They already took over a hospital and police station last night. It's being covered up by the Archios while they take care of it."

"We still can't stay here in case they ... you know."

"Just go. I was already bitten so it doesn't matter." I showed him the bite mark on my arm.

"What the hell — how?"

"The mutants are in France, too. I couldn't defend myself when they attacked the Archios. Noah fed me his blood, but I don't know how long it will last."

"He fed you his blood? What do you mean, he fed you his blood?" Lyle was rightfully shocked, but really, after what he had seen lately, that was nothing.

"Noah said their blood can heal people. Right now, it's the only thing preventing me from turning." I tried to sound casual, like I was reading the directions off a bottle of painkillers.

"Then there's still hope. Change your clothes and take whatever you need," Lyle said and dragged me away from the bed in to the hallway. "Does your father have a gun we could use? I still have mine, but no ammo."

I nodded and pointed back to a dresser in the bedroom before leaving for my room down the hall.

I stood there for a moment, thinking about if this was all a bad dream. After washing up in my bathroom as fast as possible, I grabbed clean clothes and changed into them. *This can't be happening*, I kept telling myself. *I'm going to wake up soon. I just have to play along until it's over.* I went to my closet for an old backpack from high school and began throwing in clothes.

The sound of growling and gunshots from my parents' room interrupted my packing. I got up and ran out of my room. In the hallway, I could see Lyle exiting their room and closing the door behind him.

"What happened?" I tried to push past him, but he blocked the door.

"You don't want to go in there," he said quietly. "I had to make sure they wouldn't be coming back. I'm sorry."

He was splattered all over with black blood now and the gun in his hand was shaking. "We need to go," Lyle prompted, still guarding the door.

I returned to my room to finish, but my sense of overwhelming sorrow was making it difficult to concentrate. Looking around the room I grew up in was only making things worse. A baseball bat with a significant layer of dust stood propped up in the corner. It was there more as homage to my childhood than anything else. For years, my dad took me to the batting cages on the weekends. He wasn't particularly athletic, but I always had the feeling he thought it would be some sort of an ideal all-American father-and-son bonding moment. He was the type of dad that would still dress up as Santa long after I found out Santa wasn't real, just because he thought it was the thing all good dads should do.

Something new on the wall above my bed caught my eye. It was the license plates from my first car, and they were in a frame. I had sold the car to someone in town when I moved to New York. Everybody in the city uses public transportation and I needed the extra cash, but it had killed me to give up the car after working through high school to save up for it. I didn't even realize until now that I had left the plates with the guy I sold it to. My parents went out of their way to get them back and frame them for me. This must have been the surprise my mom said they had waiting for me when I came home for the Fourth of July.

I couldn't take it anymore. Maybe it was the thought of what my parents' happy faces must have looked like while they were hanging the plates, or maybe it was the fact that they would never get to see their thoughtful surprise come to fruition. I couldn't fight off the feeling of emptiness creeping up inside me. I had no home, no family, and nowhere to go now. I dropped my bag on the floor and sat on the bed with my head in my hands, fighting the urge to cry. I could hear footsteps approaching my room, but didn't look up.

The footsteps paused at the doorway before continuing inside.

"I'm sorry." It was Lyle apologizing again. He took a seat next to me.

Hearing Lyle tell me he was sorry made me wonder if there was anything really left for me to lose after this. "I'm going to stay here." I kept my head down, not wanting him to see me with tears in my eyes again.

"You can't, it's not an option," he said, and picked my bag up off the floor.

"I thought it was over when Noah killed those people in New York and let me go. The Archios would take care of the mutants, my parents would have all the answers for my infection, and life would go back to normal. But he was right. I'll never escape this life now," I mumbled, pulling away from him as he tried to drag me by the arm.

"I know it must feel like the end. But it's not."

I had already messed up Lyle's life back in New York by getting him involved, and now there was a good chance he would be killed because of his association with me, just like my family. The best thing I could do for him now was part ways, but the little I knew of Lyle so far told me he would be too much of a good guy to just walk away.

I stood up, looked at my bag in Lyle's hand, and summoned it to my side.

"Come on, man. We can talk on the way if you're up to it." He gave me an encouraging smile.

I stepped back, eyeing the gun in the holster under his jacket. Confused, Lyle looked at me and then down at his gun. I pulled it through the air to float in front of me, pointing it at his head.

"Dorian, what are you doing?" He spoke calmly with his hands up. "If this is because of what I did in there, getting revenge won't make things better."

"This isn't about my parents. I don't want to mess up anyone else's life, so we go our separate ways here." I was going to miss Lyle's optimism.

"Dorian, you haven't messed up anyone's life. If it weren't for you I wouldn't have survived by myself back in your apartment building. I owe you my life." Lyle was holding his hand out to take the gun, but I kept backing it away just out of reach.

"I don't want to hurt you. Just get as far away from me as you can." Whether or not he really felt none of this was my fault or he was just trying to talk the gun down didn't matter. I had to scare him off. I held my hand out in front of me and knocked him onto his back down the hallway.

I stared at him, not knowing what else to do as he got back up.

"This is what they want," he groaned. "They want you vulnerable and alone, but you're not. Whoever tried to kidnap you is still out there. It's too much of a coincidence that this keeps happening around you. They infected your parents knowing you'd be coming back here. Don't just throw yourself at their mercy."

Lyle sounded like he was pleading for my life and not his own. He was throwing away a free ticket to leave all of this behind, one that I wouldn't have so nobly ignored if I was him.

"It's never going to end," I said and placed the gun to my head. "The police are being manipulated, my parents are dead, and no one can help. They'll never stop and no one around me will be safe."

"No! Dorian, don't do this," Lyle yelled. "We can get help. You aren't alone, don't waste your life like this." Then it hit me. Something Lyle said reminded me what of Noah told me before I left. *Don't waste my time by getting yourself killed.* "Dorian, listen to me," Lyle continued trying to reason with me.

I didn't know why, but Noah had risked healing me with his blood and trained me to use my powers in a way I never thought possible. If anyone could help, it was him. He taught me for a reason and it couldn't have been just because he was bored.

I surrendered the gun, placing it down on the floor between us. Lyle approached carefully with his hands out and replaced the gun in his holster.

"I'm sorry." I kept my head down, too embarrassed to look at him.

"Don't be. You're a good person and considering everything going on, you're handling it pretty well. Just promise you won't give up."

"I think I have an idea." I started to explain, but police sirens outside cut in.

"How the hell did they get here so soon?" Lyle exclaimed. I tossed him a clean shirt from the laundry to change into as we made our way downstairs.

I stopped short, and doubled back into the hall by the kitchen. Lyle grabbed a knife from the counter and put it in his back pocket. Flashlights were already shining in the back windows as the police searched the premises. A loud banging on the front door shook the house. I looked to Lyle, hoping he would have some professional insight into the situation. He motioned to go back upstairs and led the way, making sure we weren't spotted.

The banging on the door continued, followed by the voices of several police officers talking. I couldn't quite make out what they were saying, but it probably wasn't good news for us. We made it to the upstairs hall unnoticed until Lyle tripped into the laundry basket by the bathroom. He tried to catch his balance using the bookshelf on his left, but didn't see my mom's porcelain figurines. I could just imagine the noise they would make as they all fell and shattered. Through sheer will, I froze Lyle and the figurines in midair before they could make contact with the floor. I floated the figures safely back to their shelf and put Lyle back on his feet. He gave me a thumbs-up and walked carefully to my room.

My room faced the back of the house and overlooked a decent-sized lawn. Lyle immediately went to the window and checked the situation outside.

"They're going to —" Lyle didn't get to finish before the sound of the front door being kicked open startled us. "—force their way in."

"Think you can break our fall?" Lyle whispered as he opened the window. He started climbing out, not giving me much choice.

I watched as he jumped down to the patio. I had to resist the urge to check behind me when I heard the cops climbing the stairs. Halfway through his fall, I caught Lyle and levitated him to safety the rest of the way. I could hear the footsteps of the police right outside my door. Lyle was waving for me to jump from below. I wasn't sure what made me more nervous, getting caught by the police or falling to my doom. I remembered practicing with Noah and realized at least Lyle wouldn't be waiting to stab me on the ground below. I guess that was the point of Noah's unorthodox training; after that, everything else didn't seem so bad.

I held my breath and jumped down. This was getting easier and easier each time. I was able to slow my fall and glide past the patio onto the grass. Lyle ran over to me from where he was crouched against the house. He pointed out that the window was still open. I tried closing it as gently as possible, but I still didn't have the hang of fine manipulation, and the window slammed shut.

My stomach clenched and my heart sank in my chest. I heard the police shouting inside the house, but couldn't tell if it was because of the noise or the discovery of my parents' bodies. My body began to feel cold and numb and my bite wound throbbed under the bandage. I turned to Lyle, who was just staring at me. Everything was going dark and my head spun like I was going down a drain. I forced myself out of it and looked down at my arm. The veins running the length of my forearm were darkening. Lyle still stood there, but wasn't saying anything. He jumped back when I looked him in the eyes.

"Why are you looking at me like that?" I asked while holding my bad arm.

"The whites of your eyes are all black, like ... those things." Lyle looked freaked out, but regrouped after remembering our situation. "We have to move."

The backyard was fenced off and on the other side were trees that went on for a few yards before meeting up with the road. Lyle hopped the fence and I took a running jump, boosting myself farther up at the highest point. I immediately dropped like a rock after clearing the fence. There was a shooting pain behind my eyes and my ears started to ring. The sinister death rattle of the mutant creatures reverberated in my head. Whatever was inside me causing the infection was calling out. It felt like something was squirming its way through every blood vessel in my body. I was on the ground gasping for breath and feeling pins and needles over my entire body.

Lyle tried to help me up, but my body wasn't responding. I could hear his voice in the distance calling my name even though he was right there next to me. I needed Noah's blood again to fight off the infection, or else I would turn into one of those monsters. But after a minute, the painful sensation began to subside.

"Every time I use my powers, the infection gets worse. I think Noah's blood is starting to wear off," I told Lyle as I got to my feet. We started making our way through the trees as quietly as possible, as if that still mattered.

We were almost to the road when we heard gunshots ring out from behind us. At first, I thought we were being shot at, but the sound was too far back. It was coming from the house.

"We need to go back." Lyle stopped.

That was a terrible idea. "Did you forget that you're wanted? If we go back we're going to get attacked either by mutants or police. At least the cops all have guns."

"Avoiding arrest isn't more important than saving lives. I'll never get it off my conscience if they die because I didn't go back to help. Every man counts, and you have superpowers. If they're shooting, then they aren't in on this like the police in New York." Lyle started running back to the house before I could finish my extensive list of reasons not to.

The sound of gunfire continued and they were up to about thirty shots. I couldn't believe whatever the cops were fighting was taking that many bullets and they had to be at pretty close range. I ran after Lyle, wondering what they were even shooting at. Only my parents' bodies were in the house, but I thought they weren't coming back anymore after Lyle took care of them.

My question was answered soon after the gunshots had finished. A large shadow was closing in from overhead just before we reached the fence.

Lyle was still in the lead by a good ten feet. He grabbed his gun, but was only able to get one shot off before the cause of the shadow overtook him.

I could see the shape of a man twice the size of Lyle bearing down on him. He smacked the gun out of Lyle's hand and lifted him into the air by the throat. Lyle grabbed the knife in his back pocket and jammed it into his attacker's arm. The man didn't even flinch; he just used his free hand to pull the knife out and tossed it aside.

I ran up to them, shouting to get the guy's attention. I could hear Lyle gasping for air as he resorted to kicking the man as hard as he could, but still to no effect.

The man turned to face me, his murderous intent made crystal clear by his sadistic gaze. His eyes were glowing in the moonlight, and judging by the length of his facial hair he hadn't shaved in years. He was at least six foot eight and dressed in tattered jeans and long coat with an equally torn and dirty shirt underneath. Each fingernail ended in a sharpened nail and when he snarled I could see his incisors were dramatically longer than normal. This wasn't another mutant and it wasn't one of the Archios either. He was nothing like them; he was more of a hulking feral beast than a supermodel.

Aurelia had said the man who was after me used to be an Archios, but this guy certainly didn't look the part. This one had to be responsible for infecting my parents, or at least working with whoever had.

Anger boiled up inside of me. I wanted to make him pay. I wanted to kill him, but he'd already shrugged off being shot at and stabbed like it was nothing. I had to help Lyle, who was still struggling to break free, but I wasn't sure what I could do against someone his size.

The behemoth of a man was coming my way, dragging Lyle behind him. I could see the kitchen knife lying next to a tree. I tried willing it to me, but the slithering feeling in my veins began again. I heard the same eerie growling as before and so did the man. He stopped in his tracks, looking around confused for the source of the sound.

The man turned his attention back to me and smiled wickedly. He said something, but I couldn't hear anything other than the death rattle coming from what was in my veins. I could see him tighten his grip around Lyle's neck. Someone his size could have killed Lyle easily, but he seemed to enjoy toying with him and feeling him suffer. Lyle went limp on the ground and the man held him up for me to see. I wanted to shout, but couldn't open my mouth. I wanted to summon the knife to me, but had no concentration. Everything swirled again as I started to lose control and black out.

I could hear Lyle's voice yelling, but couldn't make out the words. I was strangely numb. I wasn't panicked from the attack anymore, or happy to hear Lyle's voice letting me know he wasn't dead. My heart wasn't even racing. In fact, it was surprisingly slow.

I tried to ask what happened as my vision returned. I was still standing in the same place. "Do it again!" Lyle yelled as he crawled to where his weapons were thrown. "Dorian, snap out of it! Hit him again! Quick!" Lyle was still shouting, but I didn't understand what he meant. What had I done?

The noise in my head faded, as did the cold slithering feeling in my veins. A few feet away the man was reeling in pain while holding his shoulder where his arm should be.

Lyle got up and grabbed his knife and gun. He ran over and shoved the gun in the man's mouth, firing until the clip was empty. The man howled in pain and grabbed Lyle by the leg, pulling him down. He easily overpowered Lyle and tried to sink his fangs into Lyle's neck, but Lyle stabbed him in the throat, causing him to stagger.

"Dorian, do something!" Lyle shouted at me. I just stood there, not sure what I should be doing or what that strange feeling was inside me.

The man pulled the knife out of his throat and attempted to stab Lyle in the forehead with it when I stopped him. I put my hand out, directing his movements. I could feel him struggling against my will and he was incredibly strong. I made him turn the knife to his own chest and stab himself through the heart. His eyes went dull and his body went lifeless as though someone had flicked the off switch on a homicidal machine. His tremendous carcass lay motionless on the grass with the knife sticking out of his chest.

Lyle got up once again and retrieved the knife. Instantly, the psychopath sprang up and leapt on him. Lyle turned just in time and replaced the knife in his heart, causing him to shut down like before.

"What the hell was that about?" Lyle screamed at the body, confused and furious. He kicked the guy in the stomach, but there wasn't so much as a flinch.

"I guess staking just paralyzes them." I stared down at the corpse. "Are you okay?"

"I've been better, but I'll live." Lyle cracked his neck and dusted off his jeans. "How do we kill this thing now before someone finds it and takes the knife out?"

"We should burn the body to make sure he's dead for good, but there's no way we are going back to my house now to get stuff to start a fire." It was a miracle that more police hadn't arrived by now, but I didn't want to push it.

Lyle kicked around in the dirt by some tree roots and picked up some sticks. "These are too wet. It must have rained here recently and the humidity doesn't help."

"Dorian?" he asked suddenly. "Where's the body?"

I turned around to check. The body was gone, along with our brief moment of levity. We looked at each other and then all around us.

"Let's talk about what exactly you did before, and why you didn't do more of it a lot sooner."

"I don't know. The infection took over when I was trying to get your knife. I blacked out and when I came to you were shouting at me."

"You don't remember tearing his arm off and it turning to dust?" Lyle pointed to a small pile of ashes a few feet away. "The mutant noises coming out of you? The demonic stare?" He was making me sound scarier than the mutants.

"No. I heard the noises in my head, but that's it. I didn't think I was that strong."

"Well, you saved my life again, but you weren't in control, and that's a problem. No crazy psychic powers unless we're being attacked, then feel free to go nuts."

I led the way toward the back road and kept checking over my shoulder at every moving branch. I couldn't shake the feeling that we were being watched, but Lyle didn't seem to notice as he kept talking. "I'm out of bullets, not that they did much anyway."

"I need to go back to France."

"How did I know you were going to say that? Right now you're the only link I have to figuring any of this out, so I guess I'm coming along," Lyle said as we reached the road behind my house. "Which way?"

"There's a train station a couple miles up the road this way," I said, and pointed the way to our left. "We can take it to reach the airport."

We walked in silence to the station, each of us trying to process the night's course of events. The only sound around was the chirping of crickets and the occasional breeze. The road we were on was only one lane and lined on both sides with trees. The area wasn't very well-lit. Streetlights were few and far between here. Even though this was where I had grown up, the place felt foreign to me now at night.

The laughter of a man off in the distance broke the silence. It wasn't jovial good-joke laughter. It was the maniacal "I'm going to get you" kind. We took off running the rest of the way to the train station with the sound of someone crashing through the trees after us.

A gathering of lights ahead marked our destination. Lyle checked behind us as we ran. "Yeah, don't look back," he warned.

I knew it wouldn't be good, but I looked anyway. The psycho we had just had the pleasure of meeting jumped out of the trees and was barreling down the road. I wanted to fight, but my powers were unreliable and I couldn't take the chance of hurting Lyle.

We just reached the intersection when a train was pulling up. At this time of night, the trains weren't going to wait around long if no one was on the platform. We still had to cross over the tracks and climb the platform with our new friend in pursuit.

The closing door chimes on the train sounded when we were only halfway up the stairs. It looked like our stalker gave up once we reached the top of the platform, but I wasn't convinced. Lyle held up his badge, screaming "Police!" at the ticket checker. He held the door for us, but we almost knocked the poor guy over while entering.

Lyle grabbed the guy by the shoulders and helped him regain his balance. "Tell me this train is going into Boston."

"Y-yes," he stuttered. "There's one more stop before there. What's going on?"

"Police business. I can't share more than that." Lyle took a seat right by the door with me.

The train car was empty except for an elderly couple across from us who were blissfully asleep for the ride.

"We should be there in twenty minutes," I told Lyle. I took my phone out to check flight times to Paris, but the veins in my hands got my attention first. They were noticeably darker — not completely black like before, but I also wasn't using any of my powers.

I pulled my sleeves down further, trying to cover them, and went on to check for flights. We were just leaving the station when a loud thud on the roof of the car made everyone jump. Lyle and I immediately looked at each other.

"Oh my, what was that?" asked the elderly woman, who was startled out of her nap. I didn't think telling her it was probably just a psychotic beast of a man looking to kill us all would have gone over well.

"I didn't hear anything," was the best I could come up with.

"I'm sure it was just a low branch or something from the rain the other day." Lyle to the rescue.

"What do we do?" I typed in a blank text message on my phone and showed Lyle.

"Pray for a lot of low bridges," Lyle whispered.

There were no other foreboding sounds during the rest of the trip. Either the guy hunting us was waiting to launch an ambush when we got off, or he didn't want to be spotted and had given up. The train station in Boston was always pretty busy, so I doubted he would make a scene there.

Once we arrived, Lyle ditched his empty firearm down a storm drain. Wanting to avoid any more unnecessary public transportation incidents, we took a taxi to the airport. There was no sign of our stalker, but I still couldn't shake the feeling we were being followed. Unfortunately for us, the airport was close to deserted. The online ticket checkout worked like a charm to get us on the plane, but getting to the loading gate first was nerve-wracking. The corridors of the airport were empty and the shops were closed for the night. Shadows played tricks on our mind as we hurried. Some of the metal security gates that were closed over the shops behind us banged from someone pulling on them, but no one was ever there. Our stalker was making sure we knew he wasn't gone.

With only carry-on backpacks, we easily got through the security checkpoints. It was 5:00 AM now, meaning we would get there a little after 6:00 PM. Lyle and I boarded the plane without a problem, which made things even more tense. We were waiting for something bad to happen.

We found our seats and settled in. I took the window. I was just about to close the window shade when I saw something on the runway. It was the man, and he was waving at me with the same menacing smile. I turned to Lyle, who was somehow already asleep. There was nothing I could do now but prepare for the worst once we landed.

Chapter Seven

It was dusk when Lyle woke me up to let me know we had landed. I hadn't thought I would be able to sleep at all, but I must have drifted off. I warned Lyle about what I saw on the runway back in Boston as we went through customs. We were traveling during the day, supposed bedtime for the undead, so at least we should be able to get a head start before the sun set.

"I don't suppose you know French?" I asked as we waited outside for a taxi.

"No. We're tourists. I was just going to speak slow and loud."

I felt a lot better after some sleep, but we didn't have much time until the game of cat and mouse continued. An available taxi pulled up curbside for us. I indicated where the chateau should be on my cellphone's GPS for the driver.

The sun was setting as we drove through the streets of Paris. We passed the grounds of the Eiffel Tower, meaning we still had at least an hour until we got there. I went over everything I had learned about the Archios with Lyle so he would be prepared.

The lights outside became fewer and farther apart as we crossed the city limits. Twenty more minutes in and the road turned into the winding path through the trees I remembered.

"How's that doing?" Lyle pointed to my bad arm. "You're looking kinda pale; it's making me nervous."

"More pale than usual? It feels the same really, just numb." I knew feeling nothing was probably worse than feeling pain. At least pain lets you know you're alive.

Our driver started swearing in French after we heard loud pop from the back of the car. There was another popping sound and the car wobbled off the road to a stop. We all got out and checked the tires. Sure enough, the back tires were shredded. The driver leaned into his window to call his dispatch about it.

"Sorry man, we need to keep moving. We can just walk the rest." Lyle took out his wallet and handed over cash. The driver muttered something under his breath in broken English and counted out his money. "Ready to start hiking?" Lyle asked me.

Something made a bizarre gurgling noise behind Lyle. We both looked just in time to see our driver's body torn in two at the waist. The looming figure of my least-favorite new acquaintance stepped out from the shadows, holding the two pieces in his hands. He poured the man's blood down his throat, letting it gush all over him before discarding the body. The giant man's missing arm was reattached, and steadily regaining muscle now that it had fed on fresh blood.

He took a swipe at Lyle, who rolled out of the way and threw the driver's side door open as interference. The man tore the car door off and swung it at Lyle's head, but once again Lyle dodged by diving into the car. I could see him through the window reaching for the glove box.

"Dead end," was the first thing I had heard this guy say. I saw him duck down and the next thing I knew he was flipping the car over on top of me with Lyle still in it.

I managed to jump out of the way as it landed on its side where I had just been standing. It was clear he did not want me reaching the Archios at any cost.

Lyle climbed out of the car with a gun the driver must have kept. He fired off a few shots into our would-be killer, which did little except get his attention. I knew using my powers would make me lose control from the infection and I couldn't risk hurting Lyle.

"We're not far, we need to run!" I yelled to Lyle.

He sprinted over to me as the relentless stalker pounced on the car.

"Wait!" Lyle put his arm out to stop me and finished unloading his clip into the taxi's exposed gas tank. The car burst into flames, catching the man on fire with it. "Now we run," he shouted, and took off down the road.

I could see the lights of the chateau through the trees. The sound of footprints stampeding after us helped squeeze out our last bit of adrenaline. We were in the clearing now and running out of steam. I started screaming for Noah as we passed another large fountain like the one in the rose maze.

My screams were soon answered by Noah's voice behind me. "Look who came running back."

I stopped in my tracks to see him lounging on a fountain bench. All I could do was point in the direction we came as I caught my breath. Sure enough, the stalker was still at our heels, but Noah didn't seem the least bit concerned.

"You brought a human into the lion's den, interesting." Noah turned his attention to Lyle. "Sorry, but I'm not hungry."

Lyle's eyes were completely glazed over as he stared at Noah. Seeing Lyle react like this was weird, since he had been pretty collected up to now. It made me wonder whether I had acted this obvious too.

Our huge nemesis was at the fountain sizing up Noah. "You have something I want," he snarled.

"Yeah, I hear that a lot." Noah got to his feet, looking down at his eight-pack and stretched with his hands behind his head, showing off the striation of his muscles. "Get in line."

The man growled, baring his fangs and showing his nails. Noah patted the hilt of one of his swords and smiled at him. "Now, if you wanna play rough, I guess we could work something out, but you're not leaving here in one piece."

Noah's grin widened, showing his fangs.

Our stalker wasn't having any of Noah's wiseass remarks. He rolled his shoulders back and let out a terrifying roar, but Noah was still unimpressed. He waited for the man to finish his failed attempt at intimidation and then looked over his shoulder at us.

"Don't blink."

Noah tossed one of his *wakizashi* high up in to the air and took the other in his hand before disappearing. He was moving so fast I couldn't make out anything more than faint images of him as he systematically dismembered the beast with the precision of a surgeon. Noah's opponent was nowhere near fast enough to react, let alone make an attempt to defend himself.

Noah finished him off by hopping up on the man's shoulders and catching the *wakizashi* he had tossed into the air. He used one sword to decapitate and the other to stab the heart out of the guy's chest, then leaped from the shoulders of the corpse as it fell apart.

"Told you so," he said to the remains as he sauntered back over to us.

"Jesus, that's some freakin' athleticism. No wonder you're so ripped. That was unreal," Lyle blurted out. "You were so fast, too ..."

Noah ignored Lyle's rambling and crossed his arms. "What are you doing back here, kid?"

"I need help and I don't know where else to go."

"Do you ever get tired of being so useless? I'm not your babysitter and I'm not here to take out your trash," he said, and pointed at the ashen remains.

"Relax, man," Lyle snapped out of his trance to intervene. "He just lost his parents."

"So what? That's supposed to be your area of expertise, officer." Noah's words were as sharp as his blades. I knew he was a jerk, but I couldn't believe he was being this cruel. Maybe coming here was a mistake.

"They're dead. The mutants got them."

"Oh, you mean the ones I tried teaching you how to defend yourself against? I told you, you can never escape this world. You kept whining about going back home. You led trouble right to your doorstep — and now mine."

"I'm sorry. I've lost everything and I think your blood is wearing off. I don't know what to do."

"Not my problem. But hey, you still have your friend here for now."

"Come on, Dorian. You don't have to take this, let's just leave," Lyle said, and started to walk away.

"You can go, but the human stays here."

Lyle and I looked at each other. "What? Why?" we asked in unison.

"I can't let him live now that he knows about us," Noah said. He grabbed Lyle by the neck and picked him up. "You should be honored, officer, you're about to die to the best."

Lyle reached for his gun and put it to Noah's head.

"At least he's got some fight in him," Noah smirked. "Go ahead. Take the shot."

With no other options left, Lyle fired. Noah grabbed the gun with his free hand, pointing it away before the bullet left the barrel.

"Put him down!" I demanded.

"You want me to put him down?" Noah laughed and disappeared with Lyle. "Here, catch!" His voice boomed from far across the lawn on the roof of the main chateau. He threw Lyle off and sat on the ledge, watching him fall helplessly.

I ran as fast as I could, but only Noah could have made it in time. Lyle was a few feet away from dying right in front of my eyes. I had no choice but to try and catch him with my powers. I put my hands out and focused on breaking his fall, but I could already feel the slithering sensation behind my eyes and in my veins. Just a couple of seconds more was all I needed to help him land safely. My body was going cold and numb, and a ringing in my ears deafened me. I saw Lyle land slowly on his hands and knees as the world started spinning.

"Hey! Hey! Snap out of it! Are you okay?" Lyle's voice called to me in my nightmare. "We have to get away from here."

Lyle was shaking me in a desperate attempt to bring me back to reality when my vision returned.

"This guy is out of his mind!" Lyle exclaimed.

Noah was leaning against the chateau wall, watching us from the shadows. I had had enough. I pushed past Lyle and walked up to Noah. Wiping that smug look off his face was too much to ask for, but I was determined to speak my mind at least.

"I don't know what your problem is and I don't know why, but I know you wanted me to come back here ..." My heart was pounding and my hands were shaking in frustration as I continued. I wasn't good at confrontation, especially with someone like him. "You may be a self-absorbed, arrogant narcissist, but I don't buy that everything you taught me was because you were bored. You told me not to waste your time; you wanted me to survive."

I felt light-headed and the veins in my arms were going black again as I pointed at him in anger. "You were right, is that what you want to hear? I can't escape and I paid the price." The unnerving death rattle was creeping into my head now and the wriggling under my skin returned. My vision started to cut out again. I couldn't even tell if I was still conscious or dreaming. "I have nothing left to lose; my world is crumbling around me. But here I am, so if you want me, you got me!"

It sounded like a grenade going off as everything went black. My eyesight flickered in and out and the growling in my head was a deafening scream now. In between flashes of darkness, I could see the wall of the chateau in front of me explode inward and demolish the room inside.

Noah appeared beside the hole and looked in and then back at me. "Oh yeah. Now this I can work with."

I regained consciousness to feel myself gagging. Noah was forcing blood down my throat from his wrist.

"Stop fighting it," he ordered when I tried pushing him off. "Do you want to turn into a freak after you finally found your balls?"

At his command, my body automatically stopped resisting until he was done. That power of his was getting old.

"Nice trick," he said, sounding somewhat impressed. "Is that new or have you just been pretending to be helpless up to now?"

"What happened?" I asked once he let go of me.

"You, uh, blew up the palace," Lyle said from his seat on the grass.

A sudden palpable urge compelled me to look up at one of the balconies. Aurelia was standing there, her eyes glowing in the moonlight as she watched over us. Without a word, she went back into the chateau.

"She's going to be so pissed," I said nervously. "I'm screwed."

"Nah, right before you came she told me she always wanted a huge hole blown in the side of her house." Noah's joking didn't make me feel any better. He grabbed Lyle and me and dashed up three flights of stairs and into a different ballroom, where he dumped us on our knees.

Aurelia was waiting for us in front of a gold throne. I wanted to throw up. Our nerves were soon put to ease as a kind smile from her warmed our hearts. It was that captivating aura of hers again.

"Please, rise. There is no need for such formalities."

Lyle's tongue was pretty much hanging out of his mouth and I couldn't imagine I was much better. I just hoped he remembered what I told him about her ability to read minds.

"I do not believe we have been introduced, Monsieur. I am Aurelia de Saint-Pierre," Aurelia said, and offered her hand to Lyle.

"Officer Lyle Turner of the NYPD, ma'am. At your service." He beamed and kissed her hand.

Noah snorted in laughter, but a piercing glare from Aurelia was quick to shut him up. Lyle didn't seem to notice. He was too busy puffing out his chest and flexing with his arms crossed to show off like Noah.

"Oh my, a gentleman of status," Aurelia said, and placed a hand daintily on her breast. "It is an honor to welcome you to my home, Officer Turner."

"It's my pleasure, ma'am," Lyle grinned from ear to ear. "Trust me."

"You are as delightfully charming as you are handsome, Monsieur."

I could have sworn she was blushing modestly behind the hand covering her lips. Lyle was drowning in his own hormones as he continued to flirt with her.

"Anything to see a beautiful lady such as yourself smile."

"If I may be so forward, what business do you have in France?" Aurelia asked him.

"Well ma'am, to be honest, my buddy Dorian here is going through a lot and needs some help. I understand you've got a little mutant problem too that I'd be more than happy to offer my assistance with."

"My, how very honorable of you and quite brave. I would absolutely treasure the opportunity to have a gentleman of your caliber in my company." Aurelia was right to be impressed with Lyle. He didn't have any special powers, but he was been a lot braver than I had been. My self-esteem boost from standing up to Noah was dwindling.

"A dear friend of mine has already traveled to New York," Aurelia continued. "The situation will be under control shortly."

"I think there might be more than a few people behind all this, ma'am. Dorian thought it was over when the first guy from New York was taken care of, but there was someone waiting for us in Boston, too. It's too much of a coincidence that the mutants were also found in both places."

"You are correct, Monsieur Turner, which is precisely why I wish for this ordeal to come to a quick end. If humans were to find out that my kind is the cause of these monsters, then I fear they will hunt us all."

"We have a common enemy, then. Do you know who they are or why they're doing this?" Lyle asked.

"I can only speculate that it is a less-civilized coven interested in the talents of your friend here, but I cannot imagine why."

"Speaking of that, sorry about the accident downstairs. He's having some trouble controlling himself. You know, I'm pretty good with my hands. I'd be happy to help fix up the place." Lyle was still grinning like a fool and trying to act casual as he showed off for her.

I can't believe he was using my problem for his personal gain. He wouldn't even be here if it wasn't for me, and now he was stealing the show.

"That won't be necessary, Monsieur. My people shall handle the repairs. I may, however, make use of your skills in another manner," she said and flashed a demure smile. "If you'll excuse me, I have other pressing matters to attend to. Noah will escort you to a room in the guest house should you need a place to rest during your stay."

I had almost forgotten he was still there. It was unlike him to be quiet for so long. Once Aurelia departed he signaled for us to follow him back outside.

"Man, I get vertigo just looking at her. I feel like I'm in one of those sexy perfume commercials," Lyle said, checking out every female on the way there. "I think I'm gonna like it here. I mean, *really* like it here."

"Gee, I couldn't tell."

Chapter Eight

"What about werewolves, are they real too?"

Lyle had been barraging Noah with questions for half an hour now. He was a changed man after his meeting with Aurelia. Or maybe it was all starting to sink in now that we weren't in any immediate danger.

"Yeah, they stick to the wilderness. They're seven to nine feet of muscle, fur, and claws. Unless you're looking to pick a fight with something that hits like a speeding train, I wouldn't go searching for them."

Noah was being surprisingly amicable. At least for the moment he wasn't trying to kill or berate us, except for when Lyle almost got his hand cut off for trying to touch one of the swords in Noah's room.

"See this tattoo?" Noah pointed to the large claw mark on his ribs. "I got it after I took down my first pack of those mutts."

"You went after more than one at a time?" Lyle asked. "That sounds insane, man."

"Wanted to prove to myself I could do it. Not that I had any doubts. The pack leader got a good hit in on me and since I don't scar, I had it inked instead."

I sat on the bed, barely paying attention to the conversation. Now that I had some downtime, my thoughts kept wandering to my parents no matter how hard I tried to push them out. To add insult to injury, it looked like I wouldn't even be able to give them a proper funeral.

"They're better off dead."

"What?" I looked up, realizing Noah was speaking to me.

"Your parents. They're better off," he repeated.

"Not again, man. Leave him alone," Lyle jumped in.

"I'm being serious. It could have been much worse for them," Noah said. He wasn't grinning or smirking, but he was never an easy person to read. "Like I keep telling you, you can't escape this life. Anyone close to you will be in danger."

"What you're telling me is that I have to live the rest of my life lonely and unloved in order to survive. If you're trying to cheer me up, it didn't work."

"Spare me your self-pity. Just be happy they weren't tortured or made to live out their lives in constant fear. There are things so much worse than death."

"Whatever, Noah." Even his attempts to be consoling came off as abrasive as sandpaper. "So what should we be doing? Any idea who's behind all this?"

"Vivi will be back from New York tomorrow night with information, so just hang out until then."

"I feel like I should be doing something more productive."

"Yeah, hold this." I caught a glass Noah threw at me that was lying around his room. "With your mind, stupid."

"How was I supposed to know?" I floated the glass out of my hand. Since I'd known him I didn't think he'd called me by name once; I would have been shocked if he even knew it.

"It should be your first instinct. I want you to squeeze the glass until it breaks."

This was a challenge. I had only used my powers to push, pull, or lift in one direction at a time, but squeezing would require that I apply force in all directions at once. The glass flipped and spun in the air from my uneven pressure. I felt like a thief trying to figure out a safe's combination as I listened for the sweet spot to let me know the glass was cracking. It took a few tries, but in a few minutes I crushed the glass to pieces.

"Good, that'll come in handy. Now go mourn. Get it out of your system now, because once shit gets serious I expect you to pull your own weight." Noah took out a wine bottle from the cabinet-sized refrigerator next to his bed. "Now if you'll excuse me, I have to get my drink on and watch some TV," he said, uninviting us from his room.

Lyle put his hand around his neck and looked at the bottle in disgust.

"Relax, officer, it isn't human blood. It's from one of our own. This tastes a lot better and doesn't coagulate." Noah swirled the bottle around and took a swig. "I'd offer you some, but ... I don't like you."

"Did you see the size of that flat-screen he had? Man, these guys know how to live. Where are all the cobwebs and coffins? I didn't think they'd know what a TV is," Lyle said on the way to our rooms across the hall. "Ow! Jesus Christ!"

"That's offensive." Noah had come up behind us and smacked Lyle upside the head. "And that's for telling the human I gave you my blood after I said not to." He turned and hit me upside the head too.

"Lyle's seen everything I have already, it's not like that's going to matter," I protested. "You fed me your blood right in front of him before!"

"Because I already knew you told him," Noah said, and took another swig from his bottle before going back in to his room. "Trust nobody!"

"He's gotta lighten up," Lyle said while rubbing the back of his head. "You gonna be okay?"

"I've been bitten by a mutant, cut with swords, and thrown off a roof. Getting slapped isn't a big deal."

"I meant about your parents, smartass. We haven't really had a chance to talk."

"I'm fine, just trying not to think about it."

"Well, if you change your mind I'm here for you."

It was great being able to take a hot shower. I felt as if I was staying in a five-star hotel. The guesthouse was the same baroque architecture and decor as the main chateau, only with updated amenities, such as modern bathrooms in each bedroom. I didn't see why the Archios would need all this, especially since they were so averse to having human company. The linens were also fresh and clean, as if they had recently been washed. Aurelia's servants must spend all night, every night, doing laundry and cleaning hundreds of rooms just in case she got a visitor.

I tried to avoid thinking of my parents by going over the little I had overheard of Noah's conversation with us. Waiting around for something to happen was making me anxious. The best thing I could do was prepare for the next few nights ahead.

According to Noah, there were only four ways to kill his kind for sure: sunlight, fire, decapitation, or destroying the heart. A stake through the heart only caused paralysis, as Lyle and I had learned. Holy water, crosses, garlic, ultraviolet light, and all the other legends were completely useless myths circulated for amusement.

I fought off sleep as long as possible. It was the first time since childhood that I was scared of having nightmares. I finally gave in and closed my eyes for a few minutes. The next thing I knew it was daytime.

A silver platter had been set on the table across from the bed. It was loaded with different kinds of cheeses and fresh fruits. A second platter next to it held croissants and baguettes with butter and jams. There was even a pitcher full of water and a crystal water goblet, and a cup of coffee. I wasn't sure if I was more impressed or scared that this had all been done without waking me. Now that I thought of it, after I drank Noah's blood, I was never all that hungry.

It was no caramel latte, but I downed the coffee anyway, and went to look outside. The windows were all cleverly tinted with glass that got darker the lighter it was out — technology I bet the Archios would have loved years ago.

"Hey," I called to Lyle as he walked past my door, but he didn't hear me. "Lyle!" I called again and went after him. He was going in Noah's room. What the heck was he doing?

I followed him to the doorway, not wanting to go any further. Noah was in bed sleeping peacefully with swords under his pillow and the empty bottle on the floor next to him like a drunk.

"What are you doing? Get out of there," I whispered, trying not to wake Noah. This was as suicidal as walking into a hungry bear's cave covered in meat. Lyle was at the window now and reaching for the curtains. He was going to kill Noah.

"Don't do it!" I snuck in and grabbed the curtain to stop him. "The windows are tinted anyway. You're just going to piss him off."

"So I'll open them. You heard what he said — trust no one. He's been messing with us this whole time. He's as dangerous and unpredictable as they come. This may be our only chance to get rid of him."

"Too late." It was Noah's voice. He had risen from the bed and was standing behind us with his *wakizashi* out.

"Noah, wait!" I turned and blocked his path to Lyle.

"I don't have a problem going through you," he said and went to push me out of the way.

"What's going on?" Lyle asked. "How'd I get here?"

I turned back around to him. The expression on his face was completely bewildered. "Are you kidding me? You just tried to kill Noah."

"I … no I didn't. Am I dreaming?"

"No, but now you're dead." Noah shoved me and raised his sword to attack Lyle. I put my hand out and focused on freezing the sword before it could strike. Even half-asleep in the daytime, Noah was too strong. It took so much effort that the black veins in my arms started to show.

"Let go, or you're dead next," Noah growled. I felt his words taking over my mind, but the unnatural noises from the infection filled my head, canceling them out.

"Don't kill him. There has to be an explanation," I reasoned. Lyle looked between the both of us in fright. If I didn't let go, I'd risk blowing the room and Lyle up, but if I did, Noah would kill him.

"Fine." Noah stabbed the sword into the wall next to Lyle's head. "He's telling the truth," he said, staring into his eyes. "He's clueless as always. For once that saved your life."

"I told you!" Lyle exclaimed. "I was falling asleep in bed, next thing I'm here with you two."

"I'll deal with this later." Noah dragged Lyle back to the room he was staying in by his shirt and threw him in the windowless bathroom. "Let him out, I kill you both."

He lifted an armoire like it was made of cardboard and blocked the bathroom door to trap Lyle before disappearing.

"Can I at least have that food?" I heard Lyle ask from behind the door.

"He's already gone," I told him and sat by the door. "Do you really think we can't trust him? I mean, enough that you would kill him if you could?"

"The guy's a loose cannon and he seems to have a fondness for throwing people off buildings. I can't say I wasn't hoping you'd take him out in the explosion, but after our chat I guess he was starting to be cool with me. Do you think one of the Archios here could have been controlling me?"

"They're all asleep or I'd say yes. Daytime seems to mess them up even if they're not in the sunlight. Noah was out cold for a while when we were arguing right in front of him."

"I wonder if I'll ever be able to go back. What evidence am I really going to find now to prove I didn't attack those other officers? I probably shouldn't have run." Lyle was always so optimistic that things would get better, so his doubts were out of character. Maybe he knew now how powerless it felt when someone was controlling you.

"Have you thought about what you're going to do when this is over? What brought you to New York, anyway?" he asked.

"A dumb idea. I was going to college for architecture, but got convinced to try modeling before I got too old."

"That sounds pretty fun. You must have met a lot of cool people."

"Not really. I barely got started and then this happened. I didn't get much of a chance to make any friends."

"Well, assuming New York isn't hurting when we get back, you can always pick it back up. How old are you?"

"Twenty, why? How old are you?"

"Twenty-three. I was going to say if you were twenty-one I could take you out to some of my favorite spots to get a drink and meet some girls."

"Thanks, but that's not really my scene."

"I hear ya. But bars are probably the main way people socialize in Manhattan. You get used to it after a while."

"I, uh, meant girls," I said. I shifted uneasily and got up.

"Oh." Lyle paused. "Oh! Gotcha. That's cool. You definitely moved to the right place for it."

"Yeah, I guess. I kind of just keep to myself," I said and headed for the door. "I think I'm going to take a walk."

"Did I say something wrong?"

"No." Lyle was being more casual than I had expected. "I guess I didn't think you'd be this accepting. I'm not used to talking about it with anyone."

"We've been through hell together. I'm not gonna like you any less because of who you date." Lyle sounded a little hurt that I had misjudged him. "Life would be kinda boring if we were all the same and liked the same stuff. Go ahead and do what makes you happy, as long as you're not hurting anyone. You've been holding a lot of stuff in, huh?"

It did seem really trivial now that I mentioned it. I was so used to hiding things about myself nobody knew who I *really* was.

"People always look at you differently after they find out the truth. I had childhood friends walk away and treat me like a leper. I was still the same person who played ball with them after school and video games on the weekend. We celebrated all our birthdays together for years and told each other everything. My parents always had such high expectations for me, they wanted me to be perfect and I knew they wanted grandchildren. I didn't want to disappoint them. I opened up to my friends about it first, but all they could see was a ... monster in place of the kid they grew up with. When I learned about my powers a year later I thought they might have been right."

"Those sound like assholes, not friends. A friend isn't just somebody you hang out with, they accept you for who you are. This works out great, more sexy Archios ladies for me," Lyle joked. "Since they're all so interested in you, you can be my wingman and throw a few my way."

Aurelia and Vivian were two huge exceptions. The powerful, irresistible attraction I had to them was the complete opposite of my natural feelings. It made me curious whether Noah had that effect on Lyle.

"They're all yours," I laughed. It was the first time I had felt any sort of real happiness since Boston, and I definitely needed it.

"Do you think you can give me any of that food? I'm starving," Lyle asked. I couldn't let him suffer, but if Noah found out ... But Noah had wanted me to stand up to him and be tougher.

"Stay away from the door. I have to use my powers to move the furniture he blocked it with, and I don't want to blow you up," I told Lyle.

"Then I won't be hungry anymore, at least." There was a faint noise in the hall as I let him out.

"Did you hear that?" I asked Lyle, who was busy stuffing his face. "It sounded like footsteps."

"What kind of footsteps? You said everyone should be sleeping, right?" Lyle mumbled with his mouth full.

"I don't know, but I'm going to check it out. Stay here." I pushed Lyle in the bathroom with his food and barricaded it again.

"What if it's one of those things? Come on, man. Don't be stupid," Lyle pounded on the door in protest.

"It's not like I have to worry about getting infected, and you need to save your strength for those seventeenth-century repairs you offered Aurelia." I was more curious than scared, as foolish as that sounded. The smart thing to do would be to bring Lyle for backup, but I'd endangered him enough and it would make everything more complicated if Noah found out.

The footsteps led me down a sun-dappled corridor. Judging by the casual gait of the footsteps I didn't think I was trailing a mutant. Something about being here during the day was unsettling. There was no laughter or idle chatter filling the rooms, no orchestra inviting dancers to a waltz, no servants catering to the many beautiful guests. The house was so still, so ... dead. Ironic that it took a house full of the undead to make the place seem alive.

I chased the sound down several more hallways until I was completely lost. For a guest house, it was bigger than any hotel I'd seen. Each path looked the same to me and I could have sworn I went up the same flight of stairs about three times. Shivers ran down my spine, and I felt like people were watching me from all around.

Whoever it was finally stopped moving. I approached cautiously, turning at the next intersection. A woman stared at me from behind a half-closed door. I caught a glimpse of a shadow slithering along the floor and into the room with her as she closed the door. I knew I should leave, but something was telling me to keep going.

"Hello?" I knocked lightly on the door. "Sorry I was following you. I thought you were one of those creatures that attacked here the other night."

No answer.

"I'll leave you alone, sorry again," I apologized.

I had turned to leave when I heard the door slowly open. The woman was now standing in the dark doorway, screaming in fear. A flickering light in the room showed her face. It was my mother.

"Mom?" My voice trembled as I reached out to her, but she backed into the room, still screaming like I was a monster.

"Mom, wait!" I knew this couldn't be real, but I went into the room after her. The light was coming from a TV like the one my parents had. The whole room was set up like theirs. My mom was screaming at me from the bed now and I could see my father on the phone calling for help. My skin crawled as a shadow walked through me and up to my mother.

It was Noah. I watched as my parents tried to fight him off and he overpowered them both. He injected them with something he took from his pocket and left. My mom was struggling to reach her cell phone from the nightstand.

This was how they got infected. Noah was behind this all along. He knew I'd come back if I had nothing left to run to. He followed me to Boston. He was the only one fast enough to make it there and back before me. That was why he gave me his blood and kept pushing me to learn how to fight; he just wanted to use me like I was some sword to add to his collection.

I was glad Lyle hadn't killed him. This was personal; it was my parents Noah had taken, so it was only right that I be the one to kill him. He had wanted me to have nothing left so I'd focus on him. His wish was about to come true.

The sun was already going down. I had to hurry before nightfall or I'd miss my chance. I charged down the halls as I watched the daylight fade. My heart was pounding faster and faster in rage as I passed each door.

His bedroom was close now and so was my revenge. The arrogant bastard left his door wide open, practically asking for me to finish him off. He was still asleep when I ran in. I threw open the curtain hoping it was light enough out to turn him to ash, but the sun had just set. I grabbed one of the short swords off the wall and went for his heart.

"What did I tell you about touching my stuff?" Noah grabbed the sword before opening his eyes. Time for a new plan. I'd have to force myself to lose control.

Noah completely ignored that I was trying to kill him. He got up and stretched, then went to the window and cleaned the hilt of his sword, wiping my fingerprints off with the sheets. I launched the rest of the swords from around the room at his back one after another.

"That still counts as touching," he said after catching and replacing each sword. "But you're practicing, I like it."

The cold numb feeling started spreading through my body.

"You got something you wanna say, kid? I'm sensing some more hostility from you than your usual whining."

"You killed my parents!" I shouted. The dark veins started spreading from my arm, but I was happy. I welcomed it. "Now I'm going to kill you."

"Not gonna happen. Where'd you get that stupid idea, anyway?"

It was too late. I was losing control and couldn't speak. I knew what was coming next; I'd black out and either destroy Noah or die trying.

Chapter Nine

"Why is the human unconscious on your floor?"

"The back of his head ran into my fist. Don't worry, I'm all right." I woke up facedown again to Vivian and Noah's voices.

"Might that have anything to do with the giant hole in the wall outside?"

"It might."

"What happened?" I asked as I peeled myself off the ground. It was amazing I didn't have a concussion from being knocked out so many times. Noah was kicked back on his bed watching TV without a care in the world.

"You tried to kill me," Noah said. "Now you're blocking the TV."

Everything was coming back to me now: the vision of my parents, the bedroom, and the bloody messages.

"You killed my parents." I glared at him and rubbed the back of my head.

"Yeah, you said that already."

"Noah?" Vivi questioned him with her arms crossed.

"Vi, you really think I'd go to all the way to Boston to kill a couple of humans?"

"What makes you think he killed your parents, dear?" Vivi asked.

"I saw it. I don't know how, but I had a vision of Noah turning my parents into mutants," I explained.

"A vision? Noah is not the cause of these creatures; if he was, I would kill him myself. To be candid, tainted blood provides no sustenance, so if humanity is compromised we would be starved into extinction."

"But I saw it. I heard footsteps outside Lyle's room, so I followed them and then saw a vision in one of the rooms."

"Who is Lyle?"

"Oh shit. I forgot about him," Noah said and sat up. "I got you a present, Vi. He was being annoying too, so I locked him in the room across the hall."

"Is this how you take care of matters when I'm gone?" Vivian looked like she was about to knock him out now.

"I was going to handle it after this show." Noah smiled at her with his eyes still glued to the TV.

"I have spent the past twenty-four hours impersonating everything from a government agent to a secretary, altering memories and erasing evidence, and you have not even left the bed."

"To be fair, I was also on the roof." Noah appeared behind her and placed his hands on her hips. "You seem stressed. I bet a drink would help. Let me remind you that your present is waiting."

Vivian brushed him off and headed for Lyle's room with Noah. He lifted the armoire out of the way for her and let Lyle out.

"Thanks for remembering me," Lyle grumbled.

"I didn't actually, the kid reminded me," Noah shrugged. "And thanks for the lame attempt at killing me."

"Glad you're alive," Lyle nodded to me. "What happened with the — "

I thought he had gone brain dead until I realized Vivi was standing beside me.

"Lyle, this is Vivian," I said, and moved out of the way to introduce them. I was pretty sure this would win me the title of the best wingman ever. "Vivian, Lyle's a policeman back in New York."

"Pleasure to meet you, ma'am." Lyle kissed her hand.

"*Enchanté.*" Vivian gazed at him seductively. "There is nothing I admire more than a man of honor." She traced her finger along the veins in his arms with a smile.

"I like to help in any way I can." He smiled back and flexed his bicep for her.

"You have my sincerest gratitude, Monsieur."

"Call me Lyle," he said in a complete trance.

"You are so very charming, Lyle! What a pity not all American men possess the same charisma." Vivian batted her eyelashes at him and looked over her shoulder at Noah. I could tell Lyle was in heaven right now and I had to admit I was a bit jealous, even if she wasn't normally my type. I didn't think anybody would mind her company.

"All you need is one, beautiful," Lyle said, and kissed her hand again.

"You're making me sick," Noah scoffed. "She's way out of your league. Not to mention she's older than the dirt in the garden."

"Fine by me. I prefer more mature women." Lyle was undeterred by Noah's comment.

"Don't mind Noah. If you ignore the noise that comes from his mouth he can be almost tolerable at times," Vivian shot back with a quip of her own and primped her hair in the mirror. "I find some men are slower learners than others when it comes to being a gentleman. I still have hope for him, even if it does take several lifetimes."

"Please, everyone wishes they could be me," Noah said smugly. "If you're done playing with your pet now, you can fill me in on New York."

"Oh, so now it is time for business? The Archios, along with some hired help, have slowed the outbreak from spreading, but more buildings are being condemned every night. We have done our best to make the incidents appear unrelated to anything supernatural."

"And they're buying it?" Noah asked.

"This is not my first dance, you know. The mayor and police commissioner were very convinced by my performance. I left a newspaper article in your room along with a file I think you'll find of interest. I miss the days when humans were quicker to accept whatever we told them with blind faith."

"Is there any word on a cure?" I asked.

"I'm afraid not, my dear. The only solution has been death, followed by cremation. To find a cure you would need to find the cause, which I believe to be the Strigoi."

"How'd you find that out, Vi?"

"Price had a blood contract with them in his effects. If you took time to investigate further when you were there, you would have known. The Strigoi offered him protection from the upcoming infestation in exchange for the delivery of our friend here."

"Was there anything that might link him to the police that tried to kidnap Dorian?" Lyle looked at her hopefully.

"*Non.* Monsieur Price had too many connections with humans to document them all. Why do you ask? Were they friends of yours?"

"Nah, it's nothing."

"Noah, the rest is up to you. I must go speak with Aurelia." Vivian smiled and nodded cordially to us on her way out.

"Damn, what a woman," Lyle sighed.

Noah retrieved the file Vivi left for him and returned in a second. "She's a real man-eater, all right."

"You two aren't involved, are you?" It was a little late for Lyle to be asking that now.

"Don't be stupid. Of course she wants me, but I can't be bothered with a distraction like love. She's a fellow predator and I respect her as that. Hate to break it to you, but the only thing she'd be interested in is what's in your veins, not your pants."

"She's welcome to come get some." Lyle shot me a wink. He hadn't stopped grinning since meeting her. "She just needs a real warm-blooded man."

"I'm a thousand times the man you'll ever be." Noah smirked and went back to flipping through the file. "Nothing any human can do compares to the pleasure of being fed from. Everything else is just foreplay."

"Who are the Strigoi?" I jumped in, antsy to get back on topic.

"They're a coven of mages that originated in Eastern Europe and spend their immortality reading books. Real warriors fight with swords and fists, not spells and magic wands."

"Vivian said you guys can't drink infected blood, so why would they starve themselves by turning everyone into mutants? People are going to find out it's them and they'll be hunted."

"Maybe they got tired of being a bunch of cowards, I don't know. The other covens are all jealous of us because we aren't a bunch of freaks. I've heard the bookworms conjure synthetic blood so they never have to leave their houses and deal with humans. It probably tastes like dirty water, but I doubt they know how to enjoy themselves. It's not surprising they bribed one of our people to do their legwork for them."

"You think they want Dorian because he's magical?"

"Great work, detective. Like most of us, they can read auras — light that radiates from the soul. That light can indicate how powerful or healthy someone is and if they're supernatural or not. One of them probably spotted Dorian and wanted to study him. Maybe they would have left you alone if they knew how much of a wimp really you are," Noah laughed.

"That big dude that was chasing us didn't look like the scholarly type," Lyle said.

"He's not one of them. He's an Outsider, meaning he doesn't have a coven, so he's probably just another fang for hire. Being part of a coven is an exception not a rule, especially nowadays," Noah explained. "Some Outsiders act as mercenaries, hoping they can get in good with a coven for protection or favors in the future."

"How are we going to take down an entire coven?" I asked.

"We? I'm not taking either of you anywhere after you tried to kill me. These are the real deal, not like the runt that chased you here or those mutants. You'll just get in my way."

"Slow down. You tried to kill him too?" Lyle looked at me, confused. I forgot he didn't know anything about the vision I had after I left his room. I went to explain, but Noah stopped me.

"Jealousy makes people do crazy things. You both must have been dreaming about me and couldn't deal with your feelings of inferiority." Noah was so self-absorbed it was amazing he wasn't crushed under the weight of his own ego.

"It felt too real to be a dream. And for the record, you're not my type," I said.

"I'm everybody's type."

"Forget it," I said, and rolled my eyes. "Where do we start with these Strigoi?"

"Back in New York," Vivi said, joining us again. "The situation has gotten worse in the short time since I've left. Aurelia has ordered our direct involvement with purging the city of the infected."

"How much worse are we talking about?" Lyle asked.

"There has been one outbreak after the next. During the day the city is vulnerable and it is too much for hired help and inexperienced Archios to handle on their own."

"What if they're infected, but haven't turned yet?" I asked.

"Then they won't fight back as hard," Noah added.

"What about making a cure from your blood?" Lyle asked.

"It won't work. It's not strong enough to do any more than slow down the infection for a little while. Even we are susceptible to the disease to an extent. One of our kind tried drinking from an infected and grew violently ill."

There was a sudden tremendous crash outside. It sounded like of a lot of glass shattering, followed by people screaming. Noah and Vivian immediately vanished, leaving us behind. Lyle and I went to the window to check out what was going on.

"Look." Lyle pointed to the main house. All the windows were blown out, along with many of the lights. "We've got to see if they're okay!"

An earsplitting wail ending in a woman's laughter cut through the building. Lyle said something, but my ears were still ringing from the noise. We made it outside in time to see Aurelia calmly leaving the chateau, with Vivian following close behind. Noah appeared behind them after they left and slammed the doors shut on what looked like a roiling mass of shadows.

A limousine came racing down the path to the chateau and screeched to a stop in front of the three. The driver got out to open the door for Aurelia and sped away.

"She finally throws my kind of party and I miss it," Noah was saying to Vivian as we ran up.

"What happened?" I asked them. The broken glass from the windows was covered in blood.

"Aurelia's sister, Rozalin. They don't really get along," Noah said and lay down on the grass.

A pale woman with long black hair was watching us from a window on the top floor. "That's the woman I saw before the vision of my parents. What is she?"

"A phantom that just killed Aurelia's entire dinner party," Vivian answered. "Including all of our servants."

"She's not going to follow us?" I asked.

"*Non*, she must have tethered herself to the chateau when she escaped the Underworld. She can't move too far from there."

"She must have recognized me as the biggest threat here and possessed you two to try and kill me." Noah put his hands behind his head. "I can't say I blame her."

"Great, so ghosts are real too," Lyle sighed. "I guess I'm not surprised."

"Yes, love, but there's a difference." Vivian turned to him. "Phantoms are much more formidable kinds of ghosts that have knowledge of powerful dark magic."

"I don't get why she didn't whack Aurelia; she had the chance. They've been going at this forever," Noah said.

"You haven't had the pleasure of dealing with Rozalin before like I have. She revels in chaos. Nothing would be as satisfying as the opportunity to torment her sister for eternity."

Another limo pulled up for Vivi this time.

"If you'll excuse me, I have to go find someone capable of performing an exorcism."

"Aurelia's calling to me," Noah said and opened the car door for her. "Rozalin better not touch my stuff when I'm gone. That goes for both of you too."

"What about New York?" Lyle called after them.

The limousine drove off with Vivi and Noah, leaving Lyle and me alone in front of the haunted chateau.

"It's like the whole world is in slow motion just looking at her," he said watching the limo. "All those poor Archios babes though. Now what the hell do we do? There's no way I'm staying here after that."

"I'm not sure there's anything we can do, but what if Rozalin's the one causing the mutants?"

"We should stick to the plan and go back to New York to help out there. Let the Archios deal with the ghost lady." Lyle eyed the chateau uneasily.

"Don't tell me you're scared of ghosts," I teased. "What if Vivi needs you?"

"I'm not down with things that can't be seen or hit … or killed. It freaks me out."

My mind went blank for a moment and a feeling of weightlessness came over me. *I don't remember trying to fly; what's going on?* Lyle was still talking like I was there, but I could see him below me.

"Uh, Lyle?"

Things got even more bizarre once I looked down. My body was still there and started walking on its own.

"Where are you going?" Lyle asked.

"I don't know! I thought ghost woman couldn't get us from here!"

Lyle couldn't hear my voice. I was being dragged through the air somehow. I tried flying into myself, hoping to reunite with my body, but I went right through. My body kept going until we were in the woods bordering the property.

"Dorian, stop. What are we doing all the way out here?"

I wished I could respond, but my mind was just along for the ride. The woods were pitch-black except for the headlights of a car parked nearby. Lyle stood in my way, trying to stop my body, but was pushed back with force until he hit a tree. I wasn't as concerned about him as I was about the three sets of glowing eyes we were approaching.

Chapter Ten

I'd never been the type to question the meaning of life or contemplate what came after death. Whatever happens, happens, for one reason or another. There was nothing that anyone could do to change the rules of something so fundamental, so there was no use in worrying about it.

However, after the last few nights, my philosophy was being seriously tested. Who was to say what constituted being alive and dead? After what I'd seen, could I ever again believe that clinical death truly marked the end to a life? The Archios' hearts might not beat, but they still went about their business as if nobody had clued them in that they should be six feet under.

Even when the body was destroyed, ghosts cheated the rules by escaping their final judgment, so what was death? Was death a choice? Did you simply choose to throw in the towel, fold your hand, and fade away? Was life simply the measurement of a person's will to exist?

Was it not as black and white as alive or dead, but instead a spectrum of possibilities? What gave a person that drive to keep going? Love? Hate? Hope? Or just unfinished business?

Maybe I was already dead and on my way to reunite with my parents.

What was I really still here for? I had hoped things would get better, but every step forward was followed by two steps back. I wanted revenge against those who murdered my family, but how do you take the life of something that just refuses to stay dead?

Maybe Noah was right when he said my parents were better off.

It seemed so much easier to just let go when I had nothing left to hold on to. If I closed my eyes, would it all finally stop? Noah would probably call me weak if he could hear me, but was wanting peace a weakness?

I looked on as two young men and a woman, all dressed in their eighteenth-century finest, ushered my body into a nondescript European car. They didn't seem to notice or care about Lyle as he ran over to stop them, until he got too close. The woman's eyes shone coldly as she stared into his. Lyle drew his gun, mechanically placing it to his temple.

Maybe it would be better this way for him too. We knew this was inevitable, since he chose to stay after my parents' death.

One of the men waved his hand in the air, conjuring flames that converged on Lyle. I watched his body burn on the ground as we drove out of sight. *Forgive me, Lyle. I hope you find peace.*

We traveled for hours without a spoken word. The man and woman my body sat between exchanged occasional glances as if in some silent conversation. All three of them were very noticeably undead. Unlike Noah's healthy tan or Vivian's flawless porcelain skin, these three were borderline gray and sickly, with visible postmortem veins in some places. The woman's eyes had a harsh, sinister luminescence and her fangs were clearly prominent, also unlike the Archios. Her long ringlets were grayish-white, even though she did not appear much older than the men. She wore an old-fashioned gray skirt and high-collared jacket that was clean, yet severely outdated. A silk cravat covering her neck was adorned with a blue gem and matching ribbon.

The man to my left appeared only a couple years older than Noah, possibly twenty-eight or twenty-nine at most, but nowhere near as attractive. His slate-gray eyes looked hollow against his pale, dead skin. Light blonde hair reached almost to his chin, but didn't look maintained or styled in any particular fashion. He was wearing a hooded tunic with leather pants and riding boots that reminded me of the Renaissance.

We kept driving as the sun started to rise ahead of us. I expected us to pull over or seek cover somewhere, but the driver sped up toward the sunlight instead. The other man bit down hard on his index finger to draw blood and used it to write something on his window. Arcane symbols lit up for a moment and then disappeared, turning the interior of the car as black as night. These were certainly the Strigoi that Noah and Vivian had mentioned.

The driver continued to accelerate until we were pushing ninety-five miles an hour. My out-of-body experience wasn't making me feel any safer, but the others didn't seem concerned. We attracted the attention of law enforcement, who signaled us to pull over. The driver gazed at the cop car in the rearview mirror. His eyes glowed in the dark of the car and the police immediately gave up their pursuit.

Hours passed. The signs along the side of the road were in German now, so we must have crossed the border at some point. The car was running out of gas. We pulled into a gas station. The driver opened the window a crack to give the attendant a command. The man returned to the driver's window to collect his money when he was done, but our driver had something else in mind. In one smooth move, he pulled the attendant through the open window by his hair and sank his fangs into the man's neck. The attendant was easily double the driver's size, but couldn't break free. His body stopped struggling and went limp while the driver finished his meal. I felt I should be sad at the man's slow, violent death, but it just made me wonder if he was better off too. Whatever was in store for me at our destination would probably be much worse.

The bite mark on the attendant's neck sealed with a touch of the driver's fingers before he was discarded out the window. We continued speeding down the open road for a while longer until finally turning onto a dirt path. From Noah's description of the Strigoi, I was half-expecting to wind up in a library, but we slowed down when we reached an old factory. The grass was waist-high from neglect in places alongside the path to the badly rusted-out facility. The driver took the car into the dark ruins of the building through a loading bay, which closed up once we passed.

A cloaked figure emerged from the shadow of an old jeep to greet us once we got out. "Splendid! I see you have succeeded in recovering the boy, Minerva," the cloaked man praised.

Our driver helped escort my body out while Minerva spoke. It was the first time I got a good look at him. The driver was tall and slender, probably around my age when he was turned, and he looked like he could be related to the other man with us. His clothes had a pseudo-Victorian gothic flair, giving him a much more ironically youthful image.

"Of course I have, for I am not a miserable failure such as yourself." Minerva stared ahead past the cloaked man.

"Rightfully so, Archmage, but surely you can understand how the circumstances were more challenging than we had anticipated."

"No, please explain how woefully inept you must be, when I simply walked onto the Archios' estate and took our property from right under their noses. Your incompetence disgusts me," Minerva jeered. She made a slight gesture of her hand, and the cloaked man exploded in green flames until nothing was left but the echo of his screams.

The two men from the car gave each other an unsettled look as they followed her deeper into the facility. We stopped in front of a huge metal security door. The driver stepped up to a broken-down control panel and placed his hand over it, causing the circuitry to spring to life and open the door.

We walked across several narrow catwalks in near-total darkness. Beyond a few more heavy metal doors and down a flight of stairs we reached an area with overhead incandescent lights that flickered on as we walked and then off again as we passed. This wasn't just a factory, it was an abandoned military bunker from the Cold War that the Strigoi had repurposed as a laboratory. Trailing after my body in my incorporeal form, I had no sense of smell, but if I did, I was sure this place would reek of must from the state of disrepair and neglect everything was in.

Our tour brought us to a gigantic circular room resembling a missile silo. All around, the Strigoi were busy fiddling with clockwork contraptions and reading from archaic tomes.

"Colleagues," Minerva greeted the crowd. "I have returned, victorious where others have failed in such a simple task. And now you are all of no use to me." Her audience burst into green flames that reduced them to ash in seconds. The two men we had traveled with were appalled as they watched the massacre.

"Minerva! What are you doing?" the older one shouted.

"Cleansing the cancerous disappointment this coven has suffered from for too long," she replied without the slightest hint of remorse.

"They were our allies," the younger man spoke. "When the other houses hear of this ..."

"Then I shall deal with them in the same manner if they are unable to comprehend my superiority. Prepare the subject. I will return shortly," she ordered. I was immediately drawn back into my body once she left.

The men walked me to the center of the floor, where a large circular indentation was carved and outlined in runes. I was still finding it hard to speak or concentrate. The men took a step back while the younger one magically activated another control panel that brought down a glass containment tube around me. As the feeling in my body returned, I asked myself how they expected glass to hold me. The older-looking of the two bit his finger like in the car and drew a line of runes on the glass with his blood. The bloody symbols, along with the ones on the floor surrounding the tube, lit up momentarily. I banged on the glass, but anytime I did, the runes would illuminate again, shielding it from damage.

"I can't believe what I just saw," the younger man said to his accomplice. "That fire ..."

"Soul-searing balefire from Hell. A gift from a demon," the older man stated.

"You knew about this?"

"I had my suspicions."

They completely ignored me as I banged on the glass and shouted at them to let me go. Any use of my powers and I risked losing myself to the infection. I contemplated just allowing it to take over while they continued to talk in front of me.

"Why didn't you do something about it? Pacts with demons are forbidden for good reason! We have to tell the other Archmages."

"Keep your voice down, Tristan," the older man hissed. "I had no proof and never thought it would come to this. There is nothing we can do but go forward. Now help me find a cure."

They were going to cure me? I thought I was about to be cut open and studied. The man put his hand out to me. I felt a strange pulling and then saw tiny droplets of blood leaking from the pores in my exposed skin. It collected along the glass and dripped down, pooling at the bottom, where it drained into the indentation on the other side. The man bent down and scooped up the blood in a jar.

"Curious." he questioned after tasting it. "The Archios must have given him blood?"

"That could be useful," Tristan said, watching me.

Without Noah's blood, the infection was spreading rapidly through my veins. They performed the same spell twice more, first collecting my pure blood and then a sample of the black blood. I dropped to the floor, shivering as the cold clutches of death gripped me.

"How can you be so calm about this?" Tristan asked.

The other man ignored him and read something from a tome, causing my body to seize up. Once it relaxed all the pain and shivering was gone. Whatever spell he had cast sedated me so heavily that my body lay there lifelessly while my thoughts faded in and out.

"Calm about what?" Minerva asked from behind them.

"How could you kill all of our colleagues? And demons? You know they are forbidden!" Tristan exclaimed.

"Nothing is forbidden to me. Placing needless limitations on ourselves makes us no better than mortals. We are not to be handicapped by morals and myths. The true quest for knowledge cannot be confined by such petty idealisms."

"I do not believe the source of the infection is viral, bacterial, or magical," the older man said in an attempt to change the conversation. "We took samples to begin work on a cure."

"A cure? There is no need for a cure."

"Isn't that the whole reason we reclaimed him?" Tristan asked.

"I have no use for him alive. Kill him. Once his soul has been severed from the body we will begin the infernal possession ritual."

The two men looked at each other and then at me.

"That wasn't the plan," Tristan argued. "He wasn't meant to be used as a vessel for a demon."

"The plan is what I say it is," Minerva snapped at him. She conjured a grisly-looking leather-bound book in her hand. "This has everything you need to prepare the ritual."

"The *Grand Grimoire?*" Tristan read the title out loud. "This is a demon's manuscript on making deals with the Devil."

"Good, I see you can still read. You should have no problem making preparations."

"How did you get this? Humans have kept it out of reach for centuries by sealing it in a holy place."

"The copy in the humans' possession is a fake, but we now hold the original. The author loaned it to me so we can finish our work. The Infernals whispered to me from beyond the Gates of Hell to create them an army capable of standing against the light. And that is exactly what we have done."

"Surely you cannot be comfortable with this, brother."

Tristan looked to the other man, who was doing his best to remain silent.

"See to it that everything is in order for my return later tonight," Minerva commanded. "Can you do that?"

Tristan stared down at the grimoire, thinking. "No, I won't do it. I cannot be a part of this."

"Very well," she said calmly.

Tristan caught fire, burning to cinders like the others while she watched.

"No!" the other man exclaimed and kneeled over the ashes. "He was your nephew, Minerva! Why, why would you do this?"

"He was incompetent. Take the book, Vance, unless you wish to share his fate. Have the ritual prepared by the time I return at midnight," she demanded before leaving the room in a magnificent display of fire and smoke.

Vance worked for hours in the poor lighting while I lay there unable to move or feel anything. He didn't look at me or his brother's remains once. Every so often he would glance at the jars of blood he took from me and then continue reading to himself or mixing some concoction. The anxiety of not knowing what was coming, or how bad it would be, was worse than anything I had felt up to now. I just wanted it to be over, one way or another.

"It wasn't supposed to be like this," Vance's voice spoke in my head. "But I promise your death will be swift."

"Just let me go, please! I'm really not worth all of this."

"I can't do that, or she will kill me too."

"Your brother died standing up to her because he believed what she was doing was wrong. I know you feel the same way; I could see it in your face. Don't let Tristan's death be in vain!"

He didn't respond; I wasn't even sure he was still listening. He just kept working with the same stoic expression. It figured the braver of the two brothers would die, leaving my only chance at survival barred by the one too afraid to act. Noah was always preaching that cowardice would be the end of me, but I assumed it would be my own.

After a while, he left the room with his head still stuck in the diabolical spellbook. The wriggling in my veins had been creeping up this whole time, but at a much slower rate than usual, thanks to whatever paralyzing spell he had cast.

Once he was gone, I started to regain my motor functions along with the increased spread of the infection. I got up slowly and banged on the glass for help, although I wasn't sure why I expected to get any. The vibrations from the hair-raising death rattle shook the glass around me.

I clawed frantically to get out as my body went numb again. The only feeling left in me was a brief stinging in my fingertips from the nails breaking off. There was no holding off the frenzy any longer. I didn't recognize my own face in the reflection of the glass. I was hideous; the whites of my eyes were black again, leaving just the gray ring of my iris, and my skin was covered in dark veins and dried blood from where I was bled out.

The massive steel doors opened again. I expected to see Vance, but another group of robed Strigoi entered instead. They investigated the piles of ash scattered around the room and the curious machines and notes lying around, occasionally muttering to each other in German. My body was acting on its own, twitching and jumping aggressively at them as they passed by and looked in at me. My mind was fading away in a pre-sleep state, but I could still make out a little of what was going on.

Vance marched into the room with his head down, reading, just as he had left. He seemed startled by the visitors.

"So it is true, demon worship in our very own coven!" an elderly Strigoi said, taking one look at the book Vance carried. "You know this act is forbidden. Hand over the *Grand Grimoire* and I may grant you leniency."

"No," Vance responded. "This artifact is not mine to give. If you wish to claim it you would do best to speak with the Archmage of this house, but you most certainly will come to regret it."

The group was aghast at Vance's insubordination. They chattered among themselves for a moment until the elderly man silenced them with a raised hand.

"You dare threaten a member of the Council? Contact of any kind with demons will not be tolerated, nor will your insolence. I will not have you, nor your Archmage, bring doom upon our coven over some foolish lust for power."

He raised his hand, summoning the grimoire to him from across the room, and spoke a phrase in some unfamiliar language that bound Vance in rings of light. Vance was a lost cause now, but I was more scared for myself at the moment. I felt like my tongue was trying to crawl its way out of my throat. I kept grabbing at my neck to make it stop as it drove me mad. The glass began quaking as my powers flared out of control, clashing with the magic that shielded it. My vision was almost completely obscured by pulsating darkness, but it was a single sound that mattered to me the most. A sound I heard even above the shrieking, snarling death growls. It was the sound of glass cracking.

Chapter Eleven

"We'll be taking this specimen for our own studies. Don't worry, it will be put to good use."

The leader approached my prison and gawked at me like he was at the zoo. I was overtaken by anger and an irrational hunger as I looked back at him. I wanted to ... eat him? My body was acting completely on its own. A sliver of consciousness was all that was keeping me from fading away for good. As unlikely as it might be, I was hoping I would cause at least one of them some trouble when I turned as payback for everything they had put me through.

The glowing runes dissipated from the glass. It only took a second, but I watched in slow motion as my prison shattered around me. The impact from my heightened powers continued, turning the leader into nothing more than a bloody smear before he could react.

My body stepped out of the circle and over his remains. The other mages were scrambling to wrap their heads around what they had just witnessed, but weren't fast enough to take action. Out of the corner of my eye, I could see each one of them exploding in a shower of blood as my powers raged out of control. This was more than I could have asked for. I'd been living on borrowed time since this started. Even if I were to die here, at least I would go out with a bang.

Vance was already gone. He had probably escaped during the initial chaos. The blast doors slammed shut to seal me in, but no piece of metal was about to stop my rampage now. Door after door crumpled like tin cans under my power. Each crushing blow was accompanied by a dreadful symphony of gears grinding from the door motors trying to close and the infection's eerie growls inside me.

My sudden appetite was consuming me from the inside. I could sense food where my body was going. I tore my way through the facility, not sure what I'd find in each room. Some of the rooms were libraries or arcane laboratories, and others contained more clockwork contraptions.

Down at the end of the hall was a door protected by runes I couldn't break through. On the other side, two voices were conversing. I strained to hear over the ghastly sounds emanating from me.

"I know why you're here, but the boy is our property," said Vance.

"I'm here because you jackasses thought you could bribe our people to do your dirty work and stroll up onto our land uninvited dressed like that. Oh, and the whole mutant plague has gotta stop, it's getting annoying."

That was Noah's voice! His blood was the only hope I had of returning to normal.

"We have nothing to do with those abominations. Our only concern has been reclaiming what is rightfully ours."

"Doesn't seem like he's too fond of being your little science experiment or having mercenaries sent after him. You may have bitten off more than you can chew there, champ."

"This wouldn't have happened if he hadn't been infected during his time with you."

"What's the big deal with this kid? You should be thankful; he's a lot more entertaining this way, if you ask me."

"He is a construct of biological and magical engineering. We created him to be a living psionic weapon, but he is uncontrollable in this state. He has always had this potential. I'm sure even you figured that out by now, since the Archios were so adamant about keeping him from us."

Created me? What is he talking about?

"Whatever you say. I've got my weapons strapped to my side and that's all I need," Noah boasted. "I'm just interested in one thing now, and that's ending this plague so I can go back to watching TV."

"Then the Carpathians are the ones you should be after, not us. I can't say I ever expected the Archios to look away from their luxuries long enough to notice."

"That hurts, really. But why would the Carpathians do this?"

"It's simple. The Carpathians resent humankind for forcing them into hiding. They believe they are superior and this is their attempt at population control. We decided now was the time to reclaim this specimen and all the others from the field once the plague threatened to endanger them."

There are more people out there like me?

"Others? You weren't making a weapon, you were building an army. So that's why the mutants kept going after him. The Carpathians found out what you were doing and felt threatened."

"I don't know how they could have found out. It was supposed to be a contingency plan, not a declaration of war. Archmage Minerva preached to our coven about a way to keep us safe as the world continues to fall out of our hands. Even in daylight, we would have these living weapons to watch over us. They fit in perfectly with human society, but have the power of any Ancient."

"Infection or not, I don't think he'd be on board with that plan after everything you put him through. You keep beating a dog and eventually it's gonna bite back."

"Sound advice from one whose master keeps him on a tight leash. I'm surprised you were allowed to travel this far from her hip."

"Normally I'd kill you myself, but I think the kid has earned this one."

With a big smile, Noah threw open the door. My powers took over and lifted him and Vance into the air. I had to fight the destructive urges as if I were drowning in a powerful current, desperately trying to swim to the surface. Noah transformed into a cloud of mist, making me lose my grip on him. I wanted answers and Vance had them.

"Hey buddy, it's your pal, Noah." He reformed beside me with his arm around my shoulder. "Let me introduce you to the guy who's responsible for killing your friend, sending a bounty hunter to kidnap you, and been the cause of all your troubles."

I tried to demand answers from him, but all that came out were growls and a barely intelligible "Answers."

"Wait!" Vance looked utterly terrified. "I can cure you and answer all your questions, but we must leave now. Minerva will be returning at any moment."

"So? What's she gonna do, hit me with a book?" Noah scoffed.

"She is more powerful than you think. Minerva has been consorting with a demon behind our backs and is expecting to use this specimen's body as a vessel for it."

"Hmm, never killed a demon before."

"You wouldn't stand a chance. To them, we are little more than insects. Our origin stems from their machinations during the last contest between Heaven and Hell.

"Angels, tasked by God, escorted the purest and most devout of mankind through the Gates of Heaven. Out of spite, the Demon Kings of Hell tempted man with immortality and power so they could remain on Earth as gods instead of commoners in Heaven. Those who accepted the gift received the brand of Hell upon their soul. The Demon Kings used our predecessors to drink God's flock dry and spread the curse.

"The angels struck back, vanquishing the undead, but not all of them were destroyed. God placed His own curse on those cunning enough to survive. Their bodies may never again walk in the light until they cast off their sins in the dark. Disappointed in the new frailty of their creations, the Demon Kings abandoned them as forgotten children.

"The only time a demon holds any interest in us is right before it devours our soul in Hell. Association with Infernals is forbidden because of how volatile and untrustworthy they are. Besides, weren't you only here for information on the plague?"

"I like a challenge," Noah replied, "and I could use a new trophy for my room. What's in this for you, anyway? I know how weaselly you Strigoi are. The second your hide is on the line you'll go running."

"I have a more personal stake in this than some trophy. My brother was killed because he didn't want to see Minerva use our work like this."

"Don't tell me you're getting sentimental."

"Sentimental, no. Responsible, yes. This life-form is the first of its kind, a collective progeny birthed through a fusion of sorcery and science. I cannot allow our investment in him to be lost to any affliction or Infernal."

It sickened and angered me hearing them talk as if I were some lab rat.

"Touching. How do you plan on getting out of here with him like this? I can't read his mind. I'm pretty sure he's checked out and going to kill you soon."

"He's still in there. I'll explain later, but for now you have to give him more of your blood so he'll regain control and put me down."

"Why would you think he had my blood?"

"We can discuss this later. Time is of the essence."

"Shit. I knew I was going to regret giving him that. If you made some unflattering voodoo doll of me I'll kill you myself."

"The blood of yours that I removed from him is in the ritual room. We can use that if it makes you feel better. Just hurry."

I'd never seen Noah move as slowly as he did, strolling out of the room just to get under Vance's skin, but he was back soon enough. I couldn't see him at first, but knew he was there thanks to the blood suddenly going down my throat. The dark tide churning inside me barely eased. I was too far gone for Noah's blood to fight back the infection. My head cleared enough to let me release Vance, but I felt numb and stiff as I tried to direct my body.

"Do your thing," Noah said to Vance as he turned visible.

"There is another stronghold not far from here. Unfortunately, Minerva will know all the same places to hide, so we won't have long until she finds us." Vance picked up the cursed tome at his feet and made his way out of the room. "We can take one of the vehicles upstairs."

"Take the kid and go on ahead. I can crawl faster than any car you've got. I'm gonna hang back here for a while to see if I can get the jump on the witch and her pet."

"I'm not going anywhere with him," I whispered to Noah after Vance left. "Let me help you."

"You want to fight?" Noah stared at me in disbelief. "Look, I don't know if you've lost your mind or finally found it, but I don't need your help."

I glared back at him in defiance. "Isn't that what you've been wanting me to say this whole time? The more I run and hide the more I lose, and I'm tired of it. I'm a person, not somebody's lab rat. I want to end this, one way or another."

"I don't know what the hell you are, but if you wanna do something useful go blow up some mutants in New York." As usual, Noah had to have the last word. He vanished. I didn't care what any of them said, I was still human.

The lights were on when I reached the ground floor where Noah and Vance were waiting. The room we had entered the facility from was much bigger than I had realized at first. It housed an entire fleet of abandoned ATVs and rusted tanks that were covered in decades of dust. Many of them looked to have been salvaged for scrap by the Strigoi to use in their machines.

"The tome," Minerva's voice sounded, followed by an explosion of black smoke from the catwalk above. Her hand was extended in Vance's direction as she looked down her nose at him.

"Your scheme will fail," he said, clutching the *Grand Grimoire* to his side. "You cannot hope to tame the denizens of Hell. It is a demon's nature to betray those with whom it deals."

"Your ignorance insults me, nephew. My actions are not so shortsighted; there is something much greater at hand. The eternal crusade between Heaven and Hell will soon claim the Earth as its battleground. And from the ashes, the rebirth of civilization will begin anew, as it has many times in the past. I am doing the Devil's work, and in exchange for my aid I will be granted a position of leadership."

"I'm sorry, Minerva, but I can't let you do this."

"Pity." She pointed her finger and ignited the area around him in green flames.

"First the kid, now this book. Why are women always so indecisive?" Noah made it across the room and back with Vance before he could be set on fire. Minerva gave another attempt at roasting them, but Noah evaded her just as easily, even while carrying Vance.

"Bring it on. I can do this all night long," Noah said.

Vance was sneaking away with the book as Noah and Minerva continued to intimidate each other. Now was my chance. I concentrated all my anger and released it in a pulse of energy at her that shook the catwalk. She put her hand to the side, negating my attack without even turning her head. It didn't make sense. I had been so much more powerful earlier.

"I'm through here. You can all perish together if that's what you want. I have plenty more untainted specimens to use as vessels. I won't mind reaping your souls so I don't leave empty-handed."

"Talk all you want, lady," Noah taunted. "I'm still gonna cut your head off."

I motioned to the walkway, tearing it out from under her, but failing to do her any harm again. Why wasn't I strong enough all of a sudden? Why now, when I needed it most?

"Be patient and wait your turn." Minerva scowled. "You'll have your chance to die soon enough, just like the cattle you called a family."

I had never wanted to hurt somebody as badly as I did her. Noah took the opportunity to pounce on her with his swords drawn, but was repelled by a force field similar to the one around the containment chamber. Minerva shrieked with laughter at his failure.

"Absolutely pathetic! Do you believe someone of my genius would not be prepared for such a foolhardy attack? It was I who single-handedly defeated one-half of the infamous Saint-Pierre sisters, after all. No, compared to her you are nothing!"

"You mean you're the dumbass that offed Rozalin? Out of all the Ancients, you go after the one that can keep coming back after death."

"That is precisely what I was counting on. All I needed was to light the fuse that would goad the sisters into war again. It was a simple task, knowing the hatred they hold for each other. I merely had to impersonate an Archios pretending to carry out Aurelia's orders to assassinate her sister. I knew when Rozalin returned from the grave she would waste no time in exacting her revenge. The resulting calamity at the chateau made it elementary to reclaim the boy.

"The next apocalypse is upon us, and now the covens are too busy warring amongst themselves to sense its approach. Let them all eradicate each other. Humans will be much easier to rule when the new cycle begins without their meddling."

"Yeah, yeah. Dawn of an era, a new world order, *vive la revolution*. I'm not impressed. Give me decadence and debauchery over this bullshit any day."

"She's stalling!" Vance yelled from his hiding spot behind an ATV. "She's been casting a summoning spell this whole time."

"Good, I was getting bored," Noah said while relaxing on a tank. "Somebody tell her that world domination is so one-dimensional."

Minerva raised a hand above her head, igniting the air into a giant ball of green flame. The fiery orb split into three and homed in on each of us. I dove for cover behind a stack of crates that exploded on contact with the fire and sent me flying. I lost sight of Vance, but Noah was enjoying himself by speeding around the room, taunting Minerva as she continued to hurl giant orbs of fire at him. He used her own attack against her by letting the fire follow him and crash into her barrier. I couldn't hear what they were saying to each other because of the ringing in my ears, but Minerva didn't seem at all happy that she was being outsmarted.

I spotted Vance in a corner writing something in blood on the floor that faded from view. "Any of us will die instantly if struck with the flames of Hell. The greenish balefires burn away not only the flesh, but the soul, which means no chance at an afterlife." Vance's voice spoke in my head when he noticed me watching him. "It may be the only thing capable of breaking her force field if he can keep that up before she finishes summoning."

I still couldn't trust him and wasn't about to let Noah do this on his own. Ignoring Vance's warning, I crept closer to where I could get a better view of Minerva. I tried again to attack head on, hoping to get lucky and break the barrier around her. She was unfazed, but countered with one of the giant fireballs. It was closing in faster than I could run, so I ducked under the stairs to the catwalk and let the fire collide with the stairwell.

Noah appeared next to me with his hands on his hips. "You think I could work on my tan from all this fire?"

"Vance said if you get hit by it it's instant death," I warned.

"Good thing she throws like a girl then," he shrugged.

"It's here!" Vance yelled. "We have to run!"

I peeked out from the charred stairs to see a large glowing pentagram projected on the ground under Minerva. The room rumbled and the lights flickered as a massive clawed hand reached out from the ground. Minerva smiled victoriously as the demon climbed out of the portal and towered over us. It was at least fifteen feet high, with a reddish-black hide covered in sharp spiky protrusions. The head had two huge curved horns on either side of its vaguely human face.

"Damn, I'm gonna need a bigger trophy wall," Noah said, looking up at the demon from atop an old military tank.

Minerva exchanged words with the summoned beast in some incomprehensible language. The demon's voice boomed above all else, sounding like three separate beings speaking in unison.

"It is feeding her energy. We won't be able to break her shield now. I implore you, we must retreat!" Vance called out to us again, but Minerva wasn't about to let us leave. She cast her fire out, creating walls of flame to cut off the exits.

The demon brought its fist down on the tank where Noah stood and smashed it to pieces. Noah reciprocated by unleashing a furious onslaught of slashes from all directions. He moved so fast he was only visible as a blurred image. The demon's skin wasn't taking any damage as Noah continued to deftly maneuver around the giant body, searching for a weak point. It was impressive watching his high-speed high-flying acrobatics as he evaded and countered every seemingly sluggish attack of the demon.

"The tome," Minerva demanded. She had Vance cornered on the ground floor now.

"You killed my brother," Vance said. "I can never forgive you for that, Minerva."

"I wasn't asking for forgiveness." She held out her hand for the book and advanced on him. The blood Vance had scribbled on the floor earlier lit up under her feet in the shape of a circle like the one the demon had crawled out from. A powder-blue ball of light sprang up and exploded into a freezing wind, encasing her in a block of ice.

Vance stared in anger at her for a moment and then wrote more runes in his blood on the ice. "That will hold her, but not for long," he told me as he finished.

Noah was still locked in battle with the demon and neither side was making much progress. The beast noticed Minerva's frozen body and chose to assist her instead of continuing the stalemate. Noah saw the open opportunity and vaulted at the demon's face with his swords out. He stabbed it in the eyes, dragging the blades down hard as the monster roared and flailed in pain.

"It's time we leave," Vance said, jumping into one of the ATVs that hadn't been destroyed yet.

"What? I'm not leaving him here to fight by himself," I said.

"He wanted to fight and took a calculated risk against my many attempts to advise otherwise. Remember what you said about dying in vain. If we waste this chance to escape we won't get another," Vance reasoned.

My encounters with Noah were always highly questionable at best. If his plan was to use me from the start, at least the Archios were the lesser of two evils compared to the Strigoi. I did owe him for his help; if it weren't for him I would've been alone through this.

"I've already been dead inside this whole time. Running and hiding with everyone else in control of my life isn't living. If I'm going to live I don't want it to be stained with regret."

"You can't kill it. You have to survive until the spell wears off," Vance shouted. "Our atmosphere is caustic to their kind. That's why they need a vessel. They can only survive here for so long before needing to return to Hell."

"How much longer do we have?" Noah yelled back down to Vance from his perch high up on the catwalks.

"When the portal it came in from closes, it's done," he answered.

The glowing pentagram was only about half gone, meaning we had a long road ahead of us. I called the tome to my hand and flew up near the demon's face. Its eyes had healed, but what looked like dried lava dripped from the sockets where it must have bled.

"Hey! You want the book?" I shouted and floated the demon's grimoire just out of reach. It took the bait and left off trying to unfreeze Minerva. I dashed through the air to play keepaway and buy us some time, but a ring of green fire surrounded me as soon as I landed.

"It ends here." Minerva's voice came from the flames as she walked through them. I was trapped between her, the wall, and the demon, wishing I had taken Vance up on his offer. I tried again to attack or at least throw her back, but she was still shielded.

"For a failed experiment, you are more trouble than you were worth," she hissed.

"I guess I can die happy then," I snapped back at her.

The room became a blur as I was lifted out of the fire, along the wall, and down to the other side. Noah dumped me on the floor from over his shoulder.

"You all right?" he asked as I got to my feet.

"I'm fine, thanks. Are you?"

I could barely hear his response over the sound of the demon stampeding right for us, but felt a crippling pain in my stomach. "Sorry, kid, but you're cramping my style."

I started feeling cold as the pain grew worse. I looked down and saw one of Noah's blades plunged into me. My blood leaked out all over the floor. It began to turn black as he pulled the blade out and sheathed it on his hip. He took the tome from me and held it up for everyone to see.

"Here's your stupid book if you want it so bad," he shouted and dumped it at my feet as I collapsed.

All I kept asking myself as I lay in a pool of my own blood was, why? Why did I bother staying to help him? No matter whose side I was on, I was getting the crap kicked out of me. I couldn't feel the pain anymore, just a familiar numbness. The veins in my hand blackened again as my consciousness was torn away. My body rose on its own, letting me watch through my eyes as an unwilling spectator. The hole in my abdomen sealed up using the last of Noah's blood in my system.

The stomping of footsteps was drowned out by the growls inside of me. The demon wasn't at all deterred by my presence guarding the book. It moved to knock me out of the way as Minerva watched, but its giant fist froze before it could make contact. The infection was taking control of my powers again to defend itself.

The demon reared back before striking with all its might. Once again, it was stopped in midair by an invisible wall protecting me. Noah materialized out of a cloud of mist between me and the demon. One look at him grinning sent me over the edge. Whatever was inside of me fed off my anger and struck out at him. He vanished into a cloud of mist again, but the demon stumbled backward, falling onto the vehicles and crushing them beneath its enormous frame.

Noah revealed himself standing on the fallen demon and baited me to come attack him. I walked toward them and struck again, this time throwing the demon back further until it hit the wall. The tires of the vehicles in front of me screeched as they slid back from the shock wave.

Minerva reclaimed the spellbook and spoke in tongues to the demon, who replied with a haunting laugh. It belched out a volley of fire that razed the area to cinders and then sank slowly down through a portal back to Hell. Before it disappeared completely Noah thrust his blade into its hand, drawing red-hot blood that spurted out like lava.

"No matter. I have the *Grand Grimoire*, so you can keep the wretched boy for now." Minerva was speaking to Vance from somewhere in the conflagration. Noah sauntered out with swords in hand, one of which was still sizzling from its contact with the demon's molten blood. He zoomed out of range every time I went to follow him through the gauntlet of fire until I came up behind Minerva. She was in the middle of attacking Vance when I ambushed her with an assault of my own. All the rage left in me came pouring out in one tremendous blast that obliterated her shield.

"Burn in Hell, you worthless brat!" She whirled around to face me, flames of anger burning green in her eyes. I waited to be engulfed in fire, but her facial expression went blank as she tilted her head down.

"Told you I'd cut your head off." Noah stood behind her, drawing his heated *katana* through her neck as she crumbled to dust. Vance was in shock, staring at the pile of remains. Noah bit his wrist and dodged behind me. He put his arm around my neck and the wounded wrist of his other arm to my mouth, forcing blood down my throat.

"If you're through here, can we leave?" Vance asked, picking up the tome from Minerva's ashes.

"Get off me!" I yelled at Noah after regaining control. Trying to pull his arm away was like trying to move a mountain.

"You were useless," he said, pointing to Vance. "You were less useless, which is a big improvement," he added, patting me on the back.

"I can't believe you stabbed me." I was still pissed off at him, but for some sick reason his words of approval made me feel better.

"Really? It kinda sounds like something I would do. Remember, you're still alive because of my blood. Noah giveth and Noah taketh away."

Another pentagram opened under Minerva's ashes, sending all of us jumping back. The demon's hand shot out and dragged the remains down to Hell with it before resealing the portal.

"Her end of the bargain was up," Vance said, and flipped through the tome. "The pact is fulfilled with her soul. Being condemned to eternal servitude in Hell just isn't worth the power, although it is tempting."

Noah cocked his head and stared him down. "Are you serious right now?"

"So that's it? No more demon uprising?" I asked.

"For now. Minerva's plot to unleash the Demon Kings upon the world may have been foiled, but that won't stop the cycle of war between Heaven and Hell."

"Who cares? Thanks to her, we have our own mess to deal with, and it's on your shoulders to fix it." Noah confronted Vance. "The Carpathians aren't just gonna stop pissing people off, and my place still has a ghost problem."

"I have a lot of questions for you," I said, stepping between them and addressing Vance, "First, let's start with that cure."

Chapter Twelve

"The source of the contagion is a parasite, and a particularly fascinating one I may add. While we awaited the boy's arrival, we collected a live sample to examine."

Vance led us back down to the underground laboratories to answer my questions. With Minerva gone for good there was no danger in staying here anymore, and Vance claimed he had all he needed for a cure right here.

"It is a liquid-based organism that assimilates with its host by traveling through the circulatory system to reach the brain. The black fluid in the host's veins isn't discolored blood, but the parasite itself. Once it has rooted, the parasite rapidly absorbs nutrients throughout the body causing changes in the color and texture of the victim's skin. It shuts down the host's mind so that it can direct the person to keep nourishing itself. In essence, it is reverting its victim to his or her most primitive, feral state."

"Are they undead?" I asked.

"No. In fact, the hosts are still quite alive. The brain damage caused by the parasite's assimilation only drives the victim mad. It doesn't want the host resisting the impulse to engorge itself."

"So my parents were still alive the whole time? They could have been watching when I was right there next to them?"

"Oh yes, there's no doubt about that, but they may have already lost their minds." Vance's tone made this so much more upsetting. It was like he viewed people as nothing more than bacteria in a Petri dish. "It seems that if the host doesn't feed enough to satisfy the parasite, the body will start to wither.

"I have a theory. Hosts who feed frequently enough may begin exhibiting radical mutations, such as claws, to help them harvest more food. This is likely an effect from the parasite overriding a suitable host's DNA to stimulate bone or muscle development. The cancerous growths you often see are an unfortunate side effect of aggressive mutation."

"If the infected aren't undead, why are they so hard to kill?" I asked. "I've seen them take a lot of punishment and keep going."

"The infected don't feel pain and don't require most bodily functions be intact to survive. When trauma occurs, the parasite will prevent the body from going into shock and may restore energy back to the host in order to boost cellular regeneration, for a time keeping them alive. Only when significant enough damage is dealt to compensate for this accelerated healing will the infected die."

Noah started playing with all of Vance's equipment in the room out of boredom. "You're telling me we've got to beat the parasite out of him to cure him? I should've just done that from the start."

"No. He is different from regular humans, much different. He was created to be a much more resilient life-form."

"I have a name." I'd had enough of being referred to as a test subject or some creature.

"Right, sorry, uh ..." Vance stalled.

"You're kidding, right? It's Dorian. My name is Dorian. You're saying you know everything about me but my name?"

"I didn't know either," Noah said, and raised his hand.

"Do not take offense, but your name was given to you by your mortal caretakers. It served no significance to us."

"They're called parents," I snapped. "You can claim you created me all you want, but they're the ones that raised and cared for me. Did they know what I was when they adopted me?"

"No, there was no reason to inform them. We left you for adoption overseas as an ordinary human infant. The fewer people that knew the truth, the better.

"Moving on, the parasite in you seems unable to complete its purpose even without the assistance of Noah's blood. It is having significant trouble overcoming your advanced cellular structure. We may have truly achieved genetic perfection."

"If you wanted to see perfection, I'm right here." Noah took a seat and kicked his feet up on a desk, knocking over a stack of books. "I get that you're a proud parent, but how'd you pull this off when we can't breed? Undead bodies aren't the most fertile."

"We replaced the DNA of a fertilized human egg cell with a synthetic strand fabricated through magic. The genes we used were carefully selected and spliced together from countless donors. Potential weaknesses were identified and removed throughout the embryo's gestation in an artificial womb. Every essential aspect of his being was manipulated to produce results that would take nature millions of years to match.

"Human genetic research was integral to our process. Mankind has the knowledge, but what we both lacked was the technology to go through with a project of this level. It was Minerva who pioneered this new branch of complex biological magic needed to supplement our insufficient technology. My brother engineered the artificial womb using technomancy, a unique line of sorcery dealing with clockwork machinery, and I tethered the soul to the embryo that gave him his telekinetic powers.

"Dorian was created free of all potential hereditary diseases, with a substantially more resilient immune system. He is virtually impervious to harmful mutations.

"Your speed and fighting skill may be extraordinary, but in the end you hold the same weaknesses as any of our kind."

"So if he's supposed to be your super soldier, why'd you make him such a wuss?" Noah laughed.

"We didn't bother altering personality, since we were just going to control him telepathically in the end."

"Just get to the cure," I said. Focusing on the cure was the only thing keeping me going. Maybe I would actually be able to put all this behind me and hopefully never see any of them again.

"It isn't so much a cure as it is a binding. I came up with it when studying the possession ritual from the demon tome. The spell merges two entities into one and leaves the more dominant of the two in control. Since a demon can only exist in our world for a short time in its true form, it needs a vessel. Normal humans are too fragile and our own weaknesses are easily exploitable, but Dorian has neither of those problems.

"A demon is more powerful than him, but the parasite is most likely not. Casting the same ritual should leave Dorian in control and absorb the parasite into his matrix."

"What do you mean *should?*" I demanded. "What the hell are you going to turn me into?"

"In the case that the balance isn't in your favor, you will most likely mutate beyond recognition."

"No way. I'm not doing this unless it's a sure thing."

"There are no sure things when it comes to these matters. If mankind weren't so worried about ethics based on 'what if,' they would attain a much higher quality of life.

"It is laughable how close humanity has come to manipulating evolution to their benefit, yet the petty regulations of fear and faith have held them back for years. Things like stem cells are the first step in accomplishing the magnificent feat we have achieved in creating you. The key to vitality and strength is locked away in every cell, but humans purposely turn a blind eye to it.

"I will never understand why they would rather wallow in sickness and despair than risk sacrificing a few of their own for the health of billions. You were ready to die a few minutes ago. There is no way to remove the parasite without killing the host. If you don't take risks, you will never progress."

"Fine, let's do it. What have I got to lose, right? Any idea if it'll be painful?"

"Probably, or maybe not at all. There is no way to tell until it happens, but that's the fun part of an experiment."

"You're a freak," Noah chuckled.

"Don't be so quick to criticize. I will need a blood sacrifice for the ritual and it's your blood I'm going to use. It will be the perfect catalyst to help prevent the parasite from wresting control."

"Why would I do that?"

"The same reason you gave him your blood before, I presume. I can't use mine if I'm the one casting the spell."

"I only did it to keep him under control. He's your problem now, not mine."

"Then why are you still here? Shouldn't you be off hunting the Carpathians or sitting at your master's feet?"

Noah moved his feet from the desk, kicking test tubes full of liquids to the floor on purpose. "I'm not done with you yet, that's why. How good are you at exorcisms?"

"They're simple enough spells, but if you mean the issue you're having at the chateau you can forget it. Rozalin de Saint-Pierre was one of the most powerful necromancers this world and possibly the next has ever seen. I can only imagine how much worse she is to deal with in her current state."

"You owe me." Noah stood up and got in Vance's face. "If it weren't for me you would have died up there tonight."

"I had contacted the Council of the Strigoi in hopes they would take Dorian and me into custody where we would be safe. I still would have had time to escape if you hadn't barged in."

Noah took another step closer and squinted menacingly into Vance's eyes. "If there's no reason for me to keep you around, then tell me why I shouldn't just kill you now."

"And if I were to help you, what happens to me after that?"

"Take care of my ghost problem and you have my word you'll leave in one piece. I'll give you the blood for your science project, but try anything funny and the deal's off."

It was hard deciding whether I was more nervous about the ritual being painful or having to drink blood again. The idea of drinking it made me sick, but strangely the blood never tasted bad or caused me to be sick.

The two of them were so caught up in bargaining with each other's lives I was hoping they weren't paying attention to my thoughts. The sad realization that Lyle was the third victim of circumstance popped back in my head. On my way here I had started to become emotionally detached and even envious in some sick way. Death was an easy way out. If this cure did work, what did I really have to go back to without a family? If anyone should be dead it should be me, not Lyle.

There was one thing I wanted to do if the cure worked, and that was avenge those who died, starting right here with Lyle. If Vance thought I was going to be his pet to prod and experiment on, he had another think coming.

Vance cast the blood-draining spell he had used on me to begin drawing out Noah's blood into a glass container. Noah stood there with his arms crossed, not seeming the least bit affected, but as Vance continued taking more and more blood, Noah began looking uncomfortable. He was obviously trying not to show weakness as he clenched his teeth.

I wouldn't put it past Vance to pull a fast one and take advantage of Noah's weakened state so he wouldn't have to make good on his end of the deal. With Noah weakened like this, at least he wouldn't be able to stop me from putting an end to Vance after the ritual.

Noah had lost at least a gallon or two of blood by now and was looking in rough shape. Vance finally stopped, leaving Noah staggering for a second before he disappeared.

"Is he going to be all right?" I asked.

"He needs blood, so he went to feed, no doubt." Vance dipped his fingers in the blood and began painting sanguinary hieroglyphs on the floor surrounding me. "Stand here," he instructed, and pointed to the exact center of his scrawlings.

Vance poured Noah's blood out into straight lines, forming a pentagram with me in the middle.

"You should be less concerned with what your plans are for me and more worried about what that Archios have in store for you after this," he said. So much for the element of surprise. He was reading my thoughts the whole time. "Your human friend wasn't meant to die. I burned him to break Minerva's mind control so he wouldn't shoot himself. It was my intention for him to seek help, but I suppose his body was more frail than I calculated."

"Just do the damn ritual," I said through gritted teeth.

"Do you think they are your allies?" he asked. "The Archios, I mean. You seem to have an ill-placed loyalty to them. I am curious if that would change upon discerning how rotten the cores behind their appealing veneers are."

"I don't consider anyone my ally right now, so save it. You're either an obstacle or not."

"You have quite an insurmountable obstacle blocking any path you choose from now on. There is no one on Earth more manipulative than the Archios, and they will never let you out of their grasp knowing what you are now. Whether or not you consent, you will be doing their bidding until they tire of you."

"How is that any different than what you have planned?"

"I know now that the experiment was a success. Reproducing the results will be simple and there are already others like you out there. I have no choice but to make good on my end of the bargain with Noah. He will turn on me, but if you help me survive I will forget your existence and no longer interfere in your life."

"What makes you think I'd even be able to stop Noah if I wanted to?"

Vance finished his bloody artwork in silence. When he was done he flipped through the pages of the demon tome. "Don't move from the circle prematurely or it may tear you in two," he warned, and began to read aloud in tongues.

The blood lit on fire as he spoke. Flames grew steadily around me until they were well off the ground. Demonic symbols were swirling out from the fire, licking the air and singeing my skin. I pulled away in pain, but remembered not to leave the circle. I tried to grin and bear it.

The fire kept growing until I was consumed in a raging inferno. I fought against the instinct to run as the stench of my own flesh burning away overcame me. My skin boiled and blistered down to the bone. I was screaming and covering my face when the wriggling of the parasitic creature inside me came back. It felt different this time; whatever was inside me was trying to escape by any means necessary. But the cauterizing flames prevented the creature from oozing out of my wounds. There was pressure and then movement behind my eyes. I could feel them being pushed out of their sockets and soon my vision failed. The harsh growls of the parasite mixed with my own screams until a slithering in my throat silenced me.

I had to try to leave. I was going to die either way, but I'd rather it be quick. I thought of my mom and dad and wished this would be over soon so I could be with them again. Blind and mute, I clawed my way across the floor to try and leave the circle, not knowing in which direction I was headed. I could still hear the fire surrounding me and the faint chanting in tongues. A familiar numbness claimed me. While I was still somewhat aware, the pain had ceased.

I couldn't tell if I was moving anymore, or even awake. Everything was quiet now, but there was no transition into unconsciousness. Something floated past my eyes in the darkness, leaving ripples trailing behind it. I could see myself now, but I wasn't mutilated like I had expected. There were lights scattered in the distance above me and below me. Looking around in the dark, I realized I was floating too. Wherever I was went on for quite a while.

A deep booming noise came from far off. I turned to it while covering my ears, but the noise still made me tremble. What I saw couldn't be described any better than a roughly aquatic animal the size of a moon or a planet, with three sets of eyes and rows of tentacles along its side in place of fins. The giant's call must have startled more than just me, because a group of bizarre viral-looking creatures darted past, swimming in the air like a school of fish.

I couldn't tell if I was dreaming or really in another world. A current pulled me along, making me question whether I was underwater or in outer space. Tiny wisps of light illuminated the blackness, like stars in the night sky. Still in the distance, the giant passed overhead toward what looked like a cluster of small planets. Even far away, it was so massive I felt terribly insignificant. This must be how an astronaut felt on his or her first time in space, but the living beings made this even stranger.

The current stopped and I began hurtling downward into the darkness. There wasn't anything below me. Even the wisps of light were gone.

"Is he dead? I can't read his mind," I heard Noah's voice say.

There was a bright light followed by a jarring sensation of whiplash. The world around me was gone, leaving me tumbling aimlessly through empty space. The sound of Noah's voice grew louder. I squeezed my eyes shut waiting to crash into something, but the spinning feeling stopped without any impact.

"I'm not dead," I answered, looking up at Noah, who was nudging me with his boot. "I thought I got dragged down to Hell. I had this really vivid dream. At least, I think it was a dream. I was in space or something and there were all these weird creatures."

I hopped to my feet and looked myself over. The burns were gone, the bite mark was gone, and I felt great.

"It actually worked," I whispered in awe.

"Of course it did," Vance said from his workstation. He was so absorbed in studying something he didn't even bother to look up. I still couldn't forget what he did to Lyle, but for the moment I was overjoyed to be alive and well for the first time in a while.

"What you saw wasn't Hell," Vance continued. "The parasite is not from this world or even this universe. It comes from another dimension — more specifically, a place between two dimensions, a world between worlds called the Rift. What you saw was a glimpse of its native land as you two merged."

"So, what the hell is he?" Noah asked. He was gawking at me like I was some alien.

"A critical success. Although still predominantly human, the fusion has changed enough of his genetic code to be classified as a new sub-species," Vance answered. "I ran some tests while he was unconscious and the results so far have been uncanny.

"If you remember, I mentioned the parasite's ability to stimulate bone and muscle growth. Soon after the ritual's completion, Dorian's body began to regenerate dead tissue. Even as I collected samples from him to examine, his healing factor continued to repair the damage at a rate I've never seen."

Vance fidgeted with the equipment on his table and held a glass jar to the light, looking completely enamored with the red liquid inside.

"Typically, a parasite leeches nutrients from the host in order to sustain itself. Before the ritual, I found that the parasite was taking more energy than it needed to survive. The extra energy was just disappearing, which didn't make any sense. It was then I figured out the parasite was doing more than feeding itself. It was sending that extra energy somewhere. The Rift, or something in the Rift, must send these parasites out to other dimensions to harvest food.

"When the ritual amalgamated Dorian with the parasite, it stopped the flow of energy back to the Rift, but left the gateway open. You can't read Dorian's mind because of interference caused by all that energy he is attuned to in the Rift. I'm sure you noticed his aura is already several times larger. If he could learn to channel it to fuel his own powers … well, even I could not fathom the outcome."

Vance sounded like he was no longer willing to let me just walk away. Noah looked annoyed, giving me the same squinty-eyed expression as when he read my mind. Now was my chance to at least be rid of one of them.

I glared at Vance, slamming him and the table against the wall and expecting him to die the same way the others did, but it wasn't as easy without the parasite in control. In the reflection of the glass around the room my eyes temporarily reverted to the way they looked when I was infected. Vance got up from the pile of broken beakers and splintered wood, trying to preserve what he could of his samples, with no regard for his own life. I went after him before he could try to get away, but Noah stood in the way.

"Get out of my way," I told him, keeping my focus on Vance.

"As much as I'd love to watch this happen, I still need him."

I didn't have the effect I was looking for with Vance, and I didn't even want to try it on Noah, but I wasn't about to let him interfere either.

"He's never going to leave me alone. You said it yourself; once you're part of this you can never get away. Lyle died because of him. Am I supposed to just let him keep killing friends of mine when they get in the way?"

Noah put his hands on his hips and watched Vance crawling on the ground, scooping things into little jars.

"Ah, yeah ... The cop isn't dead. I just said that to piss you off. I wanted you to attack this guy before I knew he was useful."

"I told you," Vance said, pointing at Noah. "Do you think this is the first time he's lied to manipulate you? They have you caught in their web to do their bidding."

Noah swung around and threw one of his *wakizashi* right through Vance's heart to shut him up.

"But I saw him being burned to death," I said.

"Nothing a little blood couldn't fix. Vivi is taking extra-special care of him." He walked over and lifted Vance's paralyzed body off the ground with one hand.

"What else did you lie about? How do I even know Lyle really is alive and you're not just saying that to preserve Vance?"

"I guess you'll have to follow me if you want to find out," Noah said before vanishing with Vance over his shoulder.

Chapter Thirteen

There were still a few usable cars left relatively unscathed after the battle upstairs. I was in a race against the world's fastest man, but the sunrise would soon be on my side. I pictured Lyle obliviously trying to woo Vivian, but at least he was safe for now. They'd keep him alive as bait to draw me back in, but I was sure if I didn't show up one of them would have him for a snack.

I had little doubt that Vance was also as good as dead once he finished the exorcism on Rozalin. It was one less thing for me to worry about, but my anger toward him was waning now that I knew he had told the truth about Lyle. There were still so many questions I had that only he could answer.

I sped down the highway, looking like a deranged homeless foreigner. It would be a miracle if I wasn't pulled over. My clothes were almost completely burnt off except for a dusty jacket I had found in the facility. My cell phone and wallet were destroyed, along with any ID and money I had left, and I had no idea how to speak anything but English and Lyle's tourist dialect of "louder, slower English."

To top it all off I couldn't keep my eyes on the road for more than a few seconds at a time. I kept glancing at every passing shadow, expecting to see a face looking back at me. Driving into the sunset after spending hours on the road was making me paranoid about the darkness looming ahead.

With a little luck, and a lot of missed turns and wrong exits, I got to Aurelia's estate just as night rolled in. The main house was dark inside, save for a few lights flickering on the top floor. It didn't look like anyone was home there, or at the guest house either. The grounds went on for miles in all directions. I was about to get out and walk when I finally saw lights beyond a gathering of trees.

Another house stood just off the bank of a large body of water. I ditched the car and ran to the double doors. There was no way to tell if this place was haunted now too without going inside. As lavish as the other two houses, this building was smaller, but a lot more opened up inside. The majority of the first floor formed a large common area that branched out into private rooms. Directly across the common area, two staircases gave access to the overhanging floor above.

There weren't any voices or footsteps to be heard anywhere. Upstairs, ceiling-high windows spanned the entire back wall, looking out over the water. A grand piano was surrounded by lounge chairs, end tables, and well-kept potted ferns. Not a leaf was out of place, and there was not a speck of dust anywhere. This place was too maintained to be have been abandoned for long. Just how many residents and servants lived on this estate?

A single corridor branched off from the piano area. Portraits of an ageless Aurelia attired in clothing from different time periods lined the walls. All the doors down the hall were closed except one. I entered the room to find Lyle relaxing by the fireplace.

"You're alive!" We greeted each other with the same enthusiastic shout.

"Never better, actually," Lyle said, hopping out of his seat. "I guess Noah made it to you in time."

"Sort of. It's a long story. Is he here?"

"I don't know. Didn't you two come together?" Lyle asked, and then pointed to my arm. "Your bite's gone. You look, uh, different. What's going on?"

I checked in the mirror above the fireplace. It wasn't as obvious as with the Archios, but my complexion was flawless and had a healthy glow despite still needing a tan. My hair had a shine to it, and even though it was well beyond my regular bed-head by now, it somehow looked right.

"I was cured, but I'll explain later. I have to stop Noah from killing someone and then we need to get out of here."

"Welcome back, *chéri*. You are looking well." Vivian walked in just in time to hear me announce my plan to escape. No doubt she had a leash around Lyle's neck and was ready to compel me to stay.

"Is Noah here yet?" I asked her, ignoring the pleasantries. She paused, gazing into my eyes. I knew exactly what she was trying to do. "That won't work on me anymore. Tell me where Noah is and we'll be on our way."

"He's busy at the moment. I came to offer you our hospitality on behalf of Aurelia."

"Aurelia wouldn't even look at me after I couldn't defend myself in the garden. If she's suddenly interested in me again that means Noah already told her what went on."

"Dorian, chill. Vivi's just trying to be nice. Show a little respect; she saved my life," Lyle said.

"She's using you as bait to keep me here."

"Why would she do that? Everyone here has been trying to help, even Noah. What's wrong with you?"

"He responds to hospitality with hostility. His body is healed, but the Strigoi have poisoned his mind against us," Vivi sighed. "I told you this might happen."

So that was how it was going to be. They were always one step ahead. Not only did they have Lyle here, but she had gotten him to believe my thoughts weren't my own, when it was really the other way around.

"My mind isn't poisoned. I was made in a lab by a bunch of magical lunatics who want me back now, okay? A lot happened and now they're all dead except one. Noah is going to kill him after the guy gets rid of the ghost in the chateau."

"Why are you trying to save someone who's used excessive force multiple times to try and kidnap you?" Lyle asked.

"Because that is what he was created to do," Vivi interrupted. "Even if it is the same man who almost killed his friend in a fire."

"You're twisting it. I'm doing this because I want to, not because he told me to. I have questions that only he can answer. Lyle, you have to believe me. They only want to keep me here to use me because I might be more powerful now."

"Have you already lost so much faith in humanity that you have trouble believing our help was genuine? Leave if you want, but our doors may not be open to you a third time," Vivi said.

"You're not even human."

"Neither are you, but if you don't act it then what will you become? The difference between man and monster is not what we are made of, but the choices we make."

"Come on, Lyle, let's go."

"Where do you think we're gonna go after this, Dorian?" he asked. "New York is a mess, you're homeless, and I'm a fugitive. Or did you forget that?

This is all we've got, and if you look around it's a bit of an upgrade."

"What about your family?"

"When the heat is off I'll call them to let them know I'm okay. Getting family involved will only complicate things even worse. The less they know, the better. At least this way they won't have to lie to the police for me."

"If you stay here they'll kill you once I'm gone. Don't you understand? That's why they're going out of their way to be so nice to some human."

"Some human? I see. So now you think you're better than me? Just accept that this might not be all about you for once."

"That isn't what I meant," I said apologetically. "Promise me you'll stay here at least until I come back. I need to get to Noah before it's too late."

"You can't go in there," Vivi warned. "It's too dangerous."

"I've heard that before. I should be dead five times over, but I'm still here."

"Yes, because people have helped you, whether you choose to realize that or not," she said.

"It isn't the help I have a problem with. It's the motive behind it."

I left the room and ran out of the house to the car. If Lyle wanted to stay behind with Vivian for now it was fine by me. She wouldn't pull anything while I was here if she still wanted me around, and he would be out of any immediate danger.

"He saved your life because he took pity on you." It was Vivian again, right behind me.

"Who are you talking about? Lyle?" I asked.

"Noah. He has a more personal stake in this than he'll admit."

"Enough already. I don't want to hear any more reasons why I should stay and be your pet. You're getting desperate if you think I'll believe Noah is really my friend."

"Throw your life away; it may be a shame, but I'm not telling you this for your sake." Vivi glared at me with a burning conviction in her eyes. Whether it was one of her powers or simply a dire sense of urgency in her voice, I was compelled to listen.

"I was there the night he became one of us. It was the summer of 1848 during the California Gold Rush. I was escorting Aurelia on a journey there to lay claim to the riches the land had to offer.

"Aside from the financial gain of our trip, Aurelia also had an interest in acquiring another progeny to be my successor. I had been in her service a little over four hundred years and begun to grow weary of the demanding lifestyle.

"Even in the most demure ladies' attire for the period, we drew the attention of every man around for miles. The plan was to incite a riot among the sex-starved mortals clamoring for our hand and see who had potential to be a diamond in the rough.

"It wasn't difficult to strike a match with the local drunkards at a crowded saloon on our first night there. A brawl broke out that practically engulfed the town. I had my eye on a particularly handsome young cowboy who was doing his best not to get involved in the nonsense.

"As the crowd grew more violent, several of the men tried cornering us. Noah came to our aid in the first act of chivalry that night. He fought off our would-be attackers and brought us to safety with the riot following closely behind. He seemed of clear mind, not frenzied like the rest, and continued to fight on our behalf even after taking a gunshot to the shoulder.

"Eventually he was overwhelmed by the remaining men, who beat him and left him for dead. Aurelia and I watched the scene from the shadows. After the crowd dispersed, it was just the three of us under the moonlight. The young cowboy had barely a breath in him. Aurelia knelt before him and offered him immortality in exchange for remaining by her side for eternity. No man or woman has ever been able to resist her grace, and so he accepted.

"I could see the familiar look of love in his eyes despite all the blood from his injuries as she leaned over him to seal their arrangement with her fangs.

"Aurelia charged me with raising him, and I did as I would my own. We left that very same night, with no time for goodbyes or explanations. I taught him everything about surviving in our world and all the nuances of our politics. He was a quick study, but always kept his sights on Aurelia, patiently waiting for her attention once more."

"Noah was patient once?"

"*Oui*, but I feel he expended all he had in waiting for her. He was a different man back then, but in many ways still the same. Our enemies in Europe knew just as much about war and espionage as we did. Aurelia knew that what we needed was something nobody had ever seen. The Far East was still a mystery to our kind. She instructed Noah to travel there and return only when he had mastered their art of war and combat.

"He returned a battle-hardened warrior and expected to win her praise, but she had long since forgotten him. I could sense the pain from his broken heart. He left behind his family and everything he knew to enter our world under false pretenses. Rarely do people become one of us out of choice. Noah is still young by our standards, but he has had a particularly difficult time leaving the past behind him."

This painted Noah in a completely different light, assuming Vivian wasn't making this all up. I didn't understand what her point in telling me was.

"I don't get what this has to do with me," I said.

"Noah rises every night knowing he is worth no more than the blades at his side. Personal desire is irrelevant and acts of free will are forbidden. He is a warrior that exists only to serve his master — a tragic existence that he has yet to come to terms with.

"Although he will never admit it, I feel he has taken pity on you for that same reason. He pushed you toward failure so you would not share his fate, but still you have managed to succeed."

"You let me leave after I was bitten, but Noah forced me to stick around to learn how to fly," I said.

"You were bitten because he lured the creatures to your position before disappearing into the mist. We may have released you after that, but Noah knew it wouldn't be over so easily. He was attempting to scare you off when you returned to the chateau. If he could further prove your incompetence to Aurelia, she would be more likely to become disinterested and forget about you."

"That must be why he threw Lyle off the roof. He's got some really messed-up ways of showing sympathy. I thought he was just being an asshole."

"Noah has his moments, but he also has his reasons."

"I'm not going to kill him, if that's what you're worried about," I assured her. "I just want answers from Vance."

"Hardly!" she laughed. "I'm afraid even on his worst day you still couldn't do him harm. My concern is that the odds are against him in there. I would appreciate if you don't get in the way or cause a distraction that may endanger him."

"You feel guilty that he bears your burden. You feel responsible for him. Is that what this is about?"

"My feelings are a private matter and one I'm not inclined to discuss. It is neither secret nor sin that I have an attachment to someone I have known well for centuries. Emotions are what keep us human, but I won't be judged for them."

"Jeez, sorry. I just think it's nice that there's the potential for love in a life that seems so corrupt and cutthroat."

Vivian was already walking away. I knew she heard me, even if she didn't want to recognize what I said was true.

"What can you tell me about Aurelia's sister?" I called after her.

"No amount of knowledge will help keep you alive. Just pray your lucky star does not burn out."

Great. That was encouraging.

Chapter Fourteen

There was a biting chill in the air inside the chateau. The place reeked of death, like an exhumed grave. In the darkness the shadows danced, liberated from the bodies they once stalked. Chattering voices echoed in the halls as I passed, but none seemed to have an owner, nor could I decipher what was being discussed.

The interior remained mostly intact, save for the frequent piles of blood-soaked ash littering the floors. Only the many oil paintings depicting Her Majesty were touched. As if to make a statement, the faces were gouged out and the canvas splattered with blood, possibly from the remains of her followers. Her legacy tarnished, her property seized, she was no longer welcome here.

"Admiring my work?"

It was the woman who had watched from the window the other night, the one who showed me the false vision of my parents.

"It's ... different," I replied.

This was the first time I had gotten a good look at her. She had snow-white skin and straight jet-black hair down to her knees. Her clothing was more gothic princess than her sister's lavish royalty ensemble. The only jewelry she had on was a black lace choker adorned with a simple crystal. Her billowing black dress with matching corset flowed along with her hair despite the lack of a breeze. She hovered and glided gracefully through the air, with shadows twisting and swirling around her. Her body seemed corporeal, although her clothing seemed to be made of something far less natural than cloth. The way it moved was almost like it was alive. Ignoring the ghastly atmosphere she projected and her heartless smile at the chaos she had caused, Rozalin was actually quite pretty.

"This one happens to be my favorite," she said, floating down the corridor a bit to show me another ruined portrait of her sister.

Her amber eyes and pale skin stood out against the darkened hallway. I had never encountered a ghost before, but her presence wasn't anything I could have prepared myself for. You could feel the power brimming over from her and, like witnessing a bolt of lightning, it gave me both a sense of awe and danger.

"Where are Noah and Vance?" I asked. By this time, I was positive they were either dead or hadn't made it here yet, in which case I had just foiled their ambush.

"The library downstairs," she answered. "They think me ignorant of their hiding spot while they plot against me. You can get to them by taking a right up ahead; from there you'll see the stairs. Proceed with haste! They are constantly on the move to avoid being trapped. How clever."

"Uh, thanks. I didn't think you'd really tell me." I was shocked she was being so forthcoming. She knew they were plotting against her, so why would she help me reunite with them?

"Because I want an audience for their death screams!" Rozalin exploded into a fit of hysterics and dissolved into thin air. Her laughter persisted as I raced through the building. She would manifest ahead of me every few rooms to torment me. "Run, run!" she cackled. "This way!"

I made an attempt to use my powers and knock her out, but she was unaffected. My efforts just provoked more fits of laughter and taunting.

"This calls for a celebration! A tea party! We shall have a tea party to commemorate my triumph!" I was starting to think she had completely lost it when I was blindsided by a table that came flying out from a room. "Now we need guests! You can't have a tea party without guests!"

My head was spinning. The table collided with me and smashed against the wall so hard it broke. Rozalin was floating in front of me with her hands above two ash piles. Black sparks crackled from her fingertips and ignited the ashes into similarly black flames. The ashes quivered and began reforming into humanoid shapes.

Unlike the parasite-infected humans, these shambling corpses were the very image of reanimated death. Their bodies were rotted, and muscle and bones were exposed, giving off a wafting stench of putrefaction. They lurched over the broken table, snapping their jaws at me where I was trapped underneath.

"You see! I am a better host than my dear sister!" Rozalin took one of them by the chin to peer into its empty eye sockets. "And you! You are simply gorgeous now! Don't you agree?"

Kicking the second reanimated corpse away, I fled down the hall. Rozalin was giggling behind me, bringing back all the fallen residents as she flew by until there was an entire horde chasing me. I kept running until I tripped over something in the dark. It looked like a piece of wood. I slowed down for just a second to see what it was. It was the broken table again. Somehow I had gone in a circle. It wasn't hard to believe that Rozalin was screwing with me from the start, so at the turn ahead I went the opposite way.

Two hallways later and I was back at the broken table.

This was impossible. I was wasting time no matter what path I took. I ducked into one of the rooms and blocked the door with a chair from the inside. The enthralled bodies of the former inhabitants banged against the door as I leaned against it to keep them from coming in.

"What happened to wanting me to witness you killing the other two?" I shouted at her from behind the door. The banging stopped instantly. I peeked under the door to check what was going on. The walking corpses were all gone and there was no sign of Rozalin.

"Please come back out."

I jumped back in fright as a face appeared looking back at me. It was my mother, or her face at least. Her hand reached out to me from under the door.

"That isn't funny!" I yelled.

Vivi was right. Coming here was a bad idea. I put my hand out, aiming at a window across from me, and shattered the glass. I cleared away the broken pieces around the frame to climb out safely.

I jumped down to the ground below, but when I got up, I was back in a mirror image of the room. This was getting ridiculous. Noah and Vance were probably already dead or going through the same thing. We would never find each other. I walked to the door and pushed the chair out of the way to leave.

"I can bring them back." Rozalin's voice came from another chair that faced a fireplace lit with black flames. She was sitting staring into the fire and drinking from a cup of tea.

An image of my parents formed beside me.

"No, you can't. This isn't real. None of this is," I said.

"But it is. I hold power over death itself. What you see is their souls. Trapped in the

Underworld they wait for you, refusing to pass on without the chance to say goodbye."

"I don't believe you and I don't want them back if your idea is to turn them into anything except human."

I probably shouldn't have said that. The teacup vanished from her hand. She smiled sneakily and looked at me from the corner of her eye.

"Then what we need are fresh bodies to put them in. What luck! We happen to have two right here, scurrying about my halls like vermin just waiting to be exterminated!"

"What? No. I'm turning my parents into Vance and Noah? That's just ... really weird."

"Oh, but they won't be! The bodies will take whatever form the soul projects. You can have your lovely family back, and I will strip my sister of her prized pet and the troublesome mage!"

"Why do you even need my help?" I asked. "You seem plenty powerful on your own."

"Yes, yes I am. But my power wanes the longer I am absent from the Underworld. Killing them would expend all I have left and then I would be sent back, my fun ended. I could use their souls to replenish my power. A fair trade, no?"

"Please, Dorian," my mom said. "Just give us the chance to be together again. We were waiting for you. To see your face, to share your happiness when we gave you the surprise we had planned."

There was no way this was just an illusion. How else would she know something that specific if she couldn't read my mind? Still, it didn't feel right.

"No," I turned to Rozalin. "I won't do it."

"You will regret ever rejecting me!" she wailed. My parents disappeared and the building quaked as shadows formed a maelstrom around her and hurled me out of the room. "I will make sure to use mommy and daddy's souls to fuel my vengeance!" she screamed with rage from within the walls.

What did I do? All this to answer some questions about things that didn't matter up until last night. Nothing I could do now would make up for what I had condemned my parents to. That wound hadn't even healed yet, and now it was ten times worse. But Vance and Noah were still fine. If I helped them, maybe Rozalin could be stopped before anything happened to my parents.

Walking corpses continued patrolling the house, but there was no sign of Rozalin. I was able to find the stairs going down without her interference, but the walking corpses blocked the path. I carried one of the table legs with me for protection just in case. Either I really was getting stronger or these things were a bit frailer than the parasitic mutants. Hitting them with my powers alone crippled them enough for me to get by. They continued to crawl toward me with their broken bodies. I had to use the table leg as a club to put them out of commission.

"Admiring my work?" It was Rozalin again, but her voice was coming from far away.

"Where are the others?" a man asked.

No! That was Lyle, but what was he doing here? I got off the stairs and headed back, screaming for him to get out of the house.

"This one happens to be my favorite," she repeated.

"Lyle, you have to get out! Don't talk to her!" I screamed at the top of my lungs. Again, I was lost in an endless maze. Every turn took me farther from their voices, and it didn't seem like Lyle was able to hear me at all.

"Tell me where they are or I swear to God I'll shoot!" he demanded.

What was Lyle doing? A bullet wasn't going to do anything to her. This wasn't the time to be playing good cop and read her her rights.

"God? God isn't here." Rozalin burst into a fit of laughter. "No, He stopped watching this place long ago."

Their conversation faded out. I doubled back to the stairs, but there was no way of knowing whether Noah and Vance were even there anymore. One of the zombified residents came trudging out from the ballroom where I had met Aurelia. I thought at first to avoid it, but then it might get in Lyle's way. At least if he saw the body he'd know somebody in here was still okay.

I sent the corpse reeling back. Instead of using my makeshift weapon to bludgeon it to death, I took a few steps closer and kept using my power to smash its head against the wall until its skull cracked like an eggshell and went lifeless again.

I left the table leg on the floor next to it for Lyle and finally went downstairs. "Admiring my work?" I heard Rozalin saying for a third time. There was no response, just the sound of high heels tapping on the marble floor above. "This one happens to be my favorite."

It had to be Vivian that Rozalin was trying to harass now. I already knew trying to contact her would be in vain, so I continued onward.

The basement was more than a few bookshelves; this was more of a re-creation of the New York Public Library than a typical collection. The floor had two levels and floor-to-ceiling bookcases. If it weren't for the oil lamps along the sides of the bookcases, the library would be pitch-black.

I called out for Noah and Vance, but got no reply. My voice echoed into the darkness, which seemed to extend for miles. Something slithered and wrapped around my leg, making me jump, but it was gone before I could reach down to swat it away. I stumbled over chairs and piles of books, trying to get to the other side of the library. Every few feet I'd get tangled in something that felt like a spiderweb or long strands of hair, but the next second it would disappear.

Somebody was talking from behind a door off to the left, but stopped when I got close. "Hello?" I banged on the door. "Noah? Vance?"

"Maybe if we're quiet he'll go away." That was Noah, all right.

"Open the damn door!" I shouted.

Noah opened and grabbed me by the jacket, tossing me inside and slamming the door shut. Vance sat on the floor with his tome. The room was just a storage closet lit only by a few candles, with nothing more than some boxes and a spare reading desk like the ones outside.

"What's going on?" I asked.

Noah leaned back against the door, looking disgusted. "What's it look like? We're hiding like pussies because this guy didn't come prepared."

"Never mind the fact that you staked me and dragged me here against my will. When was it that I should have made preparations?" Vance protested angrily.

"Always come prepared for battle," Noah said and pointed accusingly at him.

"I am a scholar, not a warrior, and I never claimed to be anything but!"

Noah mumbled something, but I stopped him before they dragged out their argument even longer. "Lyle and Vivi are somewhere in here, too."

"I surmised others were here," Vance said. "Rozalin has left us alone for a while, so I knew she had to be busy toying with someone else."

"She knows you're down here."

"It doesn't matter. I bought us some time by warding this room against ghosts. We'll be safe until she decides to end the game and figures out how to dispel the ward."

"So what? We just wait?"

"No one's stopping you from going back out there," Noah said.

"You sound scared," I taunted him.

"Scared? I'm not scared, I'm bored. Only magic can hurt a ghost. There's no point in trying to fight an enemy that can't be hit. I'd be swiping at air all night."

"Why do I get the feeling she wanted this to happen? I mean, what's the downside to being a ghost?" I asked. "She seems like she's having a blast."

"You were lucky enough to miss that speech, I guess," Noah said, taking a seat by the door.

"A wise observation. When one such as us ages long enough to amass the power she has, death becomes more of a metamorphosis than a finality," Vance answered. "According to Rozalin, she foresaw Minerva coming to kill her. She prepared a ritual to keep her soul here on Earth instead of being sent to the Underworld for judgment like all dead are. I'm not a master of necromancy like she is. But from my limited knowledge, for the spell to work, she would have to be wrongfully murdered, and not take her own life.

"Death only grants chances to those with unfinished business and strong emotions tying them here. They pass on when they are at peace. Whether Rozalin predicted it or not, she was killed as part of Minerva's conspiracy and did not die a natural death. Rozalin was cunning enough to cheat the system. Now she is using her spectral state along with her magic to get to her sister any way she can with little consequence."

"She said she had my parents' souls and she'd use them to fuel her vengeance. She said she would bring them back to life if I helped her."

"Impossible. Rozalin may be strong, but not enough to resurrect the dead as they once were."

"Well, is it possible for her to put their souls in *another* body?"

Vance skimmed the pages in his tome, visibly losing interest in the discussion. "I suppose so, but you'd need a soulless body to put them in."

"Like from somebody recently deceased?"

"Right, in theory. But they would be undead. I'm not a necromancer, no matter how many times I tell this lout," he said, nodding to Noah.

"What's your plan to get out of here?" I asked them.

"We lay a trap of our own. A binding circle, like the one I used in the ritual with you, only this time we will be binding her to something we can use to remove her from the building," Vance said.

"So, where is it?" I looked around the room. Noah opened the door before I got an answer.

"Just couldn't stay away, huh?" Noah jested as Vivian entered the room. She pushed past him and set a briefcase down on the desk.

"Do you understand that if you use this for anything but its intended purpose you will die, and it will be painful?" She removed a vial filled with blood from the case and handed it over to Vance. "Watch him closely," she said to Noah.

"Where are you going?" he asked.

"To cause a distraction and buy you some time." Vivi left the room and closed the door behind her.

"She's as good as dead, but at least she did her part." Vance was probably better off keeping that comment to himself. Noah grabbed him by the throat and slammed him against the stone wall so hard he left an impression. Any human would have died instantly. There was no way it wasn't extremely painful at the very least for him.

"Then you'd better work fast," Noah threatened, and dropped him.

"I'm going back out, too," I said.

"This isn't a game, kid. Don't expect help because you want to play in the haunted house."

"Lyle's in here. I'll feel better doing something."

Vance poured the contents of the vial into his hand and started finger-painting familiar arcane runes on the floor. Noah stepped away from the door and sat on the desk, never taking his eyes off of Vance.

"Whatever. It's your life. Just die with some dignity and don't get in Vivi's way."

That was funny. They both said the same thing to me, only it sounded better coming from Vivian.

Chapter Fifteen

The oil lamps around the library burned an unnatural purplish-black color now. The cold ultraviolet light from the flames was brighter than the natural version and revealed more of the enormous room. The source of what I had been tangled in earlier was now visible. Long wispy tendrils made of thick smoke and shadow intertwined with each other. They seemed to float in place benignly until I got close. Then the ghostly manifestations would reach out to me as a vine instinctively snakes toward the sun.

I avoided contact with the tendrils as I navigated the library, after finding them to be immune to my power's influence, the same as Rozalin herself. A few of them melded together from a bookcase and formed a rough image of hands grasping for me. Even more of them gathered into the shape of a featureless human face that stretched out from a long neck and followed me around every turn.

A gunshot came from upstairs, which meant Lyle was there. I tried both ignoring and dodging the apparitions as I ran to leave the library. Face after face appeared in the walls, watching as I made it to the main floor. They oozed like oil out of the stonework until the walls and floor under them were completely covered. I didn't know what else Rozalin could possibly throw at me to make me lose my nerve, but I kept telling myself to keep my head down and just ignore it.

There were many more corpses littering the ground upstairs than the couple I had previously dispatched. I doubted this was Vivian's work, so Lyle must be doing pretty well on his own. The paint and wallpaper were starting to peel from the walls, the wood rotting and metal fixtures rusting. Nothing was left untouched by the sudden decay.

I thought Rozalin would have been eager to attack the moment I left the safe room, but she hadn't made an appearance yet.

"Dorian, you have to get out of here." The ghost of my father materialized before me.

"Dad, is that... is it really you?" I approached carefully, hopefully.

"Don't come any closer. You have to run, it isn't safe."

"Dad, where's Mom? Is she with you?" I asked. "I can save you. I know how to bring you back."

"It's cold, Dorian, so cold." He faded away. But if Rozalin had spared him, maybe my mom was still all right too.

I heard another gunshot from close by and went toward it to find Lyle standing over some remains.

"Are you real?" he asked, and pointed his firearm at me.

"Yes, it's me! Don't shoot me!" I said, and put my hands up.

"I'm almost out of ammo anyway." He lowered his gun and checked the clip. I walked over and looked at the body laid out between us.

"Have you been killing these?"

"Yeah," he replied and picked up a fire poker, stabbing the head to ensure it wouldn't get back up. "You don't need superpowers to be a hero."

That hurt. I could tell he was offended by my comment about him only being human, but actually, I was a bit envious now seeing how he had cleared out the place.

"I'm sorry about what I said before. I didn't mean it to come off as insulting," I apologized.

"It's cool, don't worry about it."

"My parents are here. I know how to save us and bring them back."

Lyle stared at me in confusion. "How?" he asked.

I cringed, knowing what I was about to say wouldn't sit well with him. "I need to find Rozalin."

"Take a look around you. She's everywhere! I've had enough of this ghost bullshit. We have to be leaving, not having tea or whatever the hell she wants with us."

"She's a necromancer. She can bring my parents back. Their souls are already here. I talked with them. If I don't help her, she's going to hurt them."

"Dorian, you don't even know whether it's just one of her tricks. This lady is nuts! I've met some crazy women, but she takes the cake. This is a four-thousand-year grudge because a guy chose her sister over her. She's the poster child for needing to get the fuck over it."

"What are you talking about?"

"Vivi told me the whole story. The sisters were born around here before France even existed. Aurelia was the favorite, and everyone in their village thought she was the hottest chick ever. Some mysterious dude claiming to be from another village came to their place one night. He wanted to marry one of the sisters to make good relations between their villages, and wound up choosing Aurelia.

"Rozalin got jealous because she was always in her sister's shadow. She followed them as they left the village and witnessed the guy turn Aurelia. When Rozalin ran back to her parents they thought she was just being a drama queen, and nobody in their village believed her."

I was only half paying attention to Lyle's story. He was walking through the building brandishing the fire poker, ready to bash in anything that jumped out. I could tell he was searching for the exit and hoping the more he talked the less I'd be focused on contacting Rozalin, but she hadn't slipped my mind.

"She set out on her own to find where the guy took Aurelia," he continued. "After questioning locals in other towns, she got herself mixed up with some shady people. They were involved with black magic and taught her how to use it. Their leader fell in love with her and also revealed himself to be a rival of the man Aurelia ran off with, so he offered to turn Rozalin if she'd help kill him.

"Long story short, she did. Aurelia was furious and used her glowing eye hypnosis thing to turn all the humans against Rozalin and her Goth friends. The villagers burned down their hideout and killed Rozalin's man and all her friends. Rozalin escaped and Aurelia took over the village. Every few hundred years when Rozalin regroups —"

"Lyle?" I turned around, but he was gone. "Lyle, this is a bad time to try and be funny! Where are you?"

"I didn't much care for his version for the story," Rozalin said, floating down from the ceiling.

"What did you do with him? We don't have anything to do with Aurelia or your disagreement!"

"Disagreement? Disagreement? This is no petty spat, this is war! I have been wronged for thousands of years, stripped of everything by my very own blood while she enjoys only the best and all the false love and praise this world can offer! I once lived in her shadow, now she will die in mine."

"I totally understand, but we aren't involved with any of that! I was taken here by Aurelia's orders and Lyle followed. Killing us and hurting my family isn't going to mean anything to Aurelia!"

"I offered you a deal — quite a fair one, too. You were unwise to decline. I told you that you'd regret it."

"Bring my family back, safely, and let us all leave, including Lyle. I'll do whatever it is you want. There's no way I can kill Noah — he's too fast."

"You won't have to. I was waiting for my sister to arrive, but I see it will take a more convincing invitation. Open the door they hide behind long enough for me to enter and I will take care of them myself."

"Open the door?" Didn't she know they were preparing a trap for her in there? Could she not see in the room while that ward was up?

"Yes, boy. Once the others arrive, I will have them present Aurelia with her own progeny staked through the heart. If she does not come then I will kill them, but she doesn't have to know I plan on doing that anyway."

"Wait, what others?" I asked.

"I invited some friends of my own." She smiled and faded away. "Now go on, do as I say. There will not be another chance!"

My feet felt heavy as I walked back to the library. I was torn between taking two lives and getting two back. If I didn't go through with it, not only would I lose my parents, but Vance and Noah might never allow me to be free. It seemed like an obvious choice, but something about it wasn't sitting right with me. Who was I to choose over life and death? What would my parents think about me purposely killing two people just because of something they *might* do?

"Dorian." My mom's voice came from all around me. "Is it really true? Will we be a family again?"

She was standing in front of me now.

"Mom," I whispered. "What should I do? She wants me to kill people. I have no idea if it'll even work."

"Just do what she says, honey. Isn't the chance at being together again enough of a reason to try? They are dangerous people. The world will be better off without them."

"How do you know they're dangerous?" I asked. "I didn't even tell you who she wants me to kill."

"They're all bad people, honey, and bad people should be punished. Just remember I love you."

She disappeared, leaving me to my thoughts as I descended the stairs. Lyle was at the bottom of the stairs holding the back of his head.

"What happened?" I asked him.

"Don't sneak up on me!" He jumped and turned around. "More ghost bullshit. I fell from the ceiling and wound up here."

"Go upstairs. I'll be right behind you."

"Shouldn't we be trying not to split up?"

"Vivian is still up there somewhere by herself," I said, hoping that would persuade him. "I have to do something down here first."

"What? It's too dangerous for her to be in here."

I wasn't going to argue that she had made it to the safe room completely untouched, which was more than I could say for either of us.

"Find her and get out of here."

"We're sticking together. Last time we went separate ways I got set on fire, so come with me to find Vivi and we'll come back down if it's so important."

Talking was only wasting time. I walked away and hurried through the peculiarly-lit library.

"Hurry, Dorian." It was my mom again.

"Mom?"

"Yes, honey?"

"What's our address?" I asked.

"What does that matter? Just open the door."

"Tell me," I insisted.

"Why won't you open the door, Dorian?" Desperate frustration was building in her voice.

"Because you're not my mother," I answered. "She would never ask me to kill other people and she'd never trust somebody like you, Rozalin."

"You good-for-nothing bastard!" Rozalin's spoke from my mother's form. "Couldn't even complete a simple task, could you? At least you provided me with an ounce of amusement while I waited."

"Dorian! Come on!" Lyle shouted from behind a bookcase. Rozalin was gone, but I knew it wouldn't be for long. I joined Lyle and fled to the staircase. "What were you doing back there?" he asked.

"Buying the others some time, but the rest is up to them."

When we were halfway up the stairs something swooped down on us. Whatever it was missed me and tackled Lyle, slamming him into a desk below. A second figure descended through the air, taking me to the ground with it. These things weren't ghosts. They were completely solid and flew on giant leathery wings like a bat's. They wore little in the way of clothing except some scraps fashioned as a loincloth. Their skin was gray and pulled tight over a strong, sinewy body. Each of their fingers and toes extended into sharp claws, but it was the fangs that gave away their origin. It wasn't Noah's wolfish grin, or even the pronounced teeth of the behemoth in Boston, but a full maw of jagged razor-sharp teeth. The eyes, set deep in sockets made more noticeable by a severely exaggerated brow, were neither seductive nor bestial, but had the mad gaze of a psychopath.

Laid out flat on my back, I immediately rolled over to face Lyle when the beast that had taken me down flew off. He was not as lucky. The one was on top of him, making every effort to sink its fangs into his neck. Lyle still held the fire poker and jammed it into the monster's mouth, causing it to recoil. He kicked it hard in the stomach and scrambled away, but not far enough. It grabbed hold of him and jumped on his back, using its body weight to force him into submission.

Rozalin was deeper in the library, speaking to the second winged abomination in a language I had never heard. I stayed down, trying not to draw attention to myself. I concentrated on pushing the one off Lyle with my powers, but it stayed latched on to him.

Lyle screamed and grimaced in pain. The hideous bloodsucker sunk its fangs into Lyle's neck, pinning him to the floor as it drank. Lyle's blue eyes began to go dark as he lost the struggle. I grabbed the metal poker and aimed for its heart.

Before I could strike, Vivian appeared on the other side of them, wielding a full-length *katana* etched in a rose motif with matching crimson handle. In one move, she swept the blade up, decapitating the monster and turning it to ash.

We helped Lyle sit up as he dusted off the remains from his clothes. He went to speak, but Vivian pressed a finger to his lips and leaned in to lick the blood from his neck. She bit down on her wrist and pressed it to his mouth.

I didn't doubt she could handle herself better than she let on, but I hadn't expected her to go out of her way for us.

Lyle held his neck. When he removed his hand a moment later, the puncture marks had vanished. "I thought bites were supposed to feel good," he groaned.

"Carpathians," she said, getting up and licking her own wrist as it sealed. "Their bite is painful on purpose. They enjoy tasting fear in the blood of their prey. More are on the way to aid in their *coup d'état*. They are fewest in number of the covens, but will storm the chateau with all they have if it means a chance to topple us while our sanctuary has been compromised."

I gave Lyle my hand to help him up, feeling guilty I hadn't done more. "How'd they know to come here now?" Lyle asked.

"Because I sent for them!" Rozalin laughed from above us. "Not only did I deceive the Strigoi witch to help me shed my physical form, but I informed the Carpathians of her precious little weapon! It took but a spark to ignite their paranoia. They crawled from their crypts to lay waste to their enemies before it was too late for them.

"They are an ambitious lot who yearn for their chance to reign supreme. It was only a matter of time until the Carpathians made their move to bury the other covens and overthrow humanity. They just required a little push to draw first blood! The creatures they cooked up to infest the city overseas were some of their best yet. With the Strigoi's weapon dead, the Carpathians felt the witches would cower, and only the Archios would be left to stand in their way. That's where I came in.

"I care not for the fate of the world. I will watch with glee as the chaos I've set in motion crumbles my dear sister's empire!"

"But I'm not dead!" I shouted defiantly.

"You died along with your family, and have been nothing more than a hollow shell ever since. What good is a living weapon that lacks the will to fight? You are a failure at everything other than playing the pawn to help me start a war."

"No, you're wrong. I may have lost everything and wanted to give up when things got bad, but as long as I'm still alive I won't be anybody's puppet!"

A wicked smile curled across Rozalin's face. She vanished in time for us to see the second Carpathian flying down with claws and fangs bared. Vivian readied her *katana*, but Noah dropped down from a bookcase onto it. He grabbed both wings, pulling back until they tore from the sockets. He finished it off with his swords through its neck.

Noah touched down in the pile of ash and opened his mouth to speak, but a wave of dark flame tearing through the library stopped him. The room blurred past me for a second as Noah grabbed me and ran behind one of the bookcases for cover. Vivian had done the same for Lyle on the other side of the room.

"How do we beat her?" I asked Noah as we took cover behind the shelves. He stared at me, raising an eyebrow with a puzzled look.

"Ready to finally take my advice?"

"I'm ready to do whatever it takes to end this."

"Good. See these cases? Just like in the hedge maze, don't get trapped. Always give yourself an escape route." He pointed in the direction of the safe room. "We have to get her there. She wants you to focus on what she can do to you, not what you need to do to her. Just because you can't hit her doesn't mean she's unstoppable."

I peeked around the corner to the stairs. More of the Carpathians were joining us. "Don't worry about them, they're just a distraction," he said. "Get to the room and make her follow."

"Vivi!" He stepped out into the open and shouted. "You ready?"

"I was waiting on you," Vivian called out from her hiding spot across the library. "Do you think you can keep up, *chéri*?"

Noah was gone just in time to evade another burst of black flames from Rozalin. I crept along the outer path, keeping my eyes on the center of the room, where Rozalin was stirring up mayhem. She didn't seem too concerned with friendly fire as she let loose bolts of black lightning and flame in all directions, occasionally hitting the Carpathians as they flew by.

"Why do you run?" she laughed. "Is there nothing more delightful than the sweet embrace of death?"

Three of the Carpathians were chasing after Noah. He ran up the side of a giant column and backflipped, vaulting over them. Throwing both *wakizashi* downward, he skewered two of the Carpathians to the floor through their hearts and hopped on the back of the third. In one quick move he broke its neck, causing it to fly out of control. Noah grabbed Vivian's *katana* out of her hands as he passed and used the borrowed sword to cut his ride to pieces. He threw the *katana* back, impaling the Carpathian she was fighting, and winked at her.

"Is it not natural? Is it not beautiful?" Rozalin continued her taunting. "Why do you run from the inevitable?"

Noah dodged another of her attacks while putting an end to the two Carpathians he had staked. I heard the flapping of wings close by and readied myself for a fight, but there was no one there.

Something slithered up my leg. One of the shadowy tentacles had me snared. I heard a deep rasping voice behind me. "Parasite likes you, yes? You taste good now, yes?"

A Carpathian stood between me and the middle of the room, clicking the claws of one hand together. Over his shoulder I saw Noah wasn't far away. He was skillfully cutting his way through a crowd, sending one after another to their final grave.

"Go to hell." I held out my hand and sent him soaring backward to Noah, but he didn't make it that far. A stray bolt from Rozalin disintegrated him on contact. It wasn't exactly what I was going for, but that worked, too. I felt a twinge of excitement watching him die, but I had to tell myself it wasn't a step toward becoming like them. Up to now I had only "killed" mindless creatures.

I fought to free my leg just in time for another of the Carpathians to notice me. I stayed with my back to the wall to avoid getting hit in the crossfire.

"That's right! Shed the tiresome burden of this mortal coil and join me in everlasting death!" Rozalin was still running her mouth in the main area. She was taking so much joy in all this I couldn't help but think we were still playing right into her hands. How could any individual be so twisted and starved for attention that their only source of entertainment was making others fight to the death?

I didn't even give this next one the chance to try and intimidate me. I pinned him to the wall by exerting pressure on his head. He was a lot more resilient than anything else I had fought so far, and while he wasn't going anywhere fast, I was having a hard time doing damage.

The closer I got the tougher it was to walk against the force from my powers between us. This feeling reminded me of two magnets repelling each other. I couldn't tell whether I was hurting him or not, and his face was already so ugly it wasn't much indication. Another step and the Carpathian caught fire, thrashing wildly until he died.

"Holy shit," I said to myself, and looked around if anyone else saw what I had just done. Vance stepped out from the next row of shelves, holding his book in one hand and a fistful of fire in the other.

"Oh, it was you," I sighed. "Don't even think about sneaking away. I still have questions I need answered."

"You're welcome, and if this place wasn't sealed tight I would have already been gone." He paused and glanced down at the ashes.

"What is it?" I asked as he kneeled to inspect the pile.

A bang across the room startled me. Vivian had just spun out of the way of two Carpathians chasing her and cut the chain holding up one of the giant chandeliers. It crashed down into her pursuers, right through Rozalin, who exploded them to bits.

"Why cling to life so desperately? Such a frail and fleeting state," Rozalin mused as she floated around causing anarchy. "Soon you will all be with me enjoying an eternity with your new master."

"We found someone who likes the sound of their own voice even more than Noah," I said.

"This isn't good," Vance said, ignoring my joke. He pointed to the remains. The ashes were traveling on their own across the floor to the center of the room. I scanned the rest of the room and noticed all the remains were doing the same thing, forming one big mound under Rozalin.

"That's why she doesn't care that her own allies are dying. She's going to bring them all back under her control anyway."

"I'm not sure that's her plan," Vance disagreed. "Why sacrifice a stronger army for a weaker one? She's drawing power from all the souls of the dead, but the ashes must mean something."

Vance's eyes glazed over as he got lost in thought. I didn't think he was paying attention until he casually raised his hand to another incoming Carpathian and froze it in a sheet of ice.

"Carpathians aren't known for their intelligence," he told me, "but at times they can surprise you." He placed his hand on the block of ice and exsanguinated the frozen body, drawing the blood into himself.

"That's smart," I praised, "but we'd have to freeze them all to stop whatever she's trying to do."

Vance still wasn't listening. Instead he was writing in blood on the floor again. "We need a crystal or something like it to bind Rozalin once we trap her," he said.

I remembered the jewelry cases upstairs, but it was unlikely I'd make it that far and back again. I left Vance to his work and went to find the others. Noah was almost impossible to keep track of as he dove into one crowd of enemies, dismembered them, and then moved on to the next in mere seconds. Vivian was holding her own better than I thought would be possible in formalwear. At one time she did a somersault with her *katana* out, cut a group of the Carpathians to ribbons, and landed perfectly poised on two feet.

Rozalin spotted me and sent a blast of dark energy my way. I just barely dodged and ran for cover again. The unnatural light in the room was hurting my eyes, but I saw a shadow over me a second too late. Sharp claws went right into my shoulders from behind and I couldn't strike back without seeing who was attacking me.

There was a shout and suddenly I was released, wincing as the claws were dragged out of my body. Lyle stood over the monster, jamming his trusty fire poker into its chest. He was in considerably rougher shape than when this had started. His clothes were bloodied and torn to shreds and he was covered in cuts and scrapes.

"I hate these stupid things!" he screamed at the body as he kept stabbing it.

My arm and back hurt a lot less now. I checked the damage and watched in amazement as the wound healed shut right before my eyes. I grabbed at my back. The deep lacerations there had gone away too.

Lyle finally stopped his frenzy and stepped back with his gun out. He aimed and shot at the oil lamp above, causing the black flames to immolate the paralyzed corpse.

"You good?" he asked, and snatched the metal poker from the fire. The tip of it had caught some of the Carpathian's clothes and was still burning like a torch.

"Heads up!" Noah shouted. A body came dropping down on us, but Noah dashed underneath and cleaved it in two with a swipe of his sword. "You guys tired already or something?"

The severed torso was still moving and snarling at Noah, who put his boot on its head to hold it in place.

"I need some of Aurelia's jewelry, like a necklace or something with a crystal in it," I told him.

He decapitated the torso and put the creature out of its misery.

"This isn't really the time to explore your feminine side," he grinned.

"No, idiot! Vance needs it for the ritual."

"So go pick out something nice upstairs. I'm having fun here."

"You left Vivi by herself!" Lyle pushed past us.

"She's a big girl, she can take care of herself," Noah said calmly and pointed to a bunch of the Carpathians that had her surrounded. "Look, she's already made friends."

"We need to help her," said Lyle, but Noah grabbed my shoulder to stop me.

"Don't get involved unless you understand the situation. Watch your allies just as closely as your enemies, or an attempt to help could end in failure."

I took his advice and watched from a safe distance. The Carpathians had stopped advancing and turned on each other, clawing and biting themselves to pieces while Vivian stood in the middle of them until they were done. She delicately tiptoed over the remains and joined with Lyle.

"She's the last person in here you have to worry about," Noah finished. "She's been at this longer than me."

All but a few of the Carpathians had been defeated, but that was just as troubling as when they were swarming the place. Their ashes slunk toward Rozalin, who was still raining down destruction.

"The ashes!" I yelled. "She's collecting the ashes for something!"

Lyle and Vivian were untangling themselves from the shadowy structures reaching out for them. The black fire on the end of Lyle's makeshift torch burned them away. He threw it like a spear at Rozalin just as she launched more dark lightning at him. Vivian pushed him out of the way. Even though the poker went right through her, the flames caused Rozalin to scream in anguish.

Rozalin's laughter didn't return after that. She was seething with anger now and targeting Lyle, who was too busy looking around for Vivian. The ashes swirled around Rozalin, forming one of the ritual circles like Minerva and Vance used. She killed off the last of the Carpathians herself and added their ashes to the rest.

"Do not let her complete the circle!" Vance warned from the floor above. He cast his own magical fire at Rozalin. Right as he was climbing down to lead her to the trap, she blew up the ladder, barely missing him in the process. Vance didn't move from under the collapsed bookcases.

It was up to me now. I willed an oil lamp from its fixture and flung it at Rozalin. She caught fire momentarily and was now after me.

"I will reunite you with your family one way or another!" Rozalin screamed at me in rage.

She floated over the circle and brought it to life with dark magic. The ashes rose up to form a cloud surrounding her. It pulsated and crackled with energy, and from it came the tormented faces of all those trapped within. Everything near the cloud withered and decomposed. The closer it got, the more clearly I could hear the victims' screams of despair from inside.

I ran for the safe room, pulling more oil lamps down and chucking them at the cloud as I went. It absorbed the flames, but did not slow. The mass of darkness decayed the wood and stone supporting the building as it passed.

I vaulted over rubble and into the trap room, making sure Rozalin was still in pursuit. The doorframe and wall around it eroded instantly upon contact with the cloud. My skin was flaking off as it drew near, but regrew over and over.

For a moment I wondered what would happen to me and how bad it would hurt if Vance's trap didn't work, but I didn't have to. The floor illuminated with her inches from my face. I stepped out of the way, but she couldn't follow and her deathly cloud dissipated as the magic circle trapped her.

"You think you are so clever," she smiled. "You cannot contain death. You cannot avoid it, not forever. I will have so much fun in the Underworld when I amuse myself with your family's souls."

She was looking behind me at something. A tall, lanky figure in a full-length coat, wide-brimmed hat, and peculiar bird mask was watching us.

"What did I tell you? You cannot contain me, I *am* death! There is a war coming and when it arrives a darkness greater than you can imagine will swallow you all whole and grind your bones to dust!"

I backed out of the room, trying to keep my eyes on both her and this new person. "Now, stop gawking and release me!" she commanded the figure.

Noah and Vivian were observing from a vantage point behind the stranger. It was hunched over on a cane for support and cocked its head inquisitively at her demands.

"I said release me!" she screamed. The stranger chuckled at her from behind the mask and hobbled off with the aid of its cane. "We had a deal!" she screeched. "I will slaughter you and what's left of your pathetic coven!"

The stranger ignored her tantrum as it made its way to the stairs. Rozalin let out a deafening high-pitched wail that shattered the rest of the oil lamps and sent the library up in flames. The noise was so loud my ears were bleeding and I was seeing red. Noah, Vivian, and Vance were next to me now, but I couldn't hear if they were saying anything. Noah tore the choker from Vivian's neck and threw it in the room. Vance read an incantation from the tome and the shrieking stopped as Rozalin was sucked down into the amethyst jewel.

"Please tell me that's the last we're gonna hear from her," Lyle said from a cautious distance before coming over to us.

"I'm disappointed, Vi. You're slowing down in your old age. I killed at least twice as many as you," Noah bragged.

Vivi handed him her sword and walked over to pick up the necklace. "I did it in heels."

"What is that?" I asked, referring to a rumbling from upstairs. Noah disappeared from the library, followed by Vivi. "Come on," I waved to Lyle.

"I'll be here," said Vance as he took a seat.

With Rozalin gone, the illusions and shadows haunting the chateau went with her. The rumbling grew as we followed the sound to the front doors. Outside, Vivian and Noah stood side by side, watching as something in the distance approached.

"Stay," Noah told Vivian, and handed back her sword.

"This is hardly the time to find your sense of chivalry," she said.

The noise was almost on top of us now and we could see what Noah and Vivian were concerned about. Dozens of bodies poured out from the woods, surrounding the estate and trampling the ground as they advanced.

"You've gotta be shitting me," Lyle swore. "There are hundreds of them!"

He was right. The dozen Carpathians we first saw were only the beginning. Vivian had said they would attack with all they had, but I never thought I'd see this many in one place.

"Time to go to work." Noah left, diving head first into the fray. Blood and ash spouted up from the mob like geysers, showing where he had been as he fought against the tide. Vivian returned to safety inside the chateau, but was clearly distraught at leaving Noah to fend for himself against the impossible odds.

"I don't think even he can do this alone," I shouted to Lyle over the pandemonium.

"Aurelia's out here! They're going for her; we have to help!" Lyle pointed over to the guesthouse where she stood at the top of the steps, looking out over the battle. She was impeccably primped and manicured in yet another glamorous tiered ballgown that stuck out from all the gore and bloodshed around her.

I tried getting Noah's attention, hoping he would get to her before the Carpathians did, but it was hopeless amidst the roar of battle. Lyle and I ran as fast as we could to reach her as he yelled for her to go back inside and take cover.

One of the largest of the pack reached Aurelia before us. He was an easy seven feet of ugly. Aurelia remained completely still, ready to accept her end as he towered over her. She spoke just when he was about to strike her down.

"You dare raise a hand to me?" Even over all the racket, her words were crystal-clear and just as sharp. "*I am royalty!*"

What happened next was more unbelievable than anything I had witnessed so far. Aurelia backhanded the giant with such force that it splattered him into a rain of ash that showered his comrades. I had to check Lyle's expression to make sure what I just saw was right. He, along with the others at the foot of the stairs, was dumbstruck.

"Did you see that?" he hollered. "She just bitch-slapped a guy ten times her size!"

Aurelia remained composed and stoic as she fixed her icy gaze outward. A fierce gleam in her eyes halted the hundreds of interlopers. They stayed frozen for a moment and then mechanically turned to one another to tear out each other's hearts. In only a few seconds the entire battlefield was cleared, leaving Noah standing alone on the grass where he had been fighting. Back by the trees, the man in the bird mask was still watching. He left just as casually as he had before.

"You never let me have any fun. I was just getting warmed up," Noah said, as he strutted over, cleaning off his *wakizashi*. "What now?" he asked. "Want me to go after the hunchback?"

"We should go check on Vivi and make sure Vance is still there," I whispered to Lyle, letting Aurelia and Noah talk in private.

"That would have made things a lot easier from the start," Lyle said once we were inside.

"Yeah, it would have," I agreed, thinking back to when the creatures invaded on my first night here. If she could annihilate an army that easily, then those mutants would have been nothing to her. Was my attempt at fighting them supposed to be a test, or a source of entertainment?

Vance was right where we left him, along with Vivian, although neither one of them were making any effort to converse.

Aurelia appeared with Noah and immediately took the necklace from Vivian. "Finish off the rest," she instructed, and turned to leave.

"Everyone's pretty dead, ma'am," Lyle said looking around. "You should be safe now."

"She means us," Vance chimed in. Noah and Vivian glanced at each other before Vivian turned to accompany Aurelia.

"I gave the mage my word he could go free if he helped," Noah explained to her. Aurelia stopped and addressed him over her shoulder.

"Your word is not yours to give. Kill them. Or need I remind you it is only my word that is law?"

Noah gripped the hilt of his sword tightly and gritted his teeth at her.

"What?" I cried out. "You can't be serious! We almost died helping you!" Noah moved between her and the rest of us as she left with Vivian. "Noah, you can't do this!" I protested as he drew his swords.

Vance tugged at my arm, pulling me with him. There was a blinding light from the floor, followed by thick smoke, and I now realized what he was so busy writing during the battle.

Chapter Sixteen

"What the —? Where are we?" Lyle was trying to make sense of the run-down industrial room we had been transported to.

"I told you this would happen," Vance said, walking to his desk. "They betrayed us the moment our purpose was fulfilled. Now you see why the other covens loathe them. The Archios may play nicely for a time, but it is no different any time we play their game."

I sat on the floor, exhausted from the fight and equally tired mentally from processing what had just gone down. "I'm not really a fan of the Carpathians either."

"Is anyone gonna tell me how we got here?" Lyle asked.

"We are back in the Strigoi *arcanum* just past the French-German border, but we can't stay here long or they'll find us," Vance explained. "I knew they would double-cross us, so I prepared a quick exit that would bring us back here."

"Vivi wouldn't turn on us."

"Yeah, she would," I said to Lyle. "They're all the same. They've been using us, from the start. Vivian gave me some sob story about Noah before I went into the chateau so I'd feel obligated to help out and not get in the way of their plans. The worst part is I actually fell for it."

"I don't buy it," Lyle argued. "Maybe I just don't have as hard a time finding the good in people. I saw the look in her eyes. Vivi didn't want any part of it, and neither did Noah."

"Noah is little more than Aurelia's personal attack dog," Vance said to Lyle. "He does not want her praise and attention taken from him, so he will go to great lengths to belittle the weak in front of her. What did you really expect to happen?"

"They're all corrupt!" I added. "None of them are any better than the other. Some are prettier, some are faster, some are smarter, but they're all the same. I hate the manipulation and the mind games; it makes me sick. It's pathetic that they spend their immortality screwing each other for things that humans deal with and get over every day."

Lyle looked pissed at me for not siding with him, but he needed to hear it. We were always being dragged further away as soon as we got close to getting back to our lives. Now, in place of the Strigoi and the Carpathians, we'd have to deal with being hunted by Noah. I already knew from experience it wouldn't take him long to track us.

"Humans are no better," Vance said, seated behind his desk. "We were all human once. There is no magical curse or transformation that makes us any more rotten inside than our mortal counterparts. Time is all that changes us — not on the outside, but within. Our bodies stay forever youthful, but our minds grow sour the more we are forced to cope with surviving in this world.

All the negativity — the corruption, as you put it — poisons us as we are made to swallow it and learn from it. Many even go mad. You will be the same."

"I'm not one of you and I don't want to be," I said. "I'm happy to have an expiration date if it means I won't become as twisted as the rest of you."

"You are not quite like us, but you are not mortal either."

"What do you mean by that?" I asked.

"The ritual that fused you with the parasitic entity allowed you to harness the power of the Rift. You saw for yourself how your body recovers from cellular destruction almost instantaneously. An entire dimension, created long before this world, channels its energy through you. As long as it sustains you, your cells will never die; you will never age. I believe you may be immortal."

"People have been trying to find the key to immortality forever — you just read from some book and it's done? What's going to happen when I start outliving everyone?"

"It was a series of events none of us could have predicted at the time of your creation. From a logical point of view, we wouldn't have wanted your kind to be immortal or you would easily overthrow us, defeating the purpose entirely. It was the only way to cure the infection, however."

"What if he gets his head cut off?" Lyle asked, with a little too much interest.

"I'm not sure. Decapitation and disintegration work just fine on most anything, but there's no way of knowing for sure unless we run some tests."

"Whoa, slow down," I protested. "You're not running any 'tests' or even touching me. You've done enough."

"Can't you just undo the spell?" Lyle asked.

"There is no counter-spell. He is technically a new organism, not two parts of a whole to separate."

"What happens if I get bitten again?"

"You might mutate radically and beyond repair. Or perhaps nothing at all. Come to think of it, with your level of regeneration, you may be immune to all conventional diseases. There's no way of knowing for sure without having a control to test the variables."

"You're not experimenting on me," I said firmly. "But I do have other questions that you can answer. Who are these other people you created?"

"I don't know. Only Minerva had knowledge of each specimen. I only participated in your genesis."

"How do we know he's telling the truth?" Lyle asked me.

"We don't. We can't even be sure any of us will live long enough for it to matter, but just in case, I want that book destroyed so nobody else can be threatened with demonic possessions and experiments."

"You may be right," Vance agreed, to my surprise. "This book holds many marvelous things, but at what cost? Deals with the Devil are never a worthwhile investment in the long run; a lesson Minerva is most likely learning in Hell right now."

"How could Rozalin mimic my parents if she never met them? She did it the other night too," I asked to change the subject.

"The Carpathians' creatures infected your parents. Rozalin may have been watching from the Underworld. Depending on how long they had been infected, their souls may have already been consumed by the parasite before she could get to them."

"But if their souls got eaten, then there's no afterlife?"

"Correct," Vance nodded. "They cease to exist."

"Maybe that's better than letting Rozalin get her hands on them," Lyle said, trying to offer some solace.

"I was hoping if all of this stuff was real then maybe they are in Heaven. The parasite sends the energy it eats to that other dimension, but that dimension is linked to me now. Does that mean maybe my parents' souls are a part of me?"

"Yes, I suppose you could look at it as some form of spiritual cannibalism." That wasn't what I was getting at, but of course he took the less comforting solution. It was probably best to move on while I still had time to ask questions.

"What was the significance of giving me the power to move things with my mind? If you wanted a weapon, why not fire or something more destructive?"

"Telekinesis can have varying degrees of subtlety. Setting someone on fire when there is no natural source of fire around will surely raise suspicion. It can also be quite powerful when properly directed. There are very few limitations. I've heard stories that psychics once used telekinetic powers to aid in the construction of works such as Stonehenge and the pyramids of Egypt. Those stories sparked the inspiration for your powers."

"I got a question," Lyle spoke up. "Who was the hunchback?"

"I do not know his name. Judging by the immense size of his aura he is a progenitor of the Carpathians, an Ancient like Rozalin and Aurelia."

"So, why didn't we kill him?" Lyle asked. "We were on a roll."

Vance chuckled. "Rozalin's downfall wasn't our skill or even luck. Her own hubris led to her defeat. She trifled with us to gain her sister's attention, believing we were no threat until things got out of hand. If she wanted to, she and most other Ancients could destroy an entire army with barely a yawn."

"Good thing he left on his own then," Lyle gave a satisfied smile. "At least we don't have to see him again —"

"That may not be true," Vance continued. "I should explain further why Dorian and the others were created, aside from Minerva's scheme.

"The Carpathians resent mankind for their enforced isolation. They believe themselves to be superior to humanity. While I can't blame them, their methodology is a bit harsh for my liking.

"The outbreak in New York is not a new trick for them. The Carpathians have a penchant for pestilence and madness. During the fourteenth century, one of their progenitors concocted a particularly vile disease, coined the 'Black Death,' that nearly erased mankind from Europe. The Carpathians sought to rebalance the world back in our favor by 'culling the herd,' so to speak. Dressed as human plague doctors, like the 'hunchback,' they would travel from city to city spreading the disease.

"Of course, the Archios were up in arms when they found out. Their beautiful flock was wracked with decay and falling fast. Soon the problem became an issue of survival for even them. Only the Carpathians could drink from tainted blood without ill effects; the others would involuntarily expel it and suffer lessened symptoms of the humans' condition for a time.

"For centuries, the Strigoi had already been at ease imbibing conjured blood, so this did not affect us. It wasn't until the Carpathians drew ire from hunters seeking a reason behind the plague that we became involved. No one was safe as the human population plummeted. The Archios were being starved out and hunted and so were we. Anyone remotely supernatural was persecuted and put to death. We were burned in our sleep, along with human witches and mages who were falsely accused of involvement.

"Eventually, the remaining supernaturals and hunters pushed back the Carpathians to their mountains in the East until only a few remained. The Archios did what they do best and altered the minds of the humans to believe the origin of the plague came from the Far East. They perpetrated rumors of themselves and other supernaturals as nothing more than folktales and children's stories to falsify their existence and end the hunts against them. Since then, the Carpathians have been reestablishing their numbers and plotting another rebellion, this time targeting both humans and supernaturals alike.

"They have been quiet for centuries, but we know their grudge has only intensified over time."

"Wow, just awesome," I sighed. "You still haven't destroyed that book, by the way."

"Oh ... yes, I almost forgot," he responded hesitantly and held it up, setting it on fire in his hand.

"Let's worry about how we're going to prevent the Archios from killing us," I said.

"If I can just talk with Vivi, I'm sure we can work it out," Lyle offered.

"They will be after me first, seeing as they know I will return to the Strigoi for protection and mount a strike against them while their main sanctuary is in ruins. I have very little interest in more conflict at this point, but I will be headed somewhere safe. What the coven decides is their own right. I suggest you return to New York. The turmoil there may be exactly what you need to lose them. They won't put much effort in to chasing after you if they believe you will die on your own soon enough."

"One more thing," I said while I still had his ear. "Since the ritual I feel like I look different."

"Yes, when you use your powers, your eyes still reflect the parasite, an interesting side effect of the fusion. A tissue sample would be necessary for any further explanation."

"Besides that. I'm talking about my skin and hair and even my body. Everything just looks better, like it's all been bumped up a notch."

"Oh, that. It's just a trivial aesthetic reaction caused by the Archios blood we used as a catalyst for the spell. I wouldn't worry too much about it."

"Right." As if, out of everything that had happened, having tighter abs and clearer skin was going to make me panic.

"I must be off if I'm to have a chance at reaching the next stronghold. I surmise this will be the last time we're to meet, so I leave you with a bidding of good luck and an apology for the trouble my aunt's scheme has caused you."

I thought being rid of Vance would be a weight off my shoulders, but I actually felt kind of melancholy after getting to know him more. "It wasn't your fault, but thank you and thanks for deciding to help me. I'm sorry that it cost you getting caught up in a losing bargain with Noah, though."

"Penance perhaps, hmm? So it is ..."

"How are we getting to New York from here, dude?" Lyle asked. "We have no money and no way of getting around."

"You're free to use the vehicles upstairs. This building will be leveled to erase any evidence of our work here by tomorrow."

"Can't you just zap us there? I'm not looking forward to driving aimlessly for hours to find an airport only to get arrested for being a dirty, bloody, and penniless foreigner with nice skin."

"That was a spell from the tome I just burned." I could swear there was some sarcasm in Vance's voice, but that would mean he had a sense of humor. "The spell requires a sigil to be painted in blood ahead of time at both the desired destination and the place of casting. I had it prepared, figuring a hasty retreat would be in order."

"Well, can you conjure us up some clothes, or money, or something?" I asked him.

"No, I can't say I've ever had the need to learn magic of that sort," Vance said as he made his way out the door. "Farewell."

"Guess we better get a car," Lyle said, sounding a bit dejected.

"I'll show you where they are," I told him, leading the way upstairs.

Lyle stopped to stare at the wreckage of the containment unit as we passed by the lab I had been held in. It looked a lot worse than I realized at the time. Broken glass and twisted metal mixed with the blood-stained robes and ashes of the fallen Strigoi who thought they could keep me as their pet. "Jesus, what happened here?" he asked.

"Me."

Chapter Seventeen

Getting back to New York had been no easy task, and the kindness of strangers seemed more fictional than anything I had seen the past few days. But I couldn't blame anyone for steering clear of the two foul-smelling, mangy foreigners talking to each other about supernatural conspiracies.

Fortunately, we had found a gas station outside Frankfurt where we were able to wash up a little and get directions to the nearest airport. Lyle and I came up with a plan to make enough money for plane tickets and clean clothes at the duty-free store. Or rather, I came up with it, and after much convincing, he contributed his expertise as an officer of the law. I had no way of withdrawing money from my bank without a physical card or any form of legitimate ID. Lyle was a murder suspect, so strolling into the US Embassy wasn't going to work. We had no choice but to steal what we needed.

Officer Turner knew all the tricks that pickpockets used, and put them to good effect by distracting unsuspecting victims. We did have something normal thieves didn't, and that was telekinesis. It didn't take us long to collect enough money and I got good practice at more delicate manipulation of my powers. Resorting to this brought on a disheartening feeling, but I got used to it more quickly than I should have.

"Hey, can I talk to you about something?" Lyle asked as our train pulled away from JFK Airport. It seemed odd to me that he'd have reservations about anything by now, but I had a feeling I knew what was on his mind. In a stroke of fortunate irony, or possibly clever deception, Vivian had presented Lyle with fake passports and matching IDs for both of us right before we confronted Rozalin in the chateau. He was adamant that Vivian was trying to help us escape, but I wasn't so easily convinced.

"Yeah, what is it?"

"It's about Vivi. I get why we shouldn't trust them, but we have to look at their kind as people too. She saved my life twice. I at least owe her the benefit of the doubt. Innocent until proven guilty, remember? I know you think it's because they wanted to keep us around to help, but while you were gone and I was recovering she went out of her way to keep me company." I could tell he wanted me to ask just how out of the way she went, but I wasn't interested in hearing about their pillow talk. "Noah and Vivi aren't the ones who want us dead; it was an order they couldn't refuse."

"You're a cop. If you're given an order you don't believe in to that extreme would you follow it?"

"No, I'd do what I feel is right. But we're talking about a whole different ballgame here. You saw how they can mess with each other's minds. They're not given the choice to stand up for what they believe."

"It's not like I'm in any position to be a threat to them, if that's what you're worried about now, but you're also giving them too much credit. We're nobody to them."

"I'm not saying we're in love or that we're even friends, but I honestly feel that they're capable of some compassion. Aurelia's probably pissed about her home being trashed, and doesn't trust us any more than she does Vance."

"So she tries to have us killed? That's taking it a little far."

"If she were any other woman I'd say bring her some flowers or jewelry and work the rest out under the sheets, if you know what I mean."

"Not really," I stated flatly. Sex was the last thing on my mind right now, but judging by the childish grin on his face I could tell Lyle wasn't on the same page.

"Oh right, yeah. How's that work with two guys? Do you get each other flowers? Do you even like flowers, or is that just a stereotype?"

"Lyle, just ... just stop."

"I'm serious! How else am I supposed to know if I don't ask? You must've had a boyfriend or something before, right?"

"Not really."

I was involved with someone, but I didn't want to honor what we had with a title. It started the summer before my senior year. We met at the gym where I worked and connected over our love of baseball. He didn't seem like the type to be interested in guys; he played on the school baseball team and did hockey on the side. Everything happened so fast and he took the lead each step of the way. Soon we were texting each other like a couple and going on dates that ended in my first kiss. Seven months later and he never missed a chance to wish me goodnight and good morning, always followed by how much he was in love with me. I was so happy I didn't even mind that we had to check no one was watching when we held hands, or make sure not to walk too close together or lean in to talk to each other at dinner.

Christmas week I was at the mall shopping for his gift when I see him there at the food court. He had his arms around this girl I had never seen before. I stood there debating whether I should go up to him or not until they started kissing. I felt so betrayed I was nauseous. I wanted to ask him what was going on, but I was afraid I would start crying. They walked passed me as they left and he just looked right through me like I didn't exist.

I didn't think I'd ever hear from him again, but he texted me that night asking what I was doing as if nothing happened a few hours earlier. I asked if he was with his girlfriend and he said yes without any hesitation. Then he tells me I was a mistake, he wanted a 'real' relationship and to get married one day and have a family. I guess in the end I learned that no matter how many types of people there are in the world, heartbreak is universal.

"I'm kinda scared to see what she's gonna look like." Lyle watched anxiously as the streets flew by the train window. "The city, I mean."

"I'm more worried about the others like me. They're out there somewhere."

"Yeah, but if we stop the Carpathians they should be safe," Lyle said as we passed through the tunnel into Manhattan.

"But for how long? And how do we save an entire city?"

"We made it this far, right? There's a lot fewer of them than there were yesterday, so I'd say we're doing pretty well. Their biggest mistake was making so many enemies, but I guess history really is doomed to repeat itself."

"True. No matter how much I keep saying I don't want to fight I never seem to be able to stop. I hate feeling like everything's been predetermined for me."

"You wanted to stop Rozalin, didn't you? We all have a common enemy; it doesn't mean you're being controlled."

"I was only there to get Vance until she started messing with me about my parents. Then I wanted revenge."

"That's natural."

"But is it healthy?"

"Nothing wrong with fighting if it's for the right reason."

"I want to do the right thing. I just don't want it to turn me into something I may not like along the way," I said. Whether or not my DNA or my soul dictated if I was human, I still wanted to believe I was. I'd felt like an outcast ever since I found out I was different. I constantly repressed the thought that maybe my powers were the first step to transforming into a real monster. My fear was that when my parents and everyone else found out they would turn on me and I would be alone ... or dead.

Besides the charming facade of the Archios, I was genuinely happy to find others that were different from "normal" humans too. Now, being normal seemed so insignificant. I was fighting in a war I didn't believe in and never knew existed. For all their years of wisdom, the covens were no less close-minded than the humans they laughed at. There was no one big bad guy for us to defeat. Everyone involved had had some hand in fueling the fire that now engulfed us all. I didn't want to fight and take a side, yet my personal choice in all of this seemed not to matter. It felt inevitable that my power to cause destruction would come to define me.

"Hey man, excuse me. What's the situation like in the city right now?" Lyle asked the man who checked our tickets as we pulled into Penn Station. "I hear there's some trouble going on."

"You boys must be from out of town. You picked a bad time to go on vacation." The burly man broke out in a hoarse smoker's cough. "Sightseein' during the day is all right, but if you're lookin' for the good ol' nightlife maybe you should've gone to Vegas this time around."

"What's that supposed to mean?" I asked. It was reassuring to hear the city was still standing, but this was making me wary. We were so out of touch with the news.

"Curfew started up a few days ago. Everything shuts down after nine. If the police catch you on the street you're gonna get a hefty fine or thrown in jail overnight."

"They can do that?" I turned to Lyle.

"Sure can," the gentleman answered and began rummaging through his jacket pockets for a lozenge. "Orders from higher up. They're saying it's because of some gangs that moved in causing trouble. Hogwash if you ask me. I haven't seen any gangs and I've been here thirty years. You know what I think it really is?"

Lyle and I stared blankly, waiting for him to continue.

"Terrorists," he whispered. "I hear people been getting sick whole buildings at a time. Sounds more like that biological warfare malarkey we were hearing about all the time a few years back. That stuff got swept right under the rug, didn't it?"

"Thanks, man, we'll keep our eyes open," Lyle said as we turned to leave.

"You're quite welcome, *Officer.*"

"What did he say?" We whispered to each other and turned back around. The car door closed.

He smiled at us through the window as it pulled away.

"That was messed up," Lyle complained. "How'd he know I'm a cop?"

"What time is it?" I left to find the board with all the track times for the railroad.

"I've never seen Penn Station this empty," Lyle said, catching up to me.

The station was desolate except for a few other passengers leaving the platforms and the NYPD on patrol. All the shops were closing up for the night. It was the same weird vibe as being in a mall after hours.

"8:54." Lyle pointed to the track information. "This place really does shut down by nine. Trains don't start up again until 5:30 AM. We're not getting out of the city until morning unless we walk across the bridge, but I bet it's heavily guarded."

"We didn't come here to leave."

"Okay, badass. I was just planning ahead in case things get too crazy. I guess now you're cool with joining the fight again?" he asked.

"I'm not, I just want it over with."

"Don't worry, I won't let you turn evil," Lyle assured me as we climbed the stairs out to the street.

"I don't think it's something you can stop."

"Well, Vance did say he wasn't sure if you could live through decapitation."

I tried not to laugh. "I need new friends," I muttered under my breath.

"Oh come on, you know I'm joking. I'd try shooting you first."

"You're starting to sound like Noah," I jabbed back at him.

"Please, promise you'll shoot me if I ever get like that."

Up on 34th Street the police were ushering civilians home and directing traffic as it thinned out to just a few taxis and buses making their final rounds. The city that never slept grew quiet around us. The lights were all still in full effect, giving the empty streets an abandoned feeling.

"Move along, guys," an officer politely ordered us as we hung around taking it all in. Lyle kept his head down to avoid eye contact in case he was recognized.

"What's the curfew for?" I asked.

"Just a temporary precaution. Gangs have been active in certain areas at night. We're keeping civilians off the street until we can sort everything out."

I thanked the cop for the information and hurried off with Lyle as if we knew where we were going.

"Back in France Vivi said the Archios were working on condemning buildings. We know my apartment is one, and probably the hotel where we were sent is too. There won't be anybody left in those buildings by now, but that's ground zero. We start there and work our way out."

"One building could have hundreds of those creatures in it, not to mention we can't get caught by the police or anybody helping to clear them out. So how should we do this?" Lyle asked.

"Pick a building, dive in, and don't get caught."

"Fair enough. I had to lose my gun back in Germany, so I'm gonna need a weapon for when shit goes down."

We stuck to residential side streets as much as possible while heading uptown. Police cars were on full patrol, but mostly stuck to the major avenues. Lyle and I had to duck between buildings and behind dumpsters when the occasional patrol would pass, but we were making steady progress. The good part of the curfew was that it would be easy to hear anything going on.

A police siren ahead stopped us from trying to race across Fifth Avenue unseen. We froze, hiding around the corner and hoping they would pass, but then came the sound of a car door opening and closing.

"Sir, do you know what time it is?" we heard a female officer ask.

"Yes," a man's voice wheezed. "I'm sorry, I'm sorry. I live just up ahead. I was stuck finishing late at the office when the trains stopped and I couldn't find a taxi and ..."

I peered around the corner and spotted a portly, disheveled gentleman in his late fifties wearing an ill-fitting brown suit talking to the policewoman. He was clutching a briefcase overflowing with papers in one hand and a laptop case in the other.

"Go on home, sir. Don't let me see you out here this late again. It's for your own protection."

"Thank you, officer, thank you," the businessman obliged and set his briefcase down for a moment to wipe the sweat pouring off his brow.

"And a word of advice, sir: Try not to work so hard, it could kill you," she warned and got back in her car.

I poked Lyle and gestured to go back the way we came.

"How much do you think the police really know?" I whispered as we backtracked our way around.

"Not enough, is my guess," Lyle whispered back. "The Archios did great with containment and preventing riots, but this is something for the military to handle, not the cops."

"And yet here *we* are."

"You've got a point, but at least we know what we're dealing with."

Police presence was getting heavier as we neared my neighborhood. By East 71st most of the buildings were completely dark and boarded up or cordoned off by yellow police tape. The NYPD guarded barricades that barred access to any of the streets ahead.

"How are we gonna get past that?" I searched the area for some sort of opening, but the neighborhood was locked down.

"We go up and over," Lyle said, and pointed to a fire escape between two apartments. Lyle went first, climbing up on a dumpster to reach the ladder. I was right behind him on the second rung when the sound of heavy breathing and shuffling feet came down the other side of the alley. It sounded like only one infected person and at least we were hidden in the dark. Lyle waved me on to hurry up.

We crouched on the first landing waiting for the creature to make its way closer. I looked down at my arm where I had been bitten and remembered Vance's warning about becoming infected again.

"I don't have a weapon," Lyle reminded me. "Can you take it out by yourself?"

"Yeah, I think so. I'm still trying to get the hang of using my powers without a weapon."

"Get ready." Lyle gripped the railing tensely as the infected's shadow came around the corner of the alley.

"Wait!" He blocked me just in time. The shadow didn't belong to one of the infected. It was the businessman from before. He stumbled into the alley holding his chest and leaned against the wall to loosen his tie.

"It looks like he's having a heart attack. Keep a lookout." Lyle jumped off the fire escape and ran over to help. "Don't worry, sir, I'm a cop," he said and showed the frightened man his badge as he helped him to the ground. "You're going to be okay."

Another set of footsteps was coming from the other direction. Lyle and the man were making way too much noise. The police would be on top of us any second.

"Lyle! Police!"

"I thought you were the police," the man groaned.

"I am. I'm going to get you help." Lyle headed straight for the police, heedless of his imminent arrest. "Watch him, Dorian!"

I hopped over the railing and approached the man. I wished my dad were here. He'd know what to do.

"Oh, sorry." Lyle made an abrupt stop. A young woman dressed in yoga pants and a tank top tripped over him.

"Are you all right?" he asked her.

This was turning into a clusterfuck and we hadn't even encountered anything supernatural yet.

"Dorian!" Lyle shouted. "She's infected!"

The man at my feet did not look like he was going to make it another minute. Watching him lie there dying without knowing what to do frustrated me to the point of anger. I just couldn't let someone else die.

Lyle managed to push the woman down before she could do any damage. "Can you handle this? I'm going to take him out of here to get help."

"Yeah, go," I said, keeping my eyes on the infected woman. She was already up and starting to come for us. Her body hadn't mutated yet, but she had the telltale black veins snaking along her face.

"I know this is totally against procedure, but we have to get you somewhere safe," Lyle told the man as he helped him out of the alley.

The woman charged at me, making that nauseating guttural croak. She was pinned against the wall by my thought. I had to destroy the head, but I was having a hard time applying enough force to crush it.

The infected creature's cries were soon going to attract more of its kind. "Sssstop ..."

I could swear it was talking to me. The whites of its eyes were blackening now. "Plleeasse ..."

There it was again. This thing, this woman, was still alive. She was trying to fight the infection and watching as I killed her.

"I'm sorry!" I apologized. "I can't let you go or you'll kill people!"

It might have been me projecting, but her expression had a mounting sadness to it. She was frightened and confused, clinging to life. I knew there was no cure for her, but I couldn't find it in my heart to put the poor woman out of her misery.

The dumpster was close to us. I kept my hand out to stay focused on restraining her while I walked over to open the lid. A stagnant odor wafted out from the half-empty container. This wasn't going to be pleasant, but the choice was between dignity and death.

I willed the still flailing woman into the dumpster, guiding her through the air with my hand. Once inside, I threw the lid down and raised the bar to lock it in place. She was making a racket, banging against the metal sides of the container. I looked around to see if anyone noticed and sure enough from the apartment windows above a couple was staring down at me with phone in hand.

I ran out of the alley, staying close to the buildings to keep from being detected. There were police lights much further down the avenue, but no sign of Lyle. Headlights turned down the road toward me. I sidestepped into another alley and took cover behind some garbage cans as another cop car rolled by, shining a light between the buildings. Great. Their response time couldn't have been any more perfect when it meant me getting caught.

I snuck toward the other end of the alley, hoping to lose them on the next street.

"Man, you're a slow learner," a voice came from above. "How many times do I need to tell you? Always leave yourself an escape route."

Noah was perched above me on the railing of a fire escape. There weren't any words that would help now. I fled down the alley, but the sound of high heels on pavement cut me off.

Vivian stood in my way, sandwiching me between the two of them. Maybe if I hadn't seen her in action at the chateau I would have thought she was the easier of the two to get past, but now I knew better. Noah was wrong for once; I did still have an escape route.

I flew upward between the buildings faster than I ever thought possible. "I taught him that," I heard Noah tell Vivian below me.

"*Fantastique.* Now go get him," she said, apathetic to his gloating.

Only five more floors to reach the roof, but Noah was keeping pace right beside me. He wasn't even using his super speed, which felt a little insulting, but that was probably his point. I kept my eyes ahead of me, aiming for the roof, but it wasn't easy with him showing off his parkour tricks as he scaled the building.

Being seen didn't matter to me anymore. I landed on the roof right as Noah vaulted overhead to intercept me.

"I don't want to hurt you," I said, backing away from him.

"Don't worry, you can't." He sat on the edge of an air conditioner unit watching me. I had to stay on guard. The more I focused on him, the easier it would be for Vivian to strike from another angle.

"You must think us monsters," she said, still getting the drop on me.

"Enough mind games." I glared at her. "If you're going to try and kill me, just do it already."

"Try?" Noah scoffed. "If we were going to kill you you'd have been dead the second you got off that train."

"You've been following me all this time?"

"Sure have. We've been having fun watching you run around the city in a panic," he laughed.

"*You* were having fun, *I* have been working," Vivian corrected him.

"Why are you here if you're not going to kill me?"

"I'm positive the Carpathians' creatures will take care of that for us," Vivian answered. "We don't have to dirty our hands."

"Eventually you're gonna run out of dumpsters," Noah added.

"Vance said you'd say that. What happened to him?" I asked. "You got here fast, even for you."

"He fled to a Strigoi stronghold in Munich," Vivian replied.

"How do you know that? And why were you so certain I'd return here and die?"

"You're predictable," Noah said and got down from his seat.

"No, there's no way you knew what he said and where he'd be, and make it there and back in time," I said with rising suspicion. "Not unless you three planned this."

The silence that followed spelled it all out beautifully. "How long?" I asked.

"Since my trip with him back to France," Noah replied.

"*Oui*, and after witnessing that dreadful display of self-defense in the alley we have no choice but to report your impending death. It is as I told you; there is no need to get our hands dirty when the Carpathians will do it for us."

"I don't understand. I'm right here. You said yourselves, you could have killed me at any time."

"You don't need to understand," Noah barked. "Just shut up and get out of here."

"He deserves more than a simple dismissal, Noah."

"Wait. What about Lyle?"

"He's safe," Vivian reassured me.

"I don't trust you."

"You don't have to, but there comes a time when no matter how strong or how fast you are you'll need someone to trust." She was speaking to me, but her eyes were on Noah.

"What's that supposed to mean?" I asked looking between the both of them.

"Why did you not end the suffering of that poor creature in the alley?" Vivian responded with a question of her own.

"She was still human inside. What does that have to do with anything?"

"Did you not empathize in some way? You may think us to be monsters, but on the inside we are still just as human."

"That woman is a victim. She wasn't choosing to attack me to tie up loose ends, or get rid of me because I might be dangerous. She is being controlled, so yeah, I do empathize with her. She lost everything in a split second because she got caught up in something that had nothing to do with her, just like me and all the rest of these people. We're not living in mansions playing God with others' lives. We're trying to survive."

"We are no less victims than you, manipulated and forced to suffer tragic losses over hundreds of years. Some of us accept our place while others fight it, but our pain is all felt the same way. We do not have any choice but to obey or face a fate worse than death."

"You mean Aurelia? She may have been the one to give the order to kill, but I don't see why it makes any difference to you. You have eternal youth and beauty, live in a palace, and have powers that I've only seen in movies. Why should I believe that we mean anything to you?"

Vivian opened the briefcase she was holding and slid it across the roof to me. "What is this?" I asked, looking down at it suspiciously.

"Your proof."

I glanced around first to make sure this wasn't some kind of trap. Noah was gone. "Where'd he go?" I asked, but didn't get an answer.

The briefcase was filled with forms and a newspaper. Under that were two handguns with ammo, shoulder holsters, shooting gloves, and a combat knife. The forms had Lyle's name all over them and there was a picture of Lyle in the paper.

"What is this?" I asked again.

"Monsieur Turner's absolution. His false crimes have been purged from history and no one shall ever know of their existence. Paperwork has already been filed explaining he has been on medical leave after sustaining injuries while rescuing civilians from your apartment. That newspaper has an article detailing his heroism including sworn statements from his superiors. He will also be receiving an award."

Finally, a surprise of the good kind. "Why did you do all this? And how?"

" 'How' is very simple," she smiled. "The Archios still own this city. I did shut it down for us to work, after all! The government, law enforcement, and media have been taken over. We have members in every office, precinct, and newsroom pulling strings to allow us greater control during this crisis."

"I figured that was you."

"Monsieur Turner is selfless, courageous, and gallant. Men of his kind are a rare breed. He reminds me of another, one that I failed to save from this life years ago. I do not wish to see one more pure heart lost to our war."

She really did have a thing for him, that lucky son of a bitch. Technically, I introduced them.

"Don't amuse yourself too much," she said, noticing my smile. "My best gift to give is my absence. After tonight he will be believed dead, and we will have no reason to meddle in his life any longer. I cannot promise the same for you, as other supernatural beings will sense your power as we can. The decision is yours to make, but if you truly care for your friend, you too will leave him. What happened to your family was a tragedy, one that many of us have felt, but it doesn't have to continue if you are careful."

"Who did you lose?" I asked.

"We should speak elsewhere," she suggested. "I have a limousine waiting for me on the next street. If you'll join me I will share my story once we have reached the safety of our shelter."

"Not without Lyle," I insisted.

"Noah is retrieving him and will meet us there." Vivian collected the briefcase and walked to the ledge. With remarkable agility for someone wearing a tight skirt and business suit, she jumped down to the pavement, landed on her feet, and kept walking. Not wanting to be shown up, I dove off after her, also landing successfully.

As she said, there was a limo waiting for us one block over. One of the darkened buildings we passed was filled with sounds of violence. I opened my mouth to redirect Vivian's attention, but before I could get the words out she refuted my concern.

"We have Outsiders, hired mercenaries, clearing out the buildings we have sealed off." Getting in the limo with her was awkward after our argument. It would be my own fault if I fell into a trap after all the experience I had with them. The ride was quiet, and short. The shelter she referred to was a police station less than a mile away. Our driver escorted us to the door.

"Why a police station? I'd think a four-star hotel would suit you more," I asked.

"I prefer to travel in luxury, but this is business and I'd rather my business be secure." The station was abandoned and pitch-black until she turned the lights on and entered all the correct passcodes to bypass security. We made our way to an office on a lower level, locking all doors and security gates behind us. Inside was another briefcase and her engraved *katana* sheathed on top of a desk.

"What happened to all the police officers that worked here?"

"Reassigned to another precinct overnight while the building is closed for inspection, as per the commissioner's orders."

"You mean your orders."

"I won't take all the credit. He practically handed the keys over on bended knee without any supernatural influence. Not a wise man, but a simple one, and there is something to be said for that."

"And that is?"

"I don't know, you would have to ask his wife." Vivian busied herself with files on the office's computer while we waited.

"Shouldn't Noah be here by now?" I was starting to get nervous again. It wasn't like him to not be ten steps ahead.

She produced a cell phone from her suit jacket, although I wasn't sure how she had room for it in something so formfitting. "He's on his way," she let out a sigh after reading a message. "Trying to scare Monsieur Turner by traveling via rooftops."

No surprise there.

"You have a cell phone?" I didn't want it to come off as insulting. The Archios definitely kept with the times, but still it was kind of amusing and the tension between us was making me antsy.

"Of course, love. It's the twenty-first century," she said, so blasé that I felt stupid for asking.

I sat in a chair across the desk from her playing with the pens and paperclips by levitating them.

"It's good you are finally practicing your gift." She smiled, keeping her eyes on the computer. "When you first arrived at the chateau you were too timid to even admit you had it."

"I guess I've had my back against the wall one too many times not to," I said and showed off a little by trying to create patterns in the air with the office supplies.

"Sometimes that is the best way to find out who we truly are and what we are capable of."

"Yeah, Noah kinda simulated that a little too well back in France."

"Boys will be boys, even when they are almost two hundred years old."

Chapter Eighteen

I had never spent this much time with Vivian until now. It was almost pleasant and made me laugh inside thinking how jealous Lyle would be if he knew. She turned off the computer monitor and stepped in front of a floor-length mirror to freshen up. I couldn't keep myself from staring. If I had difficulty looking away, then Lyle was a lost cause.

"You promised to tell me your story," I reminded her. "Who was it that you lost?"

"My dearest friend, Jehanette. I was born of noble blood in France during the early 1400s. My brothers had died in the war against England before I was old enough to remember their faces. Because of this I was kept at my parents' side under close watch. My only friends growing up were the children of our servants.

"When I became of proper age I was allowed trips into town disguised as one of the servant's children while they tended to the family's errands. It was there that I became acquainted with young Jehanette. I was her senior by several years, yet she had a fire in her much like my own. We conversed on all manner of things, including the war with England. I questioned what a peasant girl would know of such diplomatic affairs, but she seemed as well-versed as any king.

"Some time later I accompanied my family to a formal gathering of nobility near Paris. I attended under instructions of my father not to speak of political matters, as it was not my place. The event quickly became an inquisition between noble houses to see where each stood on the war. Defying my father, I found it difficult to remain silent on issues I felt strongly about, such as my displeasure with our King's failure to drive out the English and restore France to its former glory.

"I caught the ear of another noblewoman, who agreed with my views and expressed the same disgust in our mandated silence due to gender. We spoke more in private. I confided my friendship with the peasant girl to her and how even she could see clearly that changes were needed.

"I was invited to stay and talk more with her. I expected my father to decline such an invitation, but after a brief meeting with her he agreed with a surprising amount of enthusiasm.

"The very next day the woman was nowhere to be found. Her servants reported she had taken ill and had requested privacy while resting in her chambers. That night, however, she greeted me in fine health and high spirits, apologizing for her absence. She spoke passionately of sending the English back across the channel and of a lovely dream where we instead ruled them.

"Our conversation took a turn to religion and the supernatural as the night drew on. I thought she was daft at first or the wine had taken hold of her, as she preached of a power to rule them all right under our noses. I politely agreed, but felt uncomfortable with the heretical discussion and excused myself for the remainder of the night.

"The noblewoman appeared in my bedchambers so inconspicuously I was certain it was a dream. Her speech from earlier continued as if there were no pause while she stood over me. A bit frightened, yet intrigued by her ambition, I agreed we had much in common and should work together to make our dreams reality.

"I knew not what deal I made. Immediately her fangs at my throat took my life from me. The blood in my veins was replaced with the divine ichor flowing from her wrist. Over the next few nights my new life was explained to me. The woman had a plan that included my peasant friend back home. As noblewomen, our presence would draw much unwanted attention, but hers would go unnoticed until the time was right. She sent me to Jehanette under the shroud of night, impersonating the saints she prayed to.

"With the ability to easily influence a mortal's mind and new angelic features, along with clever costuming, I assumed the guise of a holy spirit. I explained the plan to infiltrate our military and how to strike a critical blow to the English. While dear Jehanette marched onward with the guidance of a 'divine spirit' behind her, I worked from the shadows to manipulate the minds of all she encountered, paving an easy road to victory.

"The noblewoman's plan unfolded flawlessly. I returned to her chateau bearing the good news. While I was away I received word that Jehanette had been captured. She had taken up her own crusade, believing the silence of the Holy Spirit was a sign of displeasure at her idleness. I immediately sought to rescue my friend, but was stopped by the woman. Jehanette had played her part, she explained. Her death would close the book on any suspicion of supernatural involvement that may lead an investigation back to us. I argued to save the life of my friend as she was worth more than a few military victories. My pleas were denied. Rumors were spread that Jehanette's divine guidance was nothing more than bouts of insanity, and the charges of witchcraft were dropped. I was witness to her burning at the stake and I felt every bit of her pain as if it were my own.

"Years later I was made wise to hidden truths behind the war. After the Black Death, when many kingdoms were weakened, high-ranking Archios were given land to watch over so as to prevent any further turmoil while humanity rebuilt from the ashes. The Archios controlled both England and France at the time of war. Those in charge endeavored to expand their territories by overruling the other, which caused the war.

"Feeling betrayed that I had based my trust on a lie, I confronted my master. She confessed both kingdoms had been under her control. To her, the war was an annoyance, as is the squabbling between her children to a mother. The deaths of my brothers, my closest friend, and countless others was at the hands of the very people I served blindly.

"There was little I could do, and I was not fool enough to directly defy the progenitor of our coven. Instead, I strived to rectify the injustice tainting the legacy of my good friend's name. Using the same methods I was taught that led her to death, I coerced the Church to reexamine her trial and under new evidence I produced, her honor was restored. Since last century she has been canonized as Saint Jeanne d'Arc, La Pucelle d'Orléans."

"Here's your pet," Noah said, bursting in on our conversation and dumping Lyle on the floor.

"Perfect timing," Vivi greeted them.

"Duh." Noah pulled my chair out from under me, sat in it himself, and threw his feet up on the desk.

"Slow down a second," Lyle said, looking at the three of us. "What's going on? Should I be running for my life or not?"

"No, dumbass," Noah sighed. "If I was going to kill you I would've just let you fall from one of those buildings on the way here."

Vivi smacked Noah's feet off the desk and presented Lyle with the briefcase. "There isn't much time left to waste. This contains a copy of everything I used to absolve you from your false charges. The memories of everyone involved have already been altered to reflect the alibi I created. You can walk back into work as a hero."

Lyle was wide-eyed and speechless as he flipped through the papers. It was like watching a kid on Christmas morning open a present he had been waiting all year for. "I don't know what to say. Why did you do all this?" he asked her.

"There's no reason for you to have been involved in our mess. You've been nothing but selfless, so it was only right for me to correct the mistakes made."

"It's just who I am. I don't know how I'm ever going to repay you."

"You could take a shower," Noah mocked, while checking out his own reflection in the mirror.

"Just live your life as you would have if we had never met," she told Lyle. "There is a limousine upstairs waiting to take you to a hotel outside the city limits for the night. By dawn tomorrow this will all be over."

"No," Lyle said, firmly placing the briefcase back on the desk. "I'm not leaving until it is. This is my home and I'm here to fight for it. You already saved my life twice. I could never just walk away after that."

"The conflict ahead is no place for —" Vivi started.

"A human? I've been getting that a lot lately, but I'm still here." Lyle stepped closer to her. "If you want me gone then you're going to have to make me, because I'm not going anywhere."

"That can be arranged, monsieur." Vivi's eyes began to glow as they locked with his. Before her hypnotic influence could take effect, Lyle closed his eyes and leaned in, pressing his lips to hers. The kiss continued for several seconds as I watched in astonishment.

"Gross." Noah raised an eyebrow and walked out of the room. "I'll be outside working if you wanna join me, Vivi."

Lyle flipped Noah the middle finger and continued his impassioned embrace with Vivi. She rested her hands upon his chest while he held her face.

"I think you've made your point, Monsieur Turner," she whispered to him after finally breaking away. "Your choice is yours to make."

For the first time since I had met her, her reserved professional behavior seemed to melt just a bit before she could collect herself again.

"Meet us upstairs and I will fill you in on what lies ahead," she said, picking up her *katana* on the way out. "You'll be needing the weapons in that briefcase."

"Don't forget I was the one who introduced you to her," I joked, and tried not to laugh at his grin.

"I love New York," he said, putting on the holsters and loading ammo into his new guns. "Even when it's bad, it's good."

"You know, she probably planned on that happening the whole time. I mean, she already had it all set up with the handguns and everything."

"Even better," he laughed on our way upstairs.

"Shall we, boys?" Vivi had a map of Manhattan rolled out on a table upstairs that she and Noah were inspecting. "The areas I've circled are where the highest concentration of infected are."

The Upper West Side, Upper East Side, Penn Station, and South Street Seaport were all highlighted.

"I'm not seeing a pattern," I said. "If my apartment was ground zero, then why didn't the plague just spread outward from there?"

"The Carpathians slipped into the city from the southern docks and traveled north through the sewers to your neighborhood. Once hospitals here were overwhelmed, patients were transferred west across Central Park. After you left the city, the Carpathians began infecting people at Penn Station, allowing the plague to spread by the subway systems."

"All these people dead because of me. Why didn't they just attack directly if they knew where I was?"

"The same reason we didn't," Vivi answered. "Nobody knew what you were capable of. Rushing in ran a high risk of failure. Don't be too hard on yourself; the Carpathians had been scheming to do something like this for quite some time whether you were involved or not."

"Let's just be glad the Archios were here to help," Lyle said. "How do we end this? I don't see it all going away by dawn."

"Luckily, the infection spreads through direct fluid contact and isn't an airborne disease. Sectioning off areas and eradicating the creatures isn't much of a problem, but we have to stop the source. We've closed down the docks and sent the Outsiders in through the sewers to flush out any remaining infected for disposal.

"It's the Carpathians that are the problem. We have reason to believe there is at least a small group hiding in the city that is helping the plague spread more each night. The plan is to clear out as many infected as we can in our own small groups to lure the Carpathians out of hiding. They are going to be somewhere around a high concentration of the plague. This was their focal point, and it would make sense that their hideout is near here. The Carpathians are also going to want to stay close to watch for Dorian's return."

"You think they're in his building?" Lyle asked.

"No, we've checked there already. There are three hospitals within a few blocks. If the Carpathians wanted to stay close enough to watch for you and continue propagating the outbreak, the hospitals would make the most sense.

"We'll split up to cover more ground. Noah and I will each take a facility, you and Dorian will take the third."

"Good thing we stayed, huh?" Lyle said as he patted me on the shoulder.

"We never said we were letting Dorian leave, we just weren't going to kill him," Vivi said.

"Right as I was starting to like you too," I frowned.

"It's nothing personal, dear. Business is business, no matter how unpleasant. I wish no harm to come to either of you."

"Aren't you going to get in trouble with Aurelia, returning without our heads on a platter?" I asked.

"I'm always in trouble with Aurelia," Noah shrugged.

"Our success in driving out the Carpathians will trump her other orders. She'll surely be displeased, but investing more time in tracking you down, assuming you're even still alive, wouldn't be worthwhile. As long as Monsieur Turner keeps our existence a secret, Aurelia will not concern herself over him. Her real interest was in Dorian for his potential to become a threat, but we will try and convince her otherwise should we need to."

"What if you just ran away?" Lyle suggested.

"She does not need to be in range to exact her mental dominance over others, especially her own progeny," Vivi explained. "As with all other Ancients, her power is something we could never hope to overcome. Aurelia's machinations may be unclear to many, but once you learn how to coexist things can be quite peaceful. It may not be a perfect afterlife, but I've come to accept it. The perks even make it entertaining at times."

"You're sugarcoating it again, Vivi. It's a prison of glass walls." Noah stood up, looking disgusted. "Why won't you ever just call it what it is? We're slaves."

Vivi stared down at the map for a moment, not wanting to acknowledge his outburst. "The Carpathian in charge is known by many names, but most recently goes by The Blighted One," she continued. "He made his presence known at the chateau when Rozalin was imprisoned. If he is defeated, the others will retreat."

"The hunchback dude in the bird mask? Vance told us about him, but isn't he an Ancient too?" Lyle asked.

"Yes," Vivi answered.

"But how are we supposed to kill one?" I didn't like where this was going.

"He may not even be here," she said. "Like most Ancients, he acts through others."

"You know he's here." Noah sounded increasingly fed up.

"There is a good chance he may be," she said in resignation.

"So, what, this is a suicide mission?" I was getting pretty agitated myself. "You aren't sparing me, you're using me again."

"Sucks being expendable, doesn't it? Better get used to it." Noah stormed out, leaving the rest of us bewildered.

"Am I missing something here? That was kinda dramatic, even for him." Lyle whispered to me after waiting to make sure he was gone.

"He's bitter because Aurelia tricked him into joining the Archios to protect her."

"I could think of a lot worse and most of it just happened to us this week."

"*Non*! You haven't a clue how cruel this life can be for some of us more than others. What you have experienced in a matter of days, we endure for centuries." Vivi was not pleased with us making light of Noah's anger. "Noah is a wild horse that refuses to be tamed and it only makes his situation worse. It is no secret that he refuses to serve on bended knee, but instead of crudely flaunting her power over the mind Aurelia has made a game out of his suffering."

"How did she do that?" Lyle asked.

"By breaking his heart."

"He has one of those?" Lyle was as surprised as I was when I learned more about Noah's past from Vivi the other night.

"Noah thought he and Aurelia were going to be together as lovers when she turned him," I recalled.

"There were others, three in fact. Understand I am telling you this in confidence and only because I cannot stand to hear these comments made of him.

"Once Noah learned the true intent behind Aurelia's interest in him he began to rebel. To avoid the embarrassment of having him cause a scene at her prestigious soirees she would send Noah into Paris to keep watch on the mortal families in charge of her many business ventures.

"Noah was soon distracted by a pretty young thing that happened to be the daughter of one of these mortals. He no longer minded the meaningless chore of going to Paris. Noah even snuck out quite often to court the girl and bring her gifts of jewelry taken from Aurelia's sizeable collection. They fell in love and Noah did his best to conceal his newfound joy.

"But nothing escapes Aurelia's nigh omniscience. She sent him to Paris planning for this very situation from the start and feigned ignorance to the missing baubles. When she felt it was time to end the game she ordered Noah to kill the girl. Aurelia claimed the girl's family was responsible for stealing from her and wanted to make an example out of their daughter.

"I was there when Noah confessed everything thinking that it would change Aurelia's mind. She smiled and revealed she knew all along. It was a harsh lesson in servitude. Noah offered to return the jewelry, never see his lover again, and serve without question if the girl could be spared. Aurelia rejected the offer, even when he bargained with his own life. He fought with everything he had in him to resist what came next. It was painful to watch as Aurelia took control of his mind and sent him to murder the young girl with his bare hands.

"He returned later that night, covered in her blood, and was never the same again. For years he mindlessly followed orders without so much as a glimmer of hope left in him."

"Why don't we just kill her?" My apathy toward taking a life was growing, but I felt it too easy to justify in this case. "I mean if we're actually able to take down one Ancient tonight, why not make it two?"

"She could end us both with a snap of her wrist," Vivi stated. "Conquering Aurelia is learning to make peace with her, not attack head-on. She is not our concern right now though.

"This city, your home, needs your help. Look at it any way you want, but only a fool goes into battle assuming victory is assured. Yes, it will be dangerous, but it isn't impossible. We may not need him dead so long as we can force a retreat. Our main goal is to stop the plague."

"We came to help because people need us, not because we thought it'd be easy," Lyle proclaimed.

"Whatever, I'm getting really pissed at still being a pawn on somebody's chessboard," I said, and walked out.

The limo was waiting for us in front of the station. Far-off sounds of police sirens mixed with the occasional gunshot and commotion of a skirmish somewhere on the streets.

"Your friend is throwing you under the bus in there." Noah stepped up next to me. "He wants to go with Vivi to play the knight in shining armor."

"Jealous the attention is off you for once?"

"I don't know what jealousy feels like. I just know I cause a lot of it," Noah retorted. "I thought you should know humans aren't any better. They're more annoying than anything."

"I'm happy to still consider myself one."

Noah laughed and sat on the roof of the limo. "You're about as human as this sword," he said, unsheathing Vivi's *katana* and looking at his reflection in the blade. "And just about as replaceable."

"Doesn't sound like you're any more valuable."

"Maybe to some, but the only thing that matters to me is my self-worth."

"Not if they're holding your leash."

"Sounds like you're finally starting to understand. You'll never be free unless you overcome your fear, and you can't overcome your fear until you believe you can be free."

"So how do you start? And if you know so much, why aren't you free?"

"Eliminate your weakness, then eliminate your obstacles," he said, and swung the *katana* through the air a few times before sheathing it again. "It takes patience."

"You're the last person I'd ever think would have patience." I wanted to mention I knew about his past, but Vivi had told me in confidence and bringing that up right now would probably start something that shouldn't be happening before marching off to battle.

" 'All warfare is based on deception.' " Noah showed me the tattoo on his forearm. "Deception is an art, one that's toppled the greatest empires, but it takes time. Desire is exploitable. Show your enemies what drives you and you've shown them how to stop you. Let them underestimate you, then strike."

"But then you become exactly what you hated in the first place —deceptive and manipulative."

"Now you're thinking," he said, and pointed to me like I had unveiled some big mystery. "When you're free, will you have the strength to walk away? Or will you become weak and hide behind others?"

This was the strangest conversation I'd had, with the exception of the one about my birth. Noah seemed so enlightened, like the martial arts masters he claimed to have trained with. Was this the real him? And if so, was he only revealing it now that we were potentially headed to our deaths?

"Is that why you let Vance go?" I asked. "Because you saw him in the same situation with Minerva as you are with Aurelia?"

"I don't kill for the sake of killing. I don't need to prove I'm good at what I do, believe it or not. I know I am, and that's what matters. Vance and I had an understanding. He showed remorse for what he put you through and was a victim of it himself. The world needs more people like that. Killing them would be counterproductive."

"Vivi said that about Lyle," I remembered.

"She's a different story. Vivi gave up the fight a long time ago and buried herself in denial. It's a shame. She taught me almost everything I needed to know after I was turned. I got her this sword as a present when I returned from Japan and showed her how to use it. You should have seen her face when she saw how big it was. She couldn't keep her hands off it. Before that she was only into fencing and savate," he scoffed.

"I think Vivi feels guilty or something for not being able to prevent this life for me. Now she thinks she can save people by helping them run from their problems instead, but that only creates more weakness. You need to conquer your problems or they'll catch up to you."

I realized that Noah had no idea Vivi hinted at her feelings of regret more than once to me. I thought about what she'd said — how Noah was pushing me to fail so I'd be dismissed. But they also admitted it was to see what I could do and prepare for a fight like the one ahead. Both of them seemed to constantly live out double lives and double meanings within those lives. The fact that they held on to any shred of right and wrong and hadn't just completely given up by now said a lot for them.

"Did you ever tell her it wasn't her fault?" I asked.

"No need to. Getting emotional never solved anything. She should know by now that I don't blame her." Noah flipped a small rock up off his boot, caught it, and pitched it into the police station window.

"What the hell?" I jumped back as the glass shattered. Vivi came out not a second later, with Lyle following.

"Oh, sorry. Hope I didn't interrupt anything." Noah's smirk returned.

"I was erasing evidence." Vivi glared and walked up to the limo. She was now wearing a short red dress.

"Evidence of *what?*" he teased.

"Shall I assume you discussed with Dorian what to expect should he run into the Carpathians again?" she asked.

"What more needs to be said besides that they're ugly and need to die?" He handed her the *katana*.

"You know by now that the Carpathians' bite causes incapacitating pain. You won't be able to move or concentrate to use your powers should they get their fangs in you, so watch each other's backs. It isn't as much of a concern for you, but their blood is poisonous, meaning we can't drink from it. Lastly, they have the ability to consume flesh and bone to heal themselves. Ancients like the Blighted One have been known to do this just by coming into contact with someone."

"Sounds great," I exclaimed sarcastically. "Glad I have something of an advantage, being able to push them away."

"You're going to need to do a lot more than push, even with the infected," Noah said. He disappeared for a second, returning with an empty soda can. "Remember crushing the glass at my place? Do it again."

I crumpled the aluminum can easily and dumped it back on the ground. "Good. I hope you've been practicing," he said.

"Not since that night."

Noah shook his head. "Target your enemy's head like it's the can and crush it," he instructed.

"I've been trying to do that by pushing them against the wall, but I'm not strong enough."

"Yeah, you are." Noah opened the car door for Vivi and then left for his objective without another word.

"What happens if we run into the big boss?" Lyle asked as we got in the limo with her.

"Focus on clearing out the infected. Anything with the parasite needs to die, whether or not it has turned yet. We can't risk a breach in containment. Don't engage the Carpathians if you can help it. Noah and I will come to you to confront them together."

"We should still be going in groups of two at least," Lyle argued and took her by the hand as we drove off. "Let Dorian and I go with you."

"It isn't up for debate, *chéri*, but your chivalry is appreciated as always."

I would have felt more comfortable going as a group too, but, for whatever reason, Vivi was firm in her decision. We arrived at the hospital in a few short minutes thanks to the empty roads and Vivi's police clearance.

"Once you're inside, head down to the maintenance area to turn the power back on. You'll draw attention, but at least you won't be in the dark," she advised Lyle and I as we got out on to the sidewalk. "*Bonne chance!*"

Chapter Nineteen

I hated hospitals. I mean I *really* hated hospitals. No amount of strategically cheerful wallpaper or watercolor paintings of flowers could ever mask what goes on within those walls. Every day people came in sick and dying and every day loved ones left heartbroken.

"Are you coming?" Lyle was already past the reception desk, waiting for me.

"It smells the same. I used to visit my dad at work and I always hated how it smelled."

"Are you gonna be all right?" he asked. "You heard what Vivi said. We need to watch each other's backs, and if you're distracted …"

"I'm fine," I answered, snapping back to reality.

A visitor's map adjacent to the desk showed us a layout of the building. This facility was much smaller than a standard hospital, probably used as an off-site lab or for additional rooms during a crisis. We only had two floors above us and the basement, making this seem much more feasible than it had at first. With the power out, none of the elevators or security doors were working, and the emergency backup had to have run out days ago. There wasn't any sign of trouble so far in the main foyer. A few chairs were knocked over and papers scattered, but nothing panic-worthy.

"Good news. We got a working flashlight." Lyle held up his treasure from behind the desk.

"We should just burn the place down," I suggested as we made our way down the stairs to maintenance.

"Jesus man, what's gotten into you lately? If we burn it down the city is losing a hospital that it badly needs. The fire would spread to the rest of the quarantined buildings and then out of the area, putting everyone in danger all over again. Why not just bomb the city by that point?"

"All right, it was a bad idea. I was trying to be creative."

Lyle led the way through the basement, light in one hand, gun in the other. Everything was completely normal down here, to the point of being suspicious. Still no trace of the infected anywhere.

"Stand back." Lyle kicked in the locked door to the electrical room.

The only other room in the basement was a storage room with medical supplies and extra beds and wheelchairs. No monsters under the bed here either.

"I know we say this a lot, but what the hell is going on?"

"We got played, that's what," Lyle said, opening the circuit breaker. "There's nothing here and Vivi knew it. We're on a fool's errand to keep us away from the real action."

"I'm used to it. Your new girlfriend is a complicated woman." I had hoped referring to her as his girlfriend would make him smile and ease his anxiety a bit.

"It's no good." Lyle got half the switches back on and stopped. "There's probably a short somewhere or the circuits are overloaded from all the machines coming on at once. Let's just get out of here."

I could see how distracted Lyle was by Vivi's scheme to keep us out of harm's way. I understood his frustration, but as much as I didn't like to admit it, I agreed with her reasons. Caring about people added a whole level of risk in this life. I debated bringing up that at least he was important enough for her to protect, but figured it would probably hurt his pride.

Emergency lighting was on upstairs, as well as the obnoxious blaring of the security system. If anything was festering in or around here, it would be on the lookout for us now.

"Where are you going?" I shouted over the alarm. Lyle was marching out of the vestibule.

"Seriously, man? What did we just talk about?"

"Lyle, we didn't even check the rest of the building. We need to finish what we came here to do."

"Weren't you the one who asked me about following orders or doing what I feel is right? If there's anything here we can come back for it."

"The Carpathians are looking for me to return. I'd rather be somewhere Noah and Vivi can find us. What if they come here and we're running around the streets?"

"Fine," Lyle begrudgingly agreed and walked right by me into the hospital.

"Do you know where you're going?" I asked and ran after him.

"Security office. If the alarms are working then the cameras probably are too. We can use them to scope out the other floors so there's no surprises."

The hall to reach security wasn't much of a change in ambience from the entrance. The lack of bodies told me they were already roaming elsewhere. The dim lighting from the emergency backup was almost worse than no light at all. Shadows moved about, playing tricks on our minds as we passed. No longer could I tell myself there wasn't anything to be afraid of or rationalize the unnatural like I had back in my apartment. The need for fear was very real.

Paranoia kept getting the best of me. I peeked in every room, hoping I'd see something before it saw me. The security alarm was impairing any ability we had to hear danger coming.

I fell behind from checking rooms and had to jog to catch up with Lyle. I called out for him to wait up, but over the alarm it was no use. My foot slipped on a wet patch of blood. I caught myself with my powers, but Lyle was so set on reaching the office he didn't notice. It was strange how this was the only area in the hallway with blood like this, like it had just dropped straight down.

I soon wished I hadn't thought of that. My first reaction was to look up and I knew I wouldn't like what I'd find. Several of the ceiling tiles were missing, creating an entry for the perfect hiding place.

I caught sight of a face watching from under a desk in the room next to me. I shouted and raced to get Lyle. Of course he didn't hear me until I was on top of him. I grabbed his arm to get his attention. He responded by shoving his gun in my face.

"Don't sneak up on me like that!" he exclaimed. "I almost shot you!"

"They're in the ceiling." I pointed to where I had fallen. "And there's somebody in that room."

We waited to see if anyone would come chasing us, but nothing happened. "It was probably a dead body," Lyle said.

"I'm telling you, someone is in there. They were watching me."

Carefully, we approached the room. Lyle had his gun ready for whatever was about to jump out and I kept an eye on the ceiling, waiting to be ambushed.

"Look." Lyle tapped me and motioned under the desk.

A pair of tiny feet was sticking out in plain view. Lyle and I entered the room cautiously with our backs to the wall as we made our way around the desk. The little feet belonged to an equally little girl. She was around kindergarten age and dressed in a dirty hospital gown for kids.

"Hi there." Lyle put his gun away and crouched down to her level. "What's your name?" She didn't respond. Her big brown eyes darted between the two of us nervously.

"I'm Lyle and this is my friend Dorian. I'm a police officer." He took out his badge to show her. She snatched it from his hand and inspected it. "I'll let you hold on to that if you can tell me why you're here."

She still wasn't answering. Lyle carefully got closer and checked the hospital bracelet around her wrist.

"Emilia?" He read out loud. "Is that your name?"

Emilia wouldn't open up to us at all, but I had a pretty good feeling Lyle wasn't getting his badge back.

"Emilia, we have to get you someplace safe," Lyle told her and held out his hand. She scrunched herself back as far under the desk as she could. I looked around as Lyle continued trying to get Emilia to warm up to him. The room was an office very similar to my father's at his hospital. The decor was all different, but the layout was the same. Maybe there was some generic standard hospitals used that I didn't know about.

From the door there was a wall with a bookcase to the right. To the left was the same kind of metal filing cabinet where my dad used to keep toys in the bottom drawer for me to play with when I was little. The couch and two chairs opposite the desk were different here. I remembered taking naps on the leather couch and coloring at his desk while he was with a patient.

I looked at myself in the shattered glass of the door. I could almost see a young version of me sitting at the desk over my shoulder. In middle school I liked doing homework at my dad's desk as if it was important paperwork.

"Dorian, Emilia and I are ready to leave now." Lyle held the little girl in his arms. She was still clutching his badge and had managed to charm his flashlight from him too.

"Okay," I said and moved out of the way, letting them go first. I paused to take another look at the room, imagining myself sitting at that desk.

"Dorian? You coming?" Lyle asked impatiently.

"Sorry, yeah," I apologized, but could feel a smile on my face.

A creaking from the floor above stopped me. I stood there, letting my curiosity get the best of me again as I watched the ceiling bow. I took a step back right in time for the tiles above to collapse. One of the Carpathians crashed down from the hole, smashing the desk in half under its feet.

My focus stayed on the demolished piece of furniture. It made my heart race and my hands tremble. The smile from the happy memories it brought disappeared. Lyle was shouting something behind me, but it was drowned out by the girl's screams and the alarm in the hallway. All the noises mixed together until it was a single piercing tone in my head.

My attention shifted to the winged monster before me and an uncontrollable feeling of rage burst forth. I wasn't entirely sure I was the one in control as the Carpathian floated there. The anger boiled over to such a point that I began feeling nothing at all. Its body thrashed in the air, slamming into the walls and ceiling like a helpless ragdoll as I watched.

I couldn't hear that piercing tone in my head anymore. There was only silence now. The Carpathian continued to tumble through the room until a wall finally gave way sending it into the next office.

It wasn't Noah who took my family from me, I thought. *It wasn't Rozalin or Vance. It was you. All of you.*

I must have blacked out. I was suddenly in the next room over watching the murderer's lifeless body still being tossed against the walls, but I didn't remember moving there. Everything was hazy like I was in a dream. The creature started turning to ash in front of me. Time lurched forward and the black outs became more frequent as the scene continued.

You ruined everything. I hate you. All of you.

A heavy odor of sulfur followed by my own body beginning to shake brought the piercing noise back. As I started to regain my senses I saw the Carpathian was no more. All that was left were piles of ash scattered about the room.

"Dorian! Dorian!" Lyle was shoving me. "What is wrong with you?"

His gun was out and I could smell the residue from it having just been fired.

"It was wrecking my dad's office, so I stopped it," I told him and lowered myself to the ground. I couldn't remember at what point I started flying.

"What are you talking about? You never told me your father worked in New York." He sounded angry, but I didn't understand why.

"He doesn't. He works here in Boston."

"Dorian, we're in New York. What is going on? First you go overboard killing that thing, now you think we're in Boston? You're losing it, man."

He picked up Emilia, who was crying in the doorway, and headed down the hall. I followed them, trying to remember what I had done, but the scene was already fading from my memory.

"Uh, Lyle," I said keeping up with him this time.

"What?"

"The girl is infected."

Emilia's left arm, which she had been hiding under the desk, was covered in black veins. "I told you that back in the office," he said as he stopped and turned to me. "I said she isn't bitten so she might still have a chance."

"Then why didn't my parents? It didn't take you long to put them down."

"Oh no, don't even think about putting that on me. They had already turned by the time you were in your room. I did what I had to so you wouldn't have to." He started walking away again with Emilia. "I'm taking her to the police."

"She'll infect everyone. You heard what Vivi said."

"What do you want me to do, Dorian? Kill a little kid?" he yelled. "I'm taking her, so unless you're going to kill me too just stay here in case the others show up."

"So you're just leaving me here to die instead? I've already lost everything once and you have no idea what that feels like!" I shouted after him. "You're going to walk away from me and all of this when it's over, smelling like a rose, and never having to look back!"

"It's pretty clear you can take care of yourself. I don't know what's gotten into you since we came here, but you're falling apart when we need you most."

Lyle left me standing in the reception area and carried the child with him. He wouldn't be coming back for me.

A banging sound was coming from upstairs. We never got to the security office, but what did it really matter? I was used to surprises and wasn't in the mood to be rational.

The stairs had a trail of blood that ended abruptly on the bottom step. People must have been trying to escape and were dragged back up before they reached the reception area.

The path split off in three directions from the top of the stairs. According to the visitor's map, the hospital was one big square with a hallway down the middle that had elevators.

The nurse's station to my right was a mess of scattered patient files, medical supplies and an overturned food cart. I still hadn't found any bodies. It gave me hope that everyone escaped safely, but remembering what Vivi said about the Carpathians cannibalistic habits gave me doubt. There was also a chance that the patients and staff had been infected and were now wandering the streets for fresh victims.

Plenty of patient rooms lined this hall, and all of them had their doors open. The very first one I approached was torn off its hinges. The body of a male orderly was sprawled out on the floor. I checked the ceiling for any sign of tampering, but it hadn't been touched.

The next room was a bit more interesting. The bodies of a nurse and two orderlies facedown in their own entrails surrounded a man in a straitjacket. The bound man's face was contorted and set in rigor mortis. His legs looked dislocated, possibly from an encounter with the hospital staff, but most important was the black liquid staining his mouth and jacket. I did as Noah instructed, crushing the skull like the can of soda with my mind so he couldn't come back. My stomach turned and I had to turn away to keep from throwing up.

Something was moving in a room across the hall.

Finally. I was sick of the anticipation of waiting for someone or something to jump out at me.

A man was fully restrained by the arms and legs to his bed. His eyes were the same as mine when I used my powers and in between deafening tones from the siren I could hear his death rattle. The infected man was fighting to break free and gnashing his teeth at the air. I ended his misery and left to find another victim.

I was almost at the end of the corridor now, with only two rooms left. Both doors were closed and there was only a very thin window to see through one of them. Barely any light reached the inside of the room, but through the crack I could make out a floating figure.

The door was locked, but if it meant one of the Carpathians was inside I definitely wanted in. I tried concentrating on pushing the door in, but it was heavily reinforced. I could look for a key, but finding one in the dark amongst the mess would take all night. My only other option would be to go out the window next door and fly in from there.

I went into the other room, but a metal grating I hadn't noticed covered the window. The rest of the rooms I checked were all the same. Out the window was a courtyard below. No bodies that I could see, just plants and benches fenced in. Security floodlights lit the square space pretty well. I was about to move on when something moved by one of the bushes. Something darted out away from the light and entered the building. The infected only moved that fast when chasing someone and the Carpathians usually flew, so who could that be?

The metal grating was fastened too tight for me to pull it off using my powers. If I was able to do something as delicate as mentally lift a wallet from someone's pocket then I should be able to loosen a few screws. I noticed there was a fingernail stuck under the first screw. Apparently I hadn't been the only one who came up with this idea. It took a while, longer than it should have, but I was able to unscrew the window guard with my mind.

There wasn't a ledge to stand on and the drop was a good forty feet. Unless the patient here could fly, he wouldn't have survived that fall, but maybe he believed he could.

I moved through the air to the locked room's window. Someone was in there, all right. Whoever it was had hanged himself with his own clothes, which made it look like he was floating in the dark. Poor guy must have witnessed what was going on outside his door and tried to spare himself from suffering.

The body began to spasm as it reanimated. I had a clear view so I didn't need to go through the trouble of getting inside. I only needed to hold out my hand and focus until the body hung limp again.

Sounds of more movement came from underneath me. Another figure ran around the shadowed area of the courtyard and into the first floor. Whoever this was had to have seen me. If they were running, they were most likely not friendly.

I glided down over the fence and onto the grass of the courtyard. Like the entrance, this place was relatively untouched. The pavement past the gate was another story. Children's drawings done with sidewalk chalk were partially covered over in blood. A few playground toys were strewn about. A female nurse's body dressed in what had been cheerfully-colored scrubs lay on the ground.

My shoes stuck to the floor upon reentering the building. Of course it was blood, but worse was the black fluid of the parasite that had leaked out of its hosts. I wasn't given long to inspect the other corpses around me. The power went out again and along with it came a deafening silence after listening to the siren for so long. If somebody was in here waiting for me, the squishing sound of my shoes on the tile would certainly give me away.

I guess this must be what it's like to be six feet tall, I thought as I floated over the sticky mess, remembering the modeling agent's criticism.

The moonlight from the courtyard windows let me see a short way in front of me. The walls were decorated in bright colors with animated characters pointing out messages on bulletin boards. Each room had smaller-scale hospital beds than the floor above and crayon drawings taped to the doors.

I floated by a common area with child-sized chairs and tables. A television knocked down in the chaos was lying at someone's feet. It was a doctor, judging by his white lab coat. He hadn't heard me come up behind him and was standing facing a blank wall. This was the only person I'd seen in this hall so far; maybe he'd stayed back to help others escape.

I knew he was one of the infected, but something inside me wished he wasn't. If I was correct, he was a doctor and a hero. I gave him gentle push. He jolted to life and turned toward me. I was a bit surprised when I saw what he looked like. The doctor was skeletal, rather than mutated like the others. His gait was painfully slow and the noises coming from him now were hardly audible. Vance had said the parasite sapped the life from its victims and forced them to feed constantly. Was this doctor's will to save others so great that he resisted the urge to consume his staff and patients, turning him into this brittle husk?

It didn't seem right ending him with violence after his noble struggle. He was no threat to anyone like this.

"I'll be right back," I told him and floated down the hall in search of his office. If I placed him in there then at least he could pass away peacefully without harm to anyone.

Just beyond the nurse's station was a door with a nameplate inscribed *Dr. Frank Benoit, MD.*

No. This can't be real. How is this possible? He's never been here before. Why am I seeing this?

I went inside and closed the door behind me. It took a second for my eyes to adjust to the lights, but everything was exactly how I remembered it. I sat at the desk a moment to relax and played with the tape that had held the chair arm together since

I was in eighth grade. You'd think my dad would be able to afford a new chair on his salary.

There was an unfamiliar sound of running water from across the room. I went over by the couch and saw a small fish tank in the corner. Dad was always commenting on how he wanted one for his office, but it took him a while to get around to things like that.

The fish were odd; I was expecting something more tropical, but these were dark and alien. Looking at them reminded me of the vision I had of the Rift during Vance's ritual. They were so much bigger then. I had felt so helpless floating among them before, but now things were different.

A clang of metal out in the hall stopped my gawking. The lights went out in the office as I carefully opened the door.

"Dad?" I yelled into the hallway and floated down to where I had left him.

"What is that?" someone shouted from the direction of the play area.

I arrived to find a lanky teenage boy holding a *katana* that probably weighed more than him and a girl with bright blue hair standing over my father's decapitated body. These two must have been the ones I saw running through the courtyard.

"Oh great, they fly now too," the boy said, and held his sword up to me.

"What did you do?" I asked, looking down at the body in anger.

"You can talk?" The girl sounded shocked.

I glared at them, feeling the same rage as when the Carpathians ambushed us. Their bodies flew backward down the corridor and smashed into a wall at the end. I dashed after them, keeping them pinned. I couldn't let them leave, not after they had seen me and not after what they had done.

"We're not getting paid enough for this," the boy said to his friend, who promptly shushed him.

"Paid?" I asked, noticing the boy's fangs. "What are you getting paid for?" Were these the ones sent by the Carpathians to infect my parents?

"Killing your stupid mutant pets for easy money, that's what." The boy was wearing black skinny jeans and a hoodie with a skeleton design on it. He had long black hair covering his eyes and a lip ring like I'd seen emo and punk kids wear.

"Are you kidding? I didn't do this."

"You sure look like one of them and you called that one 'dad.' What the hell are you, anyway?"

That question caught me off guard. I was a person, what else would I be? A flying, telekinetic person with black and gray eyes, covered in blood.

"Don't worry about it," I said. "Who's paying you to kill? Are you Outsiders?" Picturing these two kids as contract killers was a stretch.

"We take offense to that," the girl spoke. "We're mercenaries. Fangs for hire."

"If these mutants aren't yours then you better not be here to move in on our contract. That money is ours!" the boy complained.

"I'm not here for money and you're not really in any position to make threats."

"Oh yeah? Well, we killed your dad!" The boy jeered and bared his fangs, trying to act tough.

"Shut up!" His friend tried again to silence him.

I thought about it for a moment. Had I really called that infected doctor back there dad? Lyle was right; I was losing my mind. These visions weren't like Rozalin's illusions. They were memories and emotions I had been holding in.

"No you didn't," I said. "I made a mistake."

"How do you mistake something like that?" he asked.

There was a sharp pain in my shoulder and I felt blood trickle down my arm. Another boy ran out from behind me to his two friends, leaving a knife in me. I winced in pain as I pulled it out.

"Should we kill him?" the girl asked. The attack had caused me to lose my hold on her and the boy. The stab wound sealed up immediately after I took the knife out.

"Fuck that! He's a whole different kind of weirdo that we're not being paid to deal with," the first boy said, watching me regenerate.

I was still stunned from the pain and finding it hard to concentrate. "Where were you?" I heard the girl ask as they ran away.

"Recon," the new boy replied. "I may have accidentally stumbled on one of those Carpathian uglies upstairs, so it might be coming for us."

I collected myself in enough time to stop the three of them from getting any further. Grabbing their legs from down the hall, I dragged them back. Meeting them halfway, I passed the office I had been in. It didn't look anything like it had before. I let the Outsiders go as I looked inside the office in bewilderment.

There was a desk and chair, a completely different style than what I had seen, but other than that nothing was the same. No fish tank or bookshelves, no couch or coat rack. It looked more like a meeting room with chairs set up in a circle by the desk. Had I imagined all of that? There wasn't even a name on the door, just the number 103.

I felt lost and confused, but didn't have time to deal with it. I heard the trio scramble down the hall, screaming at what I thought was me. A much larger Carpathian was flying through the corridor. I sidestepped into the meeting room right as it passed. The aggression I had had this whole time was gone now and replaced with a feeling of sadness. Still, I knew I would have to fight my way out of here.

The Carpathian was coming back my way. It seemed like there was a tradeoff between my conscious human emotions and the more detached, savage side. I just couldn't muster the same violence necessary to defend myself when my head was swirling with fear and doubt.

Claws out, the flying bloodsucker attempted to tackle me head-on. I placed my hands out in front of me to throw it back, but the best I got was enough force to send it off balance.

This was frustrating. I knew I could do better. Even if I could only tap into half of the monstrous side that scared Lyle off, I'd be good to go. The Carpathian walked toward me, scraping its claws against the wall and causing a horrible screech. I tried knocking it back again, but barely shoved it off its feet. It was dangerously close now and swiped at me, grazing my cheek as I leaped back.

The claws on its hands grew longer and spikes jutted out of the skin covering each arm. The Carpathian rushed after me like a bull and caught me before I could dodge again. I tumbled a few yards until a radiator stopped me. Were Noah and Vivi ever going to get here?

If I had known my powers were going to fail I would have taken that kid's *katana*. When it came close enough to try and grab me, I crawled under the its legs. The knife the other guy had stabbed me with should still be where I left it. I made a break for it, but couldn't outrun the monster. A sharp claw cut my arm to the bone. I screamed and rolled on the floor in agony. The Carpathian picked me up by the waist in one hand, curiously observing the gash seal itself.

The knife was on the floor close to us. I reached out, summoned it to my hand, and plunged it down into the monster's skull. It hissed and grabbed my arm, breaking it in half. The pain was too much. I thought I'd pass out, but my recoil triggered a glimmer of the power I wanted and sent us both flying into opposite walls.

I sat up, whimpering and rocking back and forth while my arm healed. The Carpathian wasn't turning to ash. I'd have to finish it. I crawled to retrieve the knife, but the monster was conscious again. It pulled the knife from my hand and snapped it in two. That rage was starting to build. One wide-eyed glare sent the disgusting animal through the ceiling. I floated myself to avoid putting pressure on my bad arm when getting up.

The Carpathian jumped down from the hole. Its wings were cut badly by whatever caught it on the way up. I put my hand out and yanked on one of the wings until it ripped off. A terrifying roar and glower from the bloodsucker shook me to the core.

My playmate turned its back on me and retreated to the kids' common area. There was still a piece of the knife on the ground for me to use. I couldn't see what it was doing until I got close; it was eating the carcass of the doctor to heal itself. Wings, skull, and all recovered as if nothing was ever wrong. Before it finished eating, I shot the piece of knife into the monster's heart, wedging it in deep. The large body of the monster collapsed.

I levitated over it, feeling the same detachment as before creeping up on me. This wretched creature deserved everything it had coming to it after what it had done to all these people. I flipped it over, preparing to watch its face as I broke it apart piece by piece, but saw my reflection in the broken TV screen next to it.

Emilia hadn't cried because she was scared of the Carpathian. She had cried because she was scared of me. This was what caused Lyle to leave without me. Even those three Outsiders ran in spite of us all being here for the same reason. The monster in this hospital was me.

I gave the Carpathian a quick death instead of letting my hatred take over. There was nothing left to do here now. If those three mercenaries wanted this place to themselves they could have it. I had to find Lyle and apologize.

There was a pungent smell out on the sidewalk when I exited the facility.

"They finally got to you too."

I whirled around at the voice of an old man I hadn't noticed standing there. His body odor was worse than anything I had encountered in the hospital.

"Excuse me?" I asked, not sure if I was more surprised or nauseated.

"Don't remember me, do you? I warned you they were after you, but nobody listens to me! Maybe that's what keeps me safe, helps to keep my head down."

The old man started to hobble away pushing a shopping cart full of garbage ahead of him. "Wait a minute." I stopped him. "You were on the subway."

"I've been on lots o' subways. But you're one of them now so I don't got much to say to ya. They got their fangs in ya," he laughed, wiggling his filthy long fingernails in my face. "It's gonna take them some time to clean up that mess you left in there, but don't you worry, not a drop of blood will be left!"

I squinted at him and watched his mouth as he talked, trying to ignore all the other vile distractions. Sure enough, they were there. "You have fangs. You're one of them."

He closed his lips tight, playing dumb.

"Hey, gramps." A voice called from the alley that led to the back of the hospital. "We finished the contract. Let's go cash in."

It was the kid with the *katana* and his two friends. They froze when they saw me. "That's okay kiddies, he won't bite," the unkempt man cackled.

"You know them? You knew people were after me that day on the subway and didn't tell me?" I asked.

"Sure I did. You just didn't listen, just like I said you wouldn't."

"Because you're — you're —" I couldn't think of any way not to sound offensive.

"Dirty? Crazy? Scary? A monster?" He was having too much fun filling in the blanks, but he was right. He really did warn me, and just like the other passengers I ignored him because he was so different.

"How did you know people were after me?"

"These old ears hear many things. It's easy when you're invisible to everyone around you. The more they pretend I'm not here, the more I can listen!"

"You're not that invisible if you're friends with the Archios."

"Friends?" The old hobo laughed himself into such a deep cough I was scared he'd throw up something on me. "You think someone like me would be friends with those pretty little dolls? No, old Grampy pulls his own strings, thank you very much. I can't say I don't like their money though!"

He lost himself in another fit of laughter and pulled out a beaten-up coffee tin packed full of hundred-dollar bills. One of the sacks in his shopping cart was full of these coffee cans.

"You better get moving if you want to catch up with your new friends. They're over by the park west of here."

"How do you know? Forget it. You mean Central Park?" Something in the shopping cart starting moving around. "What was that?" I tried looking in between the holes.

A face popped out and scared me half to death. It was Emilia, but if she was here, what had happened to Lyle?

"What did you do with my friend?" I shouted, ready to attack him.

"I took this little one off his hands so he could join his lady."

"Lyle would never just hand over a child to a stranger like that," I argued.

"He didn't have a choice!" the man laughed again. I was ready to lunge at him, but he put his hands up. "I don't mean like that. I simply put his mind at ease. She's safe with me."

"I don't take you for the loving, fatherly type. But let me guess, looks can be deceiving?"

"And what would you have done with her? She's got the affliction. Nothing no human could ever fix. I bet you and your Archios buddies would just kill 'er, no?"

I couldn't dispute that. He was right that she would have wound up dead one way or another.

"There's no cure, but we ain't affected like human folk."

"I thought the infected blood was still poisonous to your kind?"

"Those Archios just don't want to get their pretty bitty fangs dirty. We don't get sustenance from it — doesn't stop us from turning people. Grampy doesn't mind a little puke if it means saving this darling's life."

There wasn't anything he just said that didn't make me want to dry heave.

"Gramps, we still have one more contract left we can get done before sunrise if we leave now," the blue-haired girl said, still hanging back in the alley.

"We're goin', we're goin'," he told her.

"Why don't you come with me?" I offered. "I'm sure the Archios will pay you more than what you're making on just mutants."

The eccentric old coot cackled some more and set off down the sidewalk with the others. "There ain't no profit if yer too dead to collect it, my boy!"

Chapter Twenty

I could hear hellish snarls and rattling noises from the infected up ahead, so I had to be going the right way. Flying rooftop to rooftop was definitely breaking the supernatural code of secrecy, but I was sure anyone still in the quarantine area had worse things to worry about.

Central Park was close and so were the sounds of gunfire. Lyle was across the street, fending off a throng of the infected from atop a building. Vivi was down below, slicing through the horde in an elegant bladed dance.

The infected weren't the main problem, however. Carpathians had joined the fun and it looked like they were giving everyone trouble. They were still unarmored, but their bodies had a thick bony carapace covering vital spots and dreadful claws and spikes lined their appendages, like the one I had encountered earlier.

There were only a handful of the menacing winged bloodsuckers compared to the droves of infected mutants, but any time one of them sustained reasonable damage, they would feast on their pets to repair themselves. They were smart about it, too — attacking in packs alongside the infected and then pulling back to heal while another group took their place.

"*Assistance, s'il vous plaît!*" Vivi shouted from the riot. She had just smacked the lower jaw clear off of a Carpathian trying to bite her and didn't have much room to move among the crowd, let alone swing a sword. I flew in fast to join them, but not fast enough. Two Carpathians assisted by about ten to fifteen mutants were trying to whittle Vivi down. The distraction caused by the infected gave the Carpathians the opening they needed to counter her *katana* with their claws and slash into her midsection.

Noah dove in, stabbing his blades into the Carpathians. He threw Vivi over his shoulder and zipped up to Lyle before anyone could stop him.

"Where's my kiss?" Noah asked with a cocky smile after placing Vivi on her feet. "Nice of you to show up," he said to me as I landed, ignoring Vivi's disapproving look. "What, were you taking a nap or something?"

"You told me to wait until you came for me, so I did."

Lyle was looking at me uneasily.

"I thought it'd be obvious by now not to do what you're told," Noah said and turned to Vivi. "You need blood."

"*Non*, I'm fine."

The damage didn't look too bad, not for one of them anyway.

"Here, drink from your human." Noah picked Lyle up by the shirt collar and presented him.

"Noah, you know I hate being coddled, especially by you. It is almost as if there were something other than vanity in that head of yours."

"Drink or I'll stab him and force-feed you," he threatened. She reluctantly obliged and smiled at Lyle.

"I won't take much at all," she reassured him.

I tried to be polite and not watch, but the curiosity was too tempting. Lyle seemed to be enjoying himself by the sound of his moans. His arms were wrapped around her, and he held the back of her head while she sucked on his neck.

"Gross." Noah turned away in disgust. "I hate when my food tries to grope me." He jumped to the street, leaving Vivi to recover. "You stay here and guard them." Noah pointed up at me. "More are coming. I'll hold them off."

The infected were gathering in a circle surrounding the building. A figure in a wide-brimmed hat with a long coat and walking stick stood out from the crowd. The Blighted One had made his way here after all. I glided down into the mosh pit to join Noah.

"Now you decide to not do as you're told?" Noah said to me while keeping his eyes on the plague doctor. "Take your friend and get out of here, kid."

"No, please stay." The Blighted One spoke with a harsh Slavic accent from behind his beak-like mask of bone. "I wish to take a closer look at my work."

"I'm gonna enjoy turning you inside out!" I went to push past Noah, but he blocked me with his shoulder.

"You really don't want to be doing this right now," Noah warned.

"Oh, but I think he does. It's ingrained in his very being. He can't help himself. Such a shame the Strigoi managed to pervert my gift to you, or you would be standing with me like everyone else before you."

"You're a depraved psychopath. You've killed thousands of people, including my parents! What makes you think I'd even consider joining you? There is seriously no one I hate more than you."

"Parents? Kill? You are sorrowfully confused and your illusion of humanity is misplaced. You are no more human than any other automata conjured up by the Strigoi in the past. You were meant for one purpose and one purpose only, and that is to cause destruction. You should be thankful I gave you the power you lacked."

"I've heard this all before, and I don't care what you say. Whatever I am, I still loved my parents and nothing is going to change what you've done."

"What have I done? I have been working to forge a new world left over from the broken remnants of the past when our kind once walked free. A world where those with power rule and do not hide away from the persecution caused by weaker, lesser creatures just because they are the majority. If the mortals wish to fear us, then I will truly give them something to fear! Those I have blessed with my gift will rend mankind limb from limb until they submit to our authority."

"You sound just as insane as Minerva before we sent her packing to Hell."

"The Strigoi witch sought to bring chaos and war to the world. Where she ignorantly squandered her gift from our Dark Master, I wish to use mine to rebalance the injustice. The Archios may be satisfied hiding behind mortals, but I will not be condemned by their ignorance any longer."

"Someone's pulling your strings too then, eh?" Noah gestured in disgust. "Figures. I didn't believe all the Carpathians combined could have come up with a plan half as successful as this."

"Let's see how smug you are after my parasite melts away that false beauty. Never a greater boon could have been bestowed upon me. Our kind may have forgotten their infernal roots, but I knew one day that those who created us would return to tip the scales in our favor again. It was only a matter of time, and what is time to an immortal?"

"You really are stupid." I spoke up in spite of my own safety. "The only reason a demon gave you anything is because it probably sees how desperate you are. You're being used. Once we kill you, you're gonna get dragged down to Hell to suffer just like Minerva."

"Poor simulacrum. Don't you see? There will be no distinction between this realm and Hell. The Dark Master presented me with the parasitic entity from another dimension, one I could not reach on my own. As a representative of the Carpathians I was the perfect choice to use it by infecting the mortal population. These sorry creatures can no longer think for themselves, let alone pray to the Heavens for salvation. Without mankind's prayers the Gates of Hell will open and merge both realms unhindered.

"Minerva may have failed her task of creating suitable vessels for our masters, but I will not fail mine. I know there are others out there like you, untouched and ready for possession. When I find them ..."

He was interrupted by his own heinous laughter behind the mask.

"Maybe if you weren't such a monster in the first place you wouldn't have to hide and cry for help from a demon." I said. Anger was welling up inside of me, but I couldn't let myself slip away into that uncontrollable state like in the hospital. I had to stay level headed or I wouldn't have a chance at stopping this madman.

"Monster? You have slain countless numbers of my brood purely for being different than you. You wallow in destruction and spread hatred where I have tried to herald peace and order.

"Why do you fight against your own liberation? We all deserve to be free of humanity's oppression! They should kneel to us as kings! If you will not stand aside then we will destroy you and what remains of the Archios so we may take control of the humans again. They will hide in the shadows from us, as it should be!

"If you wish to see a monster then I will show you one. Your campaign against us ends here!"

One of the infected in the ring twitched to move toward us. Noah swung out in response, slicing it into four faster than my eyes could see. The entire horde converged on us now. The Blighted Maniac was lost in the crowd, but we could hear his laughter among the shrieks and growls.

"Be on guard. These are some of the Ancient's progeny and are far stronger than the rest." Vivian rejoined us, leaping down from above with Lyle.

A relentless sea of corrupted flesh overtook us. These mutated infected were tougher than any we had dealt with before. Even some of the Carpathians weren't this vicious. Their scythe-like appendages continuously stabbed at the four of us from all sides, making any sort of defense difficult. Noah vanished for a split second, slicing through the bodies of the infected in a spiral outward. He was buying us some room, but once one wave fell another climbed over to replace it. I had already been cut several times when I realized this may be the last time I'll have a chance to apologize to Lyle.

"In case we don't make it out of this alive, I wanted to say I'm sorry for what happened back at the hospital."

"It's fine, man. I should've never left you behind; we're like family after all the shit we've been through. I know you've been through more than any of us, but just try to hang in there."

Family. That word struck a chord. I knew my parents weren't biologically mine for years, but that didn't change how much we loved each other. Whether I was their blood or not, it didn't matter to any of us. We were still a family. Maybe I'm not doomed to be alone because of who, or what, I am. There are still good people out there who will accept the true me. Acting out in hate, fear, and anger is what will really turn me into a monster.

One of the infected's bony protrusions lodged itself in Lyle's thigh. Vivi fought to cover him while he pulled out the bone, but one managed to slip by her. It used the hooked tip of its arm to pry open Lyle's mouth while forcibly trying to vomit black fluid down his throat to infect him.

"Get away from him!" I roared. I put my hands out, smashing the infected around Lyle to pieces. He looked frightened for a moment then gave me a thumbs-up.

Noah's rampage against the Carpathians came to an abrupt stop. One of them caught him by the arm, sinking its fangs into his bicep. His face was immediately stricken with blinding pain and he was unable to move. He stood powerless against the bite, struggling merely to stay on his feet. The Carpathian gored his arm with its teeth to further open the wound until blood came spurting out everywhere.

Another of the Carpathians joined in, violently grabbing Noah by the hair and jerking his head back. Noah stayed strong, refusing to let out even the slightest scream as this one tore into his neck. Both Carpathians proceeded to gorge themselves on his blood like oversized ticks.

The first of them pried Noah's *wakizashi* from his fingers and drove it through his shoulder and twisted it in sadistically. They seemed challenged by the fact that he wouldn't cry out in agony or fall to his knees. The second one held on tightly to Noah's hair, digging into his scalp with its claws. It would occasionally pull his head back further and savagely rip a bigger gash in his neck with its fangs like an animal.

"Lyle, Noah's not looking too good," I said, fighting off a wounded Carpathian that was trying to eat one of the infected mutants for health.

"Neither are we!" he yelled as he tossed an empty gun away.

Now a third Carpathian joined in. This one looked roughly female because of its slender figure and small breasts. She flew down and straddled Noah's torso, cracking his ribs between her thighs. His incredible resolve began to waver as his knees buckled. Even he had a breaking point and the Carpathians were having fun finding it. The latest assailant dug her claws into his chest and raked them across, causing deep rivers of blood to run down his body. She licked the blood from her hands.

Still gripping him between her legs, she went in for the kill.

The female bit into his chest and began to drink from directly above his heart. All three Carpathians finally started overcoming Noah's determination and forced him down, but still he fought. His expression was filled with anguish as they continued to revel in his torment. How he ever held out this long against their torture was no small feat, but the life in his eyes was fading fast. Now semi-conscious, Noah was kneeling in a pool of his own blood as they finished him off.

"Do something before they tear him apart!" Vivi screamed from further up the street. This was the first time I had seen actual fear in her eyes. Every time she got closer to him she was intercepted by another swarm of Carpathians trying to keep them separated. A fourth dinner guest had just flown down to join the feeding frenzy around Noah.

I could be rid of him right here, both of them, and never have to worry about either one coming after me. How can I trust that they'd keep their word to let me go when this is over anyway? Even if they tried, they admitted they could never defy Aurelia. In the end it's either them or me ...

"Dorian, go." Lyle unloaded another clip into the head of a Carpathian he had staked through the heart with his knife. I could tell from the exhaustion in his face that he was running out of steam after fighting all night. If I went to help I would be leaving Lyle alone and chance losing the one person I knew I could trust.

The fourth one had its fangs in Noah's wrist, drinking out what was left of his blood with the others. It wasn't easy witnessing his downfall. I felt cruel just standing there as signs of consciousness faded from his body. This wasn't me. I'm not like them. What would my father have done if they were patients of his? He'd never have let someone die on the operating table for a crime they might commit in the future, or who they were in the past. It was a sense of honor I had trouble understanding, but that changed here.

There was no way to detach all of the Carpathians from Noah without risking them ripping off whatever body part they were fastened to. I had to distract them first and it had to be fast. There was a fire hydrant on sidewalk. If I could unscrew the metal grating on a window I could do this. It was taking a lot less effort than I thought it would with my concentration divided, but I still had to hurry.

A pain worse than anything I had felt before shot through my body. One of the Carpathians had broken off from the group around Vivi and was biting into my neck. The feeling ended as suddenly as it began. An eruption of energy shot out from me in response to the pain, turning the Carpathian to ash.

I channeled the remaining telekinetic adrenaline rush to tear the cap off the hydrant. A powerful stream of water sprayed out, scattering the Carpathians in the street. Throwing Noah to safety first, I pulled the power lines down from above, electrocuting all four of the soaking wet attackers and strangling them with the wires until their heads came off.

"Are you going to be okay?" I asked after making a lofty jump over to Noah. The sizzling pool of water between us was turned black from the Carpathians' ashes.

"I need ... blood." He limped over to me, pulling the sword from his shoulder and clutching his arm. His body was so horribly mangled it was excruciating to look at. He had lost so much blood that his wounds weren't even bleeding anymore.

I couldn't open my mouth fast enough to argue against him taking my blood. He was already behind me, grasping my face to expose my neck.

"Relax, it's not gonna hurt. Just don't be weird about it and enjoy yourself too much." There was a slight pinch as his fangs penetrated the skin. I grabbed his arm in panic, but even though badly injured he remained steadfast. A warm numbing sensation spread rapidly throughout my body. Mixed feelings of intoxication and sedation lulled me into an almost inappropriately satisfying dreamlike state. The encroaching chaos around us melted away, leaving only pleasure now as he drained out my life to restore his.

What must have only been minutes felt like hours until he was done drinking and released me. Weak in the knees and delirious, I nearly fell to the ground, but he caught me. While I watched his wounds healed, my own regeneration kicked in to replenish my veins with blood again.

"Oh, you're still alive," he said as I came to my senses. "I thought I took too much for a second there. You make a pretty good blood bag, kid. A normal human would've died losing that much blood."

Slightly reinvigorated, Noah plowed through the Carpathian army in a blur of death. Vivi rejoined me as we fought together to clean up his scraps.

"He won't admit it himself, but Noah has gained respect for you, and that's saying quite a bit." She tried speaking loud enough over the clashing of bone and blade without letting him overhear.

"Why don't you tell him how you feel so he can stop trying to impress you?" I asked.

"Impress me? Do not place blame on me for his ego!" she laughed. This was such an inappropriate time to be having this conversation, but it was all-or-nothing and possibly the last time either of us would ever get to speak our mind.

"It's pretty obvious you love him, and he's always showing off to get your attention. You're really the only one he trusts. With both of you protecting each other you could make it work."

"Unlike him, I have no issue declaring that love is a wonderful thing, but we have also both seen and felt so much misery caused by love used as leverage."

"You sound scared to try. Noah was always preaching to me about overcoming fear. He even has a tattoo about it. There's no reason the both of you can't."

"It is mostly guilt, not fear, for me. By saving his life tonight, even you did what I could not. I am reminded of it every night."

"You need to let that go. You could be free together. I don't think he blames you, but that's a conversation the two of you should be having."

"Maybe you are right," she said, looking over at him. "I may have finally found something to make these wretched nights a little more bearable and it was right in front of me all this time."

"I'm going after the hunchback," I yelled to the group.

"*Non!* Only an Ancient can kill an Ancient," Vivi insisted. "Our best chance is to eliminate his army. Let Noah and I deal with him and force his retreat."

"I was made for this, Vivi." I flew over the mob, searching for the man in the mask. It didn't take long to spot the big hat. Nothing could have made me angrier than seeing him stroll through the crowd, spinning his cane like this was a leisurely walk in the park. I got an idea immediately upon seeing a car along the street. I gave it everything I had in me and rolled the car on its side, sending it bowling through the infected and into The Blighted One.

"Tell me what crevasse you plan to crawl into should you succeed? Humanity will never accept you as the monster you are now." His voice came from under the car.

I landed on the sidewalk, waiting for his retaliation. The car budged, then flipped through the air toward me. I blocked my face with my hands and the car collided with an invisible wall erected by my powers. The Blighted One stood watching me through the soulless portholes in his mask.

"Your fight to protect the humans that will never embrace you for who you are is laughable. Do you think your Archios allies will welcome you in? No, they will bury you to keep up their charade."

The more he talked the more empowered I felt to shut him up. I threw the car back at him, but he halved it with his right arm, which had mutated into a long blade. He walked toward me, knocking half of the car away with ease. Something wriggled under the leather duster he was wearing. It tore open, revealing two sickle-like appendages sprouting from his back.

The bony mask protecting his head was too thick for me to crush. That was the most effective thing I had learned up to now. I was out of tricks sooner than I had hoped. His new sword-arm looked the most dangerous, so I focused on trying to remove it. We were caught in a tug of war, but I prevailed and yanked it from his body.

I turned it back around in the air and tried impaling him with it. The sword stuck straight through his chest and melted into him, reforming at his side. Alarmed, I flew back to rethink my strategy. Our fight traveled into Central Park and was now between just the two of us. My strongest hadn't done much but stagger him for a second and I was running out of ideas already.

The Blighted One dropped on all fours and scuttled across the ground. He climbed up a tree with the help of his extra appendages and pounced with his blade out. It missed, but on his way down the blade transformed into some sort of barbed tentacle and wrapped around my arm. With a jerk it tightened until I screamed.

I crashed to the ground and crawled away from him, feeling faint from blood loss as I left a trail behind me. He absorbed the blood from my arm just like the blade. My powers still weren't enough to throw him back, and every attempt I made didn't seem to bother him. He stopped following me momentarily and gazed at the sky. A deafening noise that reminded me of a cicada echoed from his throat. Once he was done, the sound of many feet trampling the grass came from all around. I saw infected stampeding through the trees to us and knew I wouldn't be able to do this on my own.

"The parasite may not discriminate in choosing a host, but I no longer deem you worthy of such a gift."

One of the bladed appendages from the Blighted One's back pierced between my ribs. I could no longer hold back the tears and began to choke. They mixed with the blood gurgling up in my throat and prevented me from pleading for mercy. An agonizing suction wreaked havoc inside my body. The bone scythe stuck in me rent my vital organs from their connective tissue.

"That robust flavor, I would recognize it anywhere. Bloodlust and rage, the final emotions of the oppressed. This is no work of the parasite. These are your true feelings. You want to hate, to lash out and destroy what stands in your way. You may not be human, but you are every bit as wicked."

I fought my body's urge to shut down and give in to unconsciousness. I collected myself just enough to tear the appendage from him and push him away. He recoiled, but I was still surrounded by infected bearing down on me. Before they could move in, I turned my attention to the trees above me and pulled down large branches to crush them and block their path even if only for a moment.

The Blighted One regrouped quickly and reattached his severed limb to continue his quest to harvest my insides.

"Ah, you have synergized so well with the parasite. I can taste the otherworldly energies from the Rift coursing through you. It is such a shame. You would have made an ideal successor and a wonderful instrument of destruction. It wouldn't take long before you turned that anger on mankind once they shunned you."

My heart beat erratically, traumatized by my organs rupturing. My senses failed. I held on for as long as I could, hoping maybe I was at least buying the others time to go through with their plan before I died. As my sight darkened, I had one last shot at taking the plague doctor out. Staring into his mask, I cracked the glass covering his eyes and sent the shards inward. The blood leaking from the holes let me know I was successful in bringing him at least a little more suffering. While he was definitely hurt, he still managed to heal by ingesting more tissue from me.

Vivi leaped down from the night sky, cutting off the Carpathian's siphon and removing it from my body. "Noah, keep him busy!" she shouted and carried me off to a safe place in the trees.

"I can still fight," I told her as my body started patching itself up.

"You've done enough. Take Monsieur Turner with you and leave here. I will erase his memory of everything that happened this week, including everyone he has met."

"Everyone?" I had only known him for a few days, but without Lyle I had no one left. We became friends quicker than I opened up to most people under the circumstances. I didn't think I'd have to walk away as if I never existed.

"It is for your own good as well as his. I strongly advise you continue to keep your secret and move on with your life."

"If I can't do what I was created for, then who am I? What purpose does my life really have?"

"Your life is not defined by how it began, but the paths you take along the way. It is too soon for you to end that journey so recklessly."

Vivi left me to rest away from danger and took up the fight against the Blighted One alongside Noah. My missing skin and organs were growing back now and I could feel my strength returning.

I floated to my feet when I heard a woman scream. I shot through the trees, smacking into branches as I flew past.

"NO!" Noah's roar boomed loud enough to be heard across all five boroughs. The Blighted One's rib cage had burst through its torso and engulfed Vivi. By the time I got there only her face and hand were visible as she desperately reached out to Noah.

"So much for your legendary speed!" The Carpathian laughed at Noah's frustration. He dropped his swords to try and pull Vivi out, snarling with his fangs bared and punching with all his strength. A few of the remaining infected were stabbing him in the back with their bladed arms, but he shrugged off the pain in his frenzied state. My heart sank, hearing her bones crunch and pop as she was assimilated into the monster.

"GIVE HER BACK TO ME!" he bellowed.

Noah had gone berserk with rage, and was clawing and punching to get to Vivi. He picked up one of his swords to try and cut her out, but it couldn't scratch the bony carapace protecting the Blighted One. In his anger, Noah failed to notice the mutated appendages make their move to consume him next. The two from the Carpathian's back stabbed into Noah's shoulders, holding him in place while the tentacle arm wrapped around his torso. The rib cage sprang open again like a crab's legs and extended to drag him in.

He should have transformed into mist, but he was so blinded by fury, all he did was strike senselessly at the body. I threw off the infected as soon as I flew in close enough and smashed them to bits.

Lyle ran up shouting as soon as he saw Vivi's *katana* on the grass and figured out what had happened. I pried Noah from the Blighted One before he was lost too, but he shoved me away so hard I almost broke my neck when I hit a tree. Noah dove right back in, trying to attack with the same results. I went to pull him away again, but he snarled menacingly at me to back off.

His crazed punching cracked the mask, but he was also about to be consumed. I warned Lyle to stay away. My anger was well past the boiling point so I could just imagine how Noah felt. I ripped off the Blighted One's appendages holding him. I sure as hell wasn't going to lose someone else.

The Blighted One let out an insidious chuckle from behind the broken mask. I helped Noah break the rest of the mask off, revealing the grotesque face it hid. A razor-toothed maw and two beady eyes greeted us. There was no skin, only raw muscle and bone covered in black veins, which made me think the mask actually *was* his face. Noah went to impale the hideous Ancient, but stopped before the sword struck. The Blighted One ignited in a baleful green blaze. Vivi's body fell from his chest cavity and disintegrated before it hit the ground.

"Oh — I'm sorry, did you love her?" A woman's voice cackled at Noah from behind The Blighted One who was thrashing wildly to extinguish the flames. Noah was on his knees trying to scoop what was left of Vivi into his hands.

"We killed you!" I screamed. Minerva emerged from a portal on the ground. Her new look better matched the evil soul inside her. Her eyes were bright red with cat-like irises, curved horns extended from each side of her skull, and leathery crimson wings kept her aloft before us.

"Then it should come as no surprise to you why I've returned. But, I'm not here only for you ..."

"Traitor!" The Blighted One's melting carcass hissed. "You failed our master and yet you get a second chance only to betray him?"

"On the contrary. *My* master has sent me to release you from your contract. It is you who have failed him. Your army is broken and the parasitic plague meant to contaminate mankind could have been better spread by a child with a cold. I, on the other hand, have succeeded in my task at creating perfect vessels for him. He was most pleased after seeing the destruction and resilience that this one possesses."

"My people ... will know justice. They ... will hunt you ... to the depths of Hell and back to avenge me." The Blighted One's voice faded out between the crackling flames. "We will not fall ... we will be free ..."

"Splendid. I could always make use of more sacrifices. You are no less pathetic than the witch who only sought power for something so short-sighted as revenge against her sister. There is a world ready to be taken and you pine for mere freedom."

Minerva unleashed another gout of balefire upon the Blighted One and soon his body crumbled to ash too. Noah had vanished amidst the squabbling. I was hoping he would return because right now I wasn't sure if I could do this alone.

"We've already defeated your demon once and I've only gotten stronger since then."

"You speak of that infernal fodder; an insult to compare him to my master. That was nothing more than a servant." Minerva paused and with a flap of her wing deflected Noah's aerial ambush. "That won't work twice." She smiled. "I've been looking forward to returning the favor you did me by reuniting me with my master."

Noah's eyes were still berserk with rage. He disappeared again, but Minerva caught him with her flames forcing him to transform into mist several times to avoid taking damage. Lyle took a step toward Vivi's *katana*. I couldn't let him fight even if he was willing to throw away his life to be a hero. I threw him as far away as I could without hurting him. Minerva was busy taking delight in having the upper hand on Noah this time around. Despite still being faster than her he wasn't able to get close with her constantly spraying flames in his path. Noah was unrelenting, but so was Minerva. She had yet to land a blow until he got too close and was forced to drop both his *wakizashi* as they melted from the intense heat.

I thought of what Vivi said before she died about him respecting me and the time he taught me how to fly. They weren't all bad, it was the ones that were who have been ruining it for the rest. But, I have the power to change that starting here and now. It isn't just about me and my revenge anymore. I can't let this cycle start over again. There's already enough hatred and war in the world, we don't need to add anymore fuel to the fire. Minerva and the demons' unholy crusade will only lead to genocide for both humanity and the supernatural. It won't bring balance and neither side will accept the other anymore than they do already. If I was created for destruction then that's what I'll have use to put an end to this before it can begin.

My mind was clear, centered even. I felt lucid again for the first time in a while. The anger was still there, but it wasn't in control. The world seemed to slow to a crawl around me as I honed my sights on Minerva.

The earth beneath me started to quake. It wasn't in my head though. With a wave of my hand the pavement cracked open and apartment windows shattered in a line toward Minerva. She glanced away from Noah too slowly to avoid the oncoming tsunami of cars and concrete. The green flames extinguished from around Noah instantly upon her loss of concentration as she was sent barreling down the street with the avalanche of cars.

"My nephew's pitiful sentiment to spare your life won't save you from the coming apocalypse. You and your pathetic allies will burn in hellfire with the rest of mankind."

Minerva flew into the air, throwing back all the cars in a fiery green explosion. She was many times more resistant against the direct effects of my telekinesis than anyone else I had fought. I would need to be creative to weaken her first. Water was still spraying from the fire hydrant I used earlier on the Carpathians. I angled the stream with the help of a manhole cover, but it failed to put out the oncoming flames.

"Water has no effect on the fires of Hell, fool!" She laughed.

My skin burned away in the tempest of unstoppable flames. The dead tissue reknitted itself with a temporary display of blackened blood vessels pumping life back into my body. The healing process wasn't without pain, but it caused an even greater surge of energy within me.

I flew through another burst of fire to take Minerva by surprise. We were inches apart when she flapped her wings to retreat. Everything I had stored inside me erupted outward in a shockwave that sent her ricocheting helplessly down the street.

Minerva was stopped abruptly by a sword through her heart. Noah had been waiting to greet her at just the right moment with Vivi's *katana*. He remained expressionless as he kicked her off the blade and into the flooded street. She cackled at him when he swung the beautifully engraved sword down like a guillotine.

"Soon you will bear witness to the depths of your folly! Humanity's reign is at an end and there is nothing any of you can do. Do you think such weak ideals as love and hope can break the cosmic cycle? I will return and I *will* rule —"

The malicious laughter from her severed head wouldn't cease until a gunshot finally brought us silence.

"I thought you'd be out of bullets by now." I looked over at Lyle. "I had one saved for myself. Just in case."

The same pentagram portal she came from opened beneath Minerva and returned what was left of her to Hell.

"Tell me it's over." Lyle sighed.

"For now, hopefully. Maybe even for the rest of your lifetime."

"Don't say that ..."

"It's fine. It gives me a purpose right?"

Noah bent down on one knee in Vivi's ashes holding her *katana*. "I never blamed you," he whispered to her.

He vanished in a gust of wind that swirled the ash along the street. Lyle walked up beside me as I healed away the rest of the burns. We watched the ashes dance around us until the breeze carried them away.

"I thought I wanted revenge, I thought I'd be a hero for killing everyone who wronged me, but this isn't what I imagined victory would feel like," I said, breaking the silence through a lump in my throat. "Why don't I feel like we've really won the war?"

"Heroes fight wars to end them. Only monsters fight to win, and you're no monster."

Epilogue

"Damn, Sarge, you're on fire," a young police officer exclaimed by the park gates. "Night shift just started and that's the second mugging you stopped by yourself. Someone upstairs must have really got your back."

"All about being in the right place at the right time, rookie," Lyle told him. "Hang back here a minute, all right?"

"You can't keep doing this," Lyle whispered to me as he walked up to my seat on the park bench. "People are getting suspicious."

"You mean your partner?" I peered over to where he was standing. "He looks like he hasn't even graduated high school. Anything would impress him."

"Since I've been back I'm filling my quotas for the month during the first week. I'm booking people faster than they can process them."

"And that's bad how exactly?" I asked. "We're cleaning up the streets, you're getting all the recognition. What's the problem?"

"I didn't take this job for the recognition. I appreciate what you're doing, but I'm going to get investigated if my bosses start doubting the validity of my arrests."

"Fine. I'll go help another cop who isn't so modest." I took another sip of my caramel latte and got up to leave.

"You know that's not the point, Dorian." He grabbed my arm to stop me. "I'm really glad you want to use your gift to help people, but you can't live your life in my shadow. You know you're like a brother to me. I wanna see you do your own thing and be happy."

"I am happy," I assured him. "Helping people is therapeutic and the shadows are where I feel most comfortable."

"It's been almost a year. The city has moved on, now it's time for you to. What about the modeling thing? Now's the perfect time to try that again. At least you're living with me if it falls through."

"I never wanted to do that to start with. I want to do something fulfilling."

"We'll talk more when I'm home. Go back to the apartment for now. I need to train this newbie."

"Whatever you say, Sergeant Turner."

This wasn't the first time we'd had this conversation in the past year. Lyle got his job back with an award and even a promotion, but still felt he failed to become the hero his father was. It took him a lot to get over losing Vivi and everything else we experienced. For months he talked about how he wished he was supernatural so that maybe he could have saved her. I reminded Lyle that if it wasn't for him I would have never made it out of my apartment alive that first night.

The city had returned to normal as if nothing ever happened. The very next day most of the quarantined areas were up and running with no one the wiser. It made me wonder how often this stuff happened right under our noses, like the homeless old Outsider said.

We visited my parents' graves in Boston and I used the money they left for me to contribute to an apartment I shared with Lyle. Every week we would go to the spot in Central Park where we had lost Vivi. It was depressing at first, but we both felt it necessary to not forget that there was good on the other side of the curtain, in their world.

Whenever we hung out, Lyle and I would try picking out who might be supernatural in the crowd. Somewhere out there I had brothers and sisters just like me, and I wanted to meet them. Part of me wanted the family, the companionship, and the safety in numbers for when the peace was inevitably disrupted. Part of me hoped they were as far away as possible, so I would never have to deal with the guilt of bringing them into the chaos.

After some time I started using my powers to tip the balance in the favor of good on the streets. Lyle had his new partner, but the two of us were the real team. I'd walk the darkest corners of the city looking for trouble, then call Lyle so he could make the arrest after I took care of business. I had guns and knives pulled on me so many times, but the expression on the criminals' faces when I'd bend their weapons like rubber with my mind never got old. Lyle got as much amusement out of it as I did. He would cover for me when they rambled to the police about me, saying they were intoxicated or high on some drug, but eventually all the stories that came in sounded the same and it caused tension between us. He wanted me to move on and I just couldn't let go.

There was so much out there for me to do. I wanted the road I walked through life not to be paved with the regret that I could have done more. Preventing the loss of any more good people trumped the risk of being found out for what I really was. I never admitted it to Lyle, but a very small part of me sympathized with what The Blighted One was trying to accomplish. Nobody should be forced to spend their life hiding who they are. I can understand how existing as victims of discrimination for all those years might drive someone so mad that they'd jump at the chance for the power to change it all. It made me wonder what the world would be like without the persecution of my kind, or anyone for that matter. Could mankind ever get over their hatred for those that are different?

I turned down the block to my apartment when I felt something hit the back of my head. I looked around, but there wasn't anyone else there. I was going to ignore it when I spotted something on the ground. It was a book: *The Art of War, English Edition.*

"It's a good read." A voice from behind startled me. I turned around to see Noah sitting on the hood of a car and stared at him in disbelief. "What? Still not used to my good looks?"

"I just never thought I'd see you again." There was something different about him besides his clothes. He was wearing a black sleeveless hoodie and sunglasses, with his hair tied back. "I didn't think you owned a shirt, either."

"You sound disappointed." He was talking the talk like his usual pompous self, but something was missing from the act.

"Are you okay?" I asked.

"Yeah, why wouldn't I be?" He shrugged and crossed his arms. That was it: he was still heartbroken.

"What are you doing here?" I asked to change the subject. "I thought I'd get more than a year of peace."

"I'm not here for you, I was stopping through."

"This is kind of a far trip from France to stop through. Did Aurelia send you?" I figured he was here to pay respects to where Vivi died, but it seemed out of character for Aurelia to send him here for that.

"No. So you really want to live like this?" It was his turn to switch topics now.

"Like what?" I asked, knowing he meant as a human. "I made a choice and I'm happy with it."

"Really? Because to me it looks like you haven't chosen anything. You're living between two worlds without standing firm in either one. It's like you're still afraid to be yourself. People only choose to hide if they're lazy, stupid, or afraid. Maybe even all three."

"Maybe I want peace and quiet. I don't want to live a life where I'm somebody's soldier, or their puppet, or pet. I'd think you of all people would understand that."

"I do, but how long can you keep this up until someone finds out what you are? Our kind are everywhere, and given your potential you won't go unnoticed forever."

"Then I'll move."

"So you're gonna keep retreating any time someone calls you out and drags you back into the same mess? Running and hiding aren't freedom, kid."

"What do you want me to say, Noah? What do you want from me? I'm not going back to France with you because now Aurelia thinks I might be useful again, if that's why you're here."

"Not France, and this has nothing to do with Aurelia. You don't have to worry about her anymore."

"What are you talking about? What did you do?"

"I took care of things, you'll just need to trust me. You're coming to Japan. The mountains where I trained should still be pretty isolated. Who knows, I might make something out of you yet."

"I'm not going."

"Yeah, you are. Until you're strong enough or fast enough to stop me you don't have a choice, and that's exactly my point. Live up to your potential so no one can stop you from doing what you really want or take away what's yours."

I could stop him — at least, I thought I could — but this must have been his twisted way of expressing his respect or concern for me. The only thing keeping me here was my friendship with Lyle, but if I was already drawing attention, it might cause that friendship to end tragically.

"I'll go if it means I get to kick your smug ass."

"You get to try," he laughed with a big smirk across his face. "You're gonna need every second of your immortality to even come close. First you have to admit what you're so scared of so you can get over it and move forward."

"I'm not ..." I started to disagree, but then thought about it more seriously. "I guess I don't want history to keep repeating itself every time I have people important to me. Maybe I can't hide who I am forever, but I'm worried about my inner demons taking over whenever I do lose someone I care for. I've already seen myself becoming that monster, and it scared me."

Noah was listening intently without his smirk anywhere in sight. It was more of a relief to get that off my chest than I would have imagined.

"When can we start?"